HOURGLASS

Also by Claudia Gray
Evernight
Stargazer

CLAUDIA GRAY

HarperCollins Children's Books

First published in hardback in the USA by HarperCollins Inc. in 2010
Published in paperback in the UK by HarperCollins Children's Books in 2010
HarperCollins Children's Books is a division of HarperCollinsPublishers Ltd,
77-85 Fulham Palace Road, Hammersmith, London W6 8JB

The HarperCollins website address is
www.harpercollins.co.uk

ISBN 978 0 00 735533 4

Hourglass
Copyright © 2010 by Amy Vincent

Printed and bound in England by Clays Ltd, St Ives plc

Typography by Andrea Vandergrift
1 3 5 7 9 10 8 6 4 2

First Edition

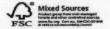

Mixed Sources
Product group from well-managed
forests and other controlled sources
www.fsc.org Cert no. SW-COC-001806
© 1996 Forest Stewardship Council

FSC is a non-profit international organisation established to promote the
responsible management of the world's forests. Products carrying the FSC
label are independently certified to assure consumers that they come
from forests that are managed to meet the social, economic and
ecological needs of present and future generations.

Find out more about HarperCollins and the environment at
www.harpercollins.co.uk/green

For Adair and Margaret Blake,
who heard the stories first

Prologue

"GET OUT," I PLEADED. "GET OUT OF TOWN FOR good. That way we don't have to kill you."

The vampire snarled, "What makes you think you could?"

Lucas tackled him, and they fell to the pavement. Those were bad odds for Lucas; short-range fighting always worked to a vampire's advantage, because a vampire's best weapons were his fangs. I ran forward, determined to help.

"You're stronger"—the vampire gasped—"than a human."

Lucas said, "I'm human enough."

The vampire grinned, a smile that had nothing to do with the desperate situation he was in and was therefore even scarier. "I heard somebody was looking for one of our babies," he crooned to Lucas. "One of the powerful ones in my tribe. Lady named Charity. Heard of her?"

Charity's tribe. A jolt of panic shivered through me.

"Yeah, I've heard of Charity. In fact, I staked her," Lucas said as he tried to twist the vampire's hand around his back. "Think

I can't stake you, too? You're about to learn different." Yet Lucas couldn't gain the advantage. They were too evenly matched. He wasn't even going to have a chance to go for his stakes. The vampire could turn the tables on him at any second.

That meant it was up to me to save him—by killing another vampire.

Chapter One

I GASPED FOR AIR SO HARD THAT MY CHEST ACHED. My face felt hot, and strands of my hair stuck to the sweaty back of my neck. Every single muscle hurt.

In front of me was Eduardo, one of the leaders of this Black Cross cell, with a stake in his hand. All around us, his vampire hunters, a ragtag army in denim and flannel, watched in silence. None of them would help me. We stood apart from them in the center of the room. Harsh overhead light painted him in stark shadows.

"Come on, Bianca. Get in the game." His voice could sound like a growl when he chose, and every word echoed off the concrete floor and metal walls of the abandoned warehouse. "This is a fight to the death. Aren't you even going to try to stop me?"

If I sprang at him in an effort to grab his weapon or knock him down, he'd be able to throw me to the floor. Eduardo was faster, and he'd been hunting for years. He'd probably killed hundreds of vampires—all of them older and more powerful than me.

Lucas, what can I do?

But I didn't dare look around for Lucas. I knew that if I took my eyes away from Eduardo for a second, the battle would be over.

I took a couple of steps backward, but I stumbled. The borrowed shoes I wore were too big for me, and one of them slipped off my foot.

"Clumsy," Eduardo said. He turned the stake between his fingers, as if imagining different angles at which to strike. His smile was so satisfied—so smug—that I stopped being scared and started being mad.

I grabbed up the shoe and flung it at Eduardo's face as hard as I could.

It smacked into his nose, and our audience burst out laughing. A few of them clapped. The tension had disappeared in an instant, and I was once more part of the gang, or so they thought.

"Nice," Lucas said as he emerged from the circle of watchers and put his hands on my shoulders. "Very nice."

"I'm not exactly a black belt." I couldn't catch my breath. Sparring practice always wore me out; this was the first time it hadn't ended with me flat on my back.

"You've got good instincts." Lucas's fingers kneaded the sore muscles at the base of my neck.

Eduardo didn't think having a shoe thrown in his face was

funny. He glared at me, an expression that would've been more fearsome if his nose weren't bright red. "Cute—in sparring practice. But if you think a stunt like that will save you in the real world—"

"It will if her opponent takes her for granted," said Kate, "like you did."

That shut Eduardo up, and he smiled ruefully. Officially, he and Kate were co-leaders of this Black Cross cell, but after only four days with them, I knew most people looked to Kate for the final word. Eduardo didn't seem to mind. As touchy and prickly as he was with everyone else, Lucas's stepfather apparently thought Kate could do no wrong.

"Doesn't matter how you knock them down as long as they fall," said Dana. "Now, can we eat already? Bianca's got to be starving."

I thought of blood—rich and red and hot, more delicious than any food could ever be—and a small shiver passed through me. Lucas saw it and put his arm around my waist to draw me close, as if for a hug. He whispered, "You okay?"

"Just hungry."

His dark green eyes met mine. If there was unease about my need for blood, there was understanding, too.

But Lucas couldn't help me any more than I could help myself. For the time being, we were trapped.

Four days earlier, my school, Evernight Academy, had been raided and burned by Black Cross. The hunters knew the secret of Evernight: that it was a refuge for vampires, a place to teach them about the modern world. That made it a target for Black Cross—a band of deadly vampire hunters, all of whom were trained to kill.

What they didn't know was that I wasn't one of the many human students who studied alongside the vampires at Evernight, unaware. I was a vampire.

Well, not a full vampire. If I had my way, that was something I would never become. But I had been born to two vampires, and despite the fact that I was a living person, I had some of the powers of a vampire and some of the needs.

Like, for instance, the need for blood.

Ever since the attack on Evernight Academy, this Black Cross cell was in lockdown. This meant that we were hiding in one secure location—namely this warehouse, which smelled like old tires and had cots for us to sleep on and oil stains on the concrete floor. People could go outside only if they were patrolling for vampires who might come after us in revenge for the attack on the school. We had to spend virtually every waking second in preparation for battles to come. I'd learned to sharpen knives, for instance, and had the very weird experience of whittling a stake. And now they'd started teaching me how to fight.

Privacy? Forget about it. I was lucky there was a door in front of the toilet. That meant that Lucas and I had almost no chance to be alone—and, even worse, that I hadn't drunk blood in four days.

Without blood, I became weak. I became hungry. The craving controlled me more and more, and if this went on much longer, I wasn't sure what I would do.

No matter what, I couldn't drink blood in front of anybody in Black Cross, save Lucas. When he had seen me bite another vampire during his year at Evernight Academy, I'd thought he would reject me forever; instead, he had overcome his Black Cross indoctrination and remained in love with me. I doubted many other vampire hunters would be capable of the same change of heart. If anyone else in the room with us right now saw me drink blood and realized the truth, I knew exactly what would happen. They would all turn on me in an instant.

Even Dana, one of Lucas's best friends, who was still cackling about my small victory over Eduardo. Even Kate, who credited me with saving Lucas's life. Even Raquel, my roommate from school who had joined me in Black Cross. Every time I looked at any of them, I had to remember: *They'd kill me if they knew.*

"Peanut butter again," Dana said as a few of us sat on the floor by our cots with our scanty dinner. "You know, seems like I remember enjoying peanut butter, once upon a long ago."

"Beats noodles with butter," Lucas said. Dana groaned. In reply to my curious glance, he added, "Last year, for a while, that was pretty much all we could afford. Seriously, every meal for a month, spaghetti noodles with butter. If I never eat that again, it'll be too soon."

"Who cares?" Raquel spread peanut butter on her bread like it was caviar. She hadn't stopped smiling for four days, ever since Black Cross first announced they'd take us in. "So we aren't dining out at fancy restaurants every night. What does it matter? We're actually doing something important. Something real."

I pointed out, "Right now, we're mostly hiding in a warehouse, eating peanut butter sandwiches without jelly three meals a day."

That didn't faze Raquel in the slightest. "It's just part of the sacrifice we have to make. It's worth it."

Dana ruffled Raquel's short black hair affectionately. "Spoken like a true newbie. We'll see what you say in year five." Raquel beamed. She loved the idea of being with Black Cross for five years, for ten, her whole life. After being stalked by vampires at school and haunted by ghosts at home, Raquel wanted nothing more than to kick some supernatural butt. As strange and hungry as the past four days had been, I'd never seen Raquel happier.

"Lights out in one hour!" yelled Kate. "Do what you've gotta."

As one, Dana and Raquel stuffed the last crusts of their sandwiches in their mouths and took off toward the makeshift shower that had been set up in the back. Only the first few people in line would have time to wash tonight, and only one or two would get warm water. Were they planning on fighting each other for a spot in line? The only alternative would probably be to share.

I felt too exhausted to think about taking my clothes off,

sweaty though I was. "In the morning," I said, half to Lucas and half to myself. "I'll have time to wash in the morning."

"Hey." His hand rested on my forearm, comfortingly warm and strong. "You're trembling."

"I guess I am."

Lucas shifted until he sat next to me. His tall frame, well-muscled but wiry, made me feel small and delicate, and his dark gold hair looked brilliant even in these dingy surroundings. His warmth made me imagine that I was in front of a fireplace in winter. As he put one arm around my shoulders, I rested my aching head against him and closed my eyes. That way I could pretend that there weren't a couple dozen people around us, talking and laughing. That we weren't in some gray, ugly warehouse that smelled like rubber. That there was nobody in the world but Lucas and me.

Into my ear, he murmured, "I'm worried about you."

"I'm worried about me, too."

"Lockdown's not going to go on much longer. Then we can get you some—something to eat, I mean—and you and I can figure out what to do next."

I understood what he meant. We were going to run away, the way we'd planned before the attack on Evernight. Lucas wanted to get away from Black Cross almost as badly as I did. But in order to do that, we'd need money, our freedom, and a chance to make plans together in private. Right now, all we could do was hang on.

When I looked at Lucas, I saw the concern in his dark green

eyes. I put my hand to his cheek and felt the rough scrub of beard stubble. "We'll make it. I know we will."

"I'm supposed to be the one taking care of you." He kept studying me, as if he could somehow find the answer to our problems in my face. "Not the other way around."

"We can take care of each other."

Lucas embraced me tightly, and for a few seconds, I didn't have to pretend we were anywhere else.

"Lucas!" Eduardo's voice echoed against the concrete and metal. We looked up to see him nearby, arms folded across his chest. Sweat made a dark V on the front of his T-shirt. Lucas and I drew away from each other. It wasn't that we were ashamed, but nobody could kill a romantic mood faster than Eduardo. "I want you to walk the perimeter on the first shift tonight."

"I went two nights ago," Lucas protested. "It's not my turn yet."

This only made Eduardo's scowl blacker. "Since when do you start whining about turns, like a kid on the playground who wants the swings?"

"Since you stopped even pretending to be fair. Back off, okay?"

"Or what? You'll run to your mommy? Because Kate wants to see some proof of your dedication, Lucas. We all do."

He meant, because of me. Lucas had broken Black Cross rules many times so that we could be together—more than the others in this cell knew.

Lucas wasn't backing down. "I haven't had a full night's

sleep since the fire. I'm not spending another night in the drainage ditch outside, waiting for nothing."

Eduardo's dark eyes narrowed. "At any second, we could have a vampire tribe on our trail—"

"And whose fault would that be? After your stunt at Evernight Academy—"

"Stunt?"

"Time out!" Dana, fresh from her shower and smelling strongly of cheap soap, held her hands in a T between Lucas and Eduardo. Her long braids fell over the thin, damp towel looped around her neck. "Chill, okay? In case you lost count, Eduardo, it's actually my turn to take a shift tonight. I don't feel so tired anyway."

Eduardo never liked being vetoed, but he couldn't refuse a willing volunteer. "Suit yourself, Dana."

"Why don't I bring Raquel out with me?" she suggested, smoothly steering the conversation away from Lucas. "My girl's chomping at the bit to do more."

"Raquel's too new. Forget it." Apparently Eduardo felt better for having been able to put his foot down. He stalked off.

"Thanks," I said to Dana. "Are you sure you aren't too tired?"

She grinned. "What, do you think I'm going to be dragging butt tomorrow like Lucas did today? No way."

Lucas pretended to punch her arm, and she mock-sneered at him. They pretty much gave each other hell all the time without meaning a word of it. I thought that Dana might be Lucas's best friend. Certainly only a real friend would take a perimeter-search shift, which involved—as Lucas put it—a whole lot of stooping, a whole lot of mud, and almost no sleep.

Soon everyone around us was preparing for bed. The only privacy any of us had was the "wall"—actually a bunch of old sheets hung over a clothesline—between the men's half of the room and the women's. Lucas and I were both right up against the sheet, separated only by a few inches and one thin cotton cloth. Sometimes I was reassured by the fact that he was so close; other times, the frustration made me want to scream.

It's not forever, I reminded myself as I changed into the borrowed T-shirt I slept in. The pajamas I'd escaped in had been ruined in the fire; the only thing I wore that belonged to me was the obsidian pendant I'd gotten from my parents that hung around my neck at all times, even when I was in the shower. The jet brooch Lucas had given me while we were first dating was tucked into the small bag they'd given me. I didn't think of myself as especially materialistic, but losing nearly everything I'd ever owned had been a blow. So I treasured the few things I had left.

When Kate called "Lights out," somebody flipped the switch almost that instant. I burrowed under the thin, army-style blanket over my folding cot. It wasn't soft, and it definitely wasn't comfortable—cots *suck*—but I was so exhausted that any chance to rest was welcome.

To my left, Raquel was already asleep. She slept better here than she ever had at Evernight.

To my right, invisible behind the slowly rippling white sheet, was Lucas.

I imagined the outline of his body, what he looked like lying down on his cot. I fantasized about tiptoeing to his side and sliding in next to him. But we'd be seen. I sighed, giving up the idea.

This was the fourth night I'd done that. And, just as I'd done the other four nights, once I stopped being frustrated about my inability to be with Lucas, I started worrying.

Mom and Dad have to be okay, I told myself. I remembered the blaze too well—the way the flames had leaped up around me and the thickness of the smoke. It would've been easy to get lost, to get trapped. Fire was one of the only ways to truly kill a vampire. *They have centuries of experience. They've been in worse trouble before. Remember what Mom told you about the Great Fire of London? If she made it through that, she could make it out of Evernight.*

But Mom hadn't made it out of the Great Fire. She'd been terribly injured and near death; my father had "rescued" her by turning her into a vampire like himself.

I hadn't exactly been on great terms with my parents lately. That didn't mean I wanted them to be hurt. Just the thought of them weak and injured—or worse—made me sick to my stomach.

They weren't the only ones I was worried about. Had Vic been able to get out of the burning school? What about Balthazar?

As a vampire, he might have been targeted by Black Cross—or by his psychotic, vengeful sister, Charity, who had nearly prevented me, Lucas, and Raquel from escaping. Or what about poor Ranulf? He was a vampire, but one so gentle and unworldly that it was easy to imagine the hunters of Black Cross wiping him out.

I didn't know how any of them were. I might never know. When I chose to leave with Lucas, I'd known that was a risk I'd have to take. That didn't mean I liked it.

My stomach growled, hungry for blood.

Groaning, I turned over in my cot and prayed for sleep. That was the only way to silence the fears and hungers inside—at least for a few hours.

I reached out for the flower, but even as my fingertip touched the petal, it blackened and withered.

"Not for me," I whispered.

"No. Something better," said the ghost.

How long had she been there? It seemed as though she'd always been by my side. We stood together on the grounds of Evernight Academy as dark clouds roiled overhead. Gargoyles glared down at us from the imposing stone towers. The wind blew strands of my dark red hair across my face. A few leaves, caught in the gale, blew through the aquamarine shadow of the ghost. She flinched.

"Where's Lucas?" Somehow he was supposed to be here, but I couldn't remember why.

"Inside."

"I can't go in there." It wasn't that I was afraid. For some reason, it seemed impossible for me to walk inside the school. Then I realized why it was impossible. "This can't be real. Evernight Academy was burned in a fire. It doesn't exist now."

The ghost cocked her head. "When you say 'now,' when do you mean?"

"Feet on the floor!"

The shout awakened us every morning. Even as I blinked my eyes, groggily trying to recall the dream that already had begun to slip away, Raquel bounded from her cot, strangely energized. "Come on, Bianca."

"It's just breakfast," I grumbled. Peanut butter on toast wasn't worth rushing for, in my opinion.

"No, something's happening."

Bleary and confused, I stumbled to my feet to see that the Black Cross hunters around me were already on guard. My exhaustion told me that it couldn't possibly be morning yet. Why had they hauled us out of bed in the middle of the night?

Oh, no.

Dana ran in and yelled, "Confirmed! Arm up, now!"

"The vampires," Raquel whispered. "They've come."

Chapter Two

INSTANTLY THE ENTIRE ROOM SPRANG INTO action. All around me, Black Cross hunters were grabbing crossbows, stakes, and knives. I slid into my jeans, my whole body tense.

There was no way I was joining this fight. None. I might have decided never to become a vampire, but that didn't mean I was ready to join a crew of vampire-slaughtering zealots. Besides, the vampires coming after us now wouldn't be the mad killers who gave the undead a bad name. They would be from Evernight Academy, seeking only what they saw as justice for what happened to the school—and, possibly, trying to save me.

But what if they tried to hurt Lucas? Could I stand by while they attacked the man I loved?

Next to me, Raquel took up a stake with shaky hands. "This is it. We have to be ready."

"I'm not—I can't—" How could I explain this to her? I couldn't.

Lucas emerged from the men's half of the room, his shirt untucked and his dark gold hair still mussed from sleep. "You two are *not* getting involved in this," he said. "You're not trained." His eyes met mine, and I knew he understood the other reasons I couldn't take part.

Raquel looked furious. "What are you talking about? I can fight! Just give me a chance!"

Ignoring her, Lucas grabbed our arms and started towing us toward the back of the warehouse. "You're both coming with me."

"The hell I am." Raquel broke free and ran to the metal door, which banged as she pushed her way through. Lucas swore under his breath as he started after her. I followed them, more in shock than anything else.

Outside, the sky was the flat gray that preceded dawn. Hunters in various states of undress shouted to one another to take position. Knives gleamed in the moonlight, and I heard the creaking and clicking of crossbows being loaded. Kate crouched on the gravel, her arms in front of her like a runner and her head cocked in a way that told me she was relying on her hearing to gauge the risk. I looked out over the field surrounding us—high and unkempt with uncut brush. To most humans, it would have looked entirely still. With my sharper vision, I could see flickers of movement coming closer. We were being surrounded.

"Mom," Lucas said softly, "somebody should guard Bianca and Raquel in the warehouse. They can't fight yet, and they'll be looked at as—traitors, something like that. The vampires would target them."

From his place at the corner of the lot, a crossbow in his hands, Eduardo said, "Running away now?"

Lucas's jaw tightened. "I didn't say *I* should be the one. But somebody ought to be with them just in case."

"Just in case the vampires get through? Best way to prevent that is by having all our fighters at the front," Eduardo shot back. "Unless you're simply looking for an excuse."

One of Lucas's hands balled into a fist, and for a moment I thought he might hit Eduardo. Calling Lucas a coward was manifestly unfair, but this wasn't the time to argue about it. I put a hand on his arm, trying to calm him.

It was Kate who intervened, though. "Eduardo, can it. Lucas, get them in the warehouse." She never looked away from the horizon, from the attackers she knew were coming. "We need all three of you to start packing our supplies. Fast as you can."

Eduardo turned to her. "No way are we running from this, Kate."

"You like fighting more than you like staying alive," Kate said, never meeting his eyes. "But I try to think like Patton. I don't run this group so everyone can die for the cause. I run it so the vampires have to die for theirs."

The shapes in the brush all rustled as one, moving closer. Lucas tensed, and I realized he could see them in the dark as well as I could. Ever since I'd first drunk his blood, he'd developed the first stirrings of vampiric power. That meant he knew what I knew: We didn't have much time. Minutes, maybe.

"Raquel, come on," Lucas said, but she stubbornly remained by Dana's side, shaking her head.

"This isn't safe," I tried. "Please, Raquel, you could be killed."

Her voice trembled as she answered, but she said only, "I'm done with running."

Dana set aside the crossbow she'd been loading and faced Raquel. Her entire body seemed to vibrate with energy. She had been the one to spot the vampires, the one who had known about the danger longest—and she was already in battle mode. Yet she spoke gently to Raquel. "Packing up our stuff isn't running. Okay? It's something we need to do, because we're going to have to get out of here, either after the fight or during it."

"Not if we win," Raquel began, but stopped when she saw Dana's expression.

"They know our location now," Lucas said. "More vampires will come. We've got to run. Help us get ready to run. That's the best thing you can do right now."

Raquel never looked away from Dana as her face shifted from determination to resignation. "Next time," she said. "Next time I'll know how to fight."

"We'll be in this together next time," Dana agreed. Her gaze shifted to the brush and the pursuers. Nobody needed vampire senses to know how close they were now. "Get your butt out of here."

I grabbed Raquel's hand and pulled her back into the warehouse. After a few days being confined here, always with dozens of people around, I felt weird seeing it almost empty. The blankets were disheveled, and some of the cots had been tipped over in the rush. Still in shock, I started folding a blanket.

"Screw the blankets." Lucas headed toward the weapons lockers. Almost everything had been taken by the hunters, but there were still a few stakes, arrows, and canisters of holy water. "We get the ammo ready. The rest we can replace."

"Of course." I should have thought of that. But how could I? My brain was stuck, like when the needle of Dad's record player caught in the scratches of his old jazz records: *Are my parents outside? Is Balthazar? Will Black Cross kill people that I care about, people who are probably only trying to rescue me?*

Outside I heard a shout—then a scream.

All three of us froze. The noise swelled outside from a few cries to a roar, and the metal wall of the warehouse thudded. It wasn't a body—a rock, maybe, or a misfired arrow—but Raquel and I jumped.

Lucas shook it off fastest. "Pack this stuff up. When they call for us, we're gonna have about two minutes to get our gear into the vans. That's it."

We got to work. It was difficult to concentrate. The cacophony outside frightened me, not only because of my fear for the others but also because it reminded me powerfully of the last Black Cross battle I'd witnessed: the burning of Evernight. My back still ached from the fall I'd taken while running across the flaming roof, and I imagined I could still taste smoke and ash. Before, I'd been able to comfort myself by thinking that it was all over—but it wasn't. As long as Lucas and I were stuck with Black Cross, the battles would always follow us. Danger would always be near.

With every shout, every thud, Lucas seemed to get more worked up. He wasn't used to staying out of fights; he was more likely to start them.

Trunk shut, locked, moving on. Do they want to take the wood that hasn't been carved into stakes yet? Surely not—they can get wood anywhere, right? I kept trying to figure it out, working as fast as I could. Next to me, Raquel was simply grabbing armfuls of junk and dumping it into boxes without even checking to see what it was. She probably had the right idea.

Something slammed hard into the metal wall again, and I gasped. Lucas didn't tell me it was going to be all right; instead, he grabbed a stake.

At that moment, two sprawling figures burst through one of the side doors. Even my vampire senses couldn't tell me which was my own kind and which was the Black Cross hunter, because they were too tangled together—a blur of motion, sweat, and snarled curses. They staggered toward us, oblivious to our presence, only to their life-and-death struggle. The half-open door behind them showed a sliver of light, and let the screams come through even louder.

"Do something," Raquel whispered. "Lucas, you know what to do, right?"

Lucas leaped forward, farther and faster than a mere human should've been able to, and swung his stake into the fray. Instantly one of the figures froze; the stake had paralyzed the vampire. I looked at his still face—green eyes, fair hair, features frozen in horror—and felt a flash of sympathy for him in the instant before the Black Cross hunter slid a long, broad blade from his belt and severed his opponent's head with a single stroke. The vampire shuddered once, then crumbled to oily dust upon the floor.

The vampire had been an old one, then; there was very little left of the mortal man he'd been. As the others stood there, looking down at the remains, I could only wonder if this had been one of my parents' friends. I hadn't recognized him, but whoever he'd been, he'd come here in the belief he was helping me.

"How did you even do that?" Raquel said. "That was, like, superhuman." She meant it only as a compliment, and luckily the Black Cross hunter was too exhausted and relieved to notice that Lucas had just called upon vampire power.

My eyes sought Lucas's. I was relieved to see no triumph there, only a plea for understanding. When he'd been forced to choose, he had to protect his fellow hunter. I got that. What I didn't get was what would have happened if this vampire had been my mother or father.

Eduardo leaned in through the open doorway, panting but somehow exhilarated by the fight. "We've pushed them back. Won't have long before they return, though. We've got to load up now."

"Where are we going?" I asked.

"Someplace we can do real training. Get you new recruits

into shape." Eduardo glanced at me as he spoke, and although he didn't look friendly, he looked—well, like possibly he hated me less. Now that I was a potential soldier, maybe he finally saw me as useful. But then his grin changed, becoming more cynical as he turned toward Lucas. "You won't have any more excuses to run from a fight next time."

Lucas looked like he might punch Eduardo in the jaw, so I grabbed his hand. His temper sometimes threatened to get the better of him.

"Come on, people!" Kate called from outside the warehouse. "Let's move!"

Chapter Three

WITHIN TWENTY MINUTES, EVERYONE HAD PILED into Black Cross's ramshackle armada of old trucks, vans, and cars. Lucas and I made sure to get into the van Dana was driving, and Raquel took the shotgun seat. With the rest of the van piled high with the group's gear, we were on our own for the trip.

"Where are we going, anyway?" I shouted to Dana, over the wailing on the radio.

Dana pulled out, to join the caravan. "Ever been to New York City?"

"You're kidding, right?" Nobody was kidding. Lucas gave me a confused look, like he couldn't understand why I thought that was weird. I tried to explain. "You guys carry around all these weapons and go out to attack vampires. In a big city like that, don't people—you know—*notice*?"

"Nope," Dana said. "She's never been to New York before."

Raquel laughed as she thumped on the dashboard in sync with the song. "You're gonna love it, Bianca," she promised. "My sister Frida used to take me to Manhattan once a year. There are all these crazy galleries, art so bizarre you can't believe anybody ever dreamed it up."

"We're not going to have a lot of time to spend in museums," Dana said. Raquel's drumming faltered, but only for a moment; as soon as the chorus started over, she was pounding the dash as hard as ever.

"It still seems weird," I said to Lucas. "How are we even supposed to find space there?"

He said, "We have friends in New York. It's home to one of the biggest Black Cross cells in the world, and they have a pretty extensive support network."

"In other words," Dana called over the music, "those guys are rolling in dough."

I joked, "What, do they live in penthouses?"

"Not hardly," Lucas said, "but you ought to check out their arsenal. I think there are some armies that don't have the fire-power the New York cell's got."

"How come the New York cell is so big?" I asked. Despite the seriousness of our situation, I could feel my spirits rising with every mile we drove. It felt so good to be on the move. "Why aren't they like all the rest of you?"

"Because New York is a city with a serious vampire problem." Lucas looked grim. "The vampires got there almost as soon as the Dutch did, back in the 1600s. They're entrenched in that area—massive power, major influence. That Black Cross cell needs all the resources it can get to stand up against them. Actually, that was our first cell in the New World. At least, that's what they tell us. It's not like we show up in the history books."

I thought about vampires in old New Amsterdam, and then I thought about Balthazar and Charity, who had been alive then. When Balthazar had told me about growing up in Colonial America, I had thought it sounded so unfathomably old, so mysterious and impressive. It was weird to think that Black Cross went that far back, too.

Raquel must have been thinking along similar lines, because she asked, "Is that when Black Cross was founded? The sixteen hundreds?"

Dana laughed at her. "Try a thousand years before that."

"Get out," I said. "Really?"

"Started in the Byzantine Empire," Lucas said. I tried hard to remember who the Byzantines were—I thought maybe they were what came after the Roman Empire, but I wasn't sure. I imagined Mom's disgust if she knew how vague I was about this: some history teacher's daughter I made. "At first, Black Cross was the guard for Constantinople. But soon it spread throughout Europe, then into Asia. Went to the Americas and Australia along with the explorers. Apparently the kings and queens used to insist on at least one hunter traveling on every expedition."

That last bit especially caught my attention. "Kings and

queens? You mean—like, the government knows about you guys?" I tried to imagine Lucas as a sort of paranormal Secret Service agent. It wasn't that much of a stretch.

"Not so much, anymore." Lucas leaned his forehead against the window on his side. The highway rippled by, so fast the side of the road was a blur. "You guys—I mean, you guys know that vampires basically went underground not long after the Middle Ages."

I gave Lucas the wide-eyed look that means, *Shut up, will you?* He looked appropriately apologetic. Obviously, he'd nearly said *you guys went underground*—in other words, he had come close to referring to me as a vampire in front of Dana and Raquel. It had been only a slip of the tongue, but that was all it would take.

Luckily, neither Dana nor Raquel had caught it. Raquel said, "So vampires fooled everybody into not believing in them. That meant they could move more freely—and that Black Cross wouldn't be as powerful anymore. Right?"

"You got it, smarty-pants." Dana frowned at the road ahead of us. "Damn, but Kate's got a lead foot. Does she want us all to get speeding tickets? We can't break formation!"

Lucas pretended he didn't hear her bitching about his mother. "Anyway, we don't get big grants from the crown anymore. There are people who know what we do. Some of those people have money. They keep us afloat. That's pretty much how it is."

I imagined Lucas as the figure he might have been in the

Middle Ages—resplendent in a suit of armor, honored for his hard work and bravery with feasts in the greatest courts in the land. Then I realized how much he would've hated that, dressing up and making nice at fancy parties.

No, I decided, *he belongs right here, right now. With me.*

"Hey," Dana said. "At eleven o'clock. Check it out."

Then I saw what she was calling our attention to: the shape of Evernight Academy on the horizon.

We weren't that close. Evernight was far from any highway, and Kate and Eduardo weren't foolhardy enough to drag us onto Mrs. Bethany's turf again. But Evernight had a distinctive silhouette, since it was an enormous Gothic building with towers high up in the hills of Massachusetts. Even at this distance, with the school no more than a craggy outline, we recognized it. We were far enough away that the damage from the fire was invisible. It was as if Black Cross had failed to touch the school at all.

"Still standing," Dana said. "Dammit."

"We'll get it someday." Raquel flattened one hand against her window, like she wanted to punch through the glass and knock the school down herself.

I thought of my mother and father, and it occurred to me that maybe they were nearby. This moment, right now, was possibly as close as I would ever be to my parents again.

I'd become so angry with them during my last days at Evernight. They had never told me that the wraiths played a role in my birth, or that they might be coming for me someday because of that. For a year I'd been literally haunted by ghosts that seemed to think they owned me, and I still didn't know what that might mean. My parents had also refused to tell me if I had any choice other than becoming a full vampire someday. After meeting some of the vampires who truly were insane killers, I'd decided to try to find out whether it was possible for me to live out a normal life as a human being.

I still don't know the truth. What's going to happen to me? Not having any answers was so terrifying that I tried not to think about it, but dark uncertainty tugged at me nearly all the time now.

Yet as I looked up at the school, both my fear and my anger faded. I remembered only how loving Mom and Dad were and how close we'd been not that long ago. So many things had happened to me just in the past couple of days, and none of it seemed entirely real if I couldn't tell my parents about it. I felt a powerful, almost overwhelming urge to leap out of the van and run toward Evernight, calling for them.

But I knew I could never go back to the ways things were before. So much had changed. I'd been forced to choose a side, and I'd chosen humanity, life—and Lucas.

Lucas caught a lock of my hair between his fingers, gently testing whether or not I needed comfort. I leaned my head against his shoulder, and for a while we rode on without anybody talking, only the music playing. Every mile marker we passed reminded me of how far we had come from the last home I'd had and the person I used to be.

We stopped to get gasoline and take bathroom breaks occasionally, but we took a longer rest only once during the drive, for lunch.

While Dana and Raquel joined the horde of people crowding into a fast-food Mexican place, Lucas and I begged off to walk to a diner down the street. Of course we wanted a few minutes alone, but even more than I needed to be with Lucas, I needed to eat—more specifically, to drink.

The first thing Lucas said when we were walking away from the crowd along the side of the road, sort of alone at last, was, "How hungry are you?"

"So hungry I can hear your heart beating." And it seemed to me I could taste Lucas's blood on my tongue. Probably better not to mention that. The sunlight bore down on me hard, harsh now that I'd been without blood for several days. I'd never done without for so long before.

"You think the diner—maybe the raw meat would have some blood, we could sneak back there—"

"That wouldn't be enough. Besides, I know what to do." I stood still, watching the swaying grass beside the highway, which lashed back and forth in the currents of passing cars. A robin pecked at the dirt, searching for worms amid the bottle caps and cigarette butts.

"Bianca?"

I could see nothing but the robin and think of nothing but its blood. *Bird's blood is thin, but it's hot.*

"Don't watch," I whispered. My jaw ached. My fangs slid into my mouth, sharp points scraping against my lips and tongue. Though we stood in the brilliant sunshine, everything around me seemed to go dark, as though the robin were in a spotlight, moving in slow motion.

Vampire quick, I pounced. The bird fluttered in my hands for only a moment before I bit into its flesh.

Yes, that's it, blood! I drank the few sips of blood the robin had to offer, eyes shut in delight. When it was shriveled and dead in my hands, I let it drop as I wiped my mouth with the back of my hand. Only then did I realize I had just done that right in front of Lucas. Shame hit me as I thought how savage I must have looked, and how disgusted Lucas must be.

But when I hesitantly raised my eyes to him, Lucas had turned away—just like I'd asked him to. He hadn't seen. Sensing that I was done, he turned back around and smiled at me gently. When he saw the fear I felt, he shook his head.

"I love you," he murmured. "That means I'm not just here for the pretty parts. I'm here no matter what."

Alight with relief, I took his hand and walked with him to the diner. We were broke, and I wore clothes that didn't fit me, and we were on the side of a highway in the middle of nowhere— but in that moment I felt more beautiful than any princess or supermodel or anything. I had Lucas, who loved me no matter what. That was all I needed.

We ate fast at the diner. Lucas was starving, and I needed

regular food, too. Between mouthfuls of French fries, we tried to work out what else we might do with our precious few moments of free time.

"Can we find an Internet café, maybe? I could e-mail my parents."

"No. N. O. First of all, there's no way we'd find an Internet café out in the sticks. Second, you're not e-mailing them. You can call once you know where they are, but not from a cell, or anything else that can be traced back to us. You can send a letter. But no e-mail. That's another Black Cross order we're not disobeying."

Lucas claimed there was a difference between disobeying orders and breaking stupid rules, but right that second, I couldn't see it. Whatever. I knew another way to find out what had gone down the night Evernight burned.

At first I wanted to use Lucas's cell phone, but he pointed out that Black Cross would then be able to track the call. Luckily, once we were done eating, we found a bank of pay phones at the side of the diner. The first two I picked up had no dial tone, and the third's cord had been cut, but the fourth worked okay. I smiled in relief as soon as I heard the dial tone. O for operator. "Collect," I said, reading off the number I wanted from Lucas's cell phone contacts list. "Say that it's Bianca Olivier."

Silence followed. "Did she hang up?" I said.

"There's a pause with collect calls." Lucas stood next to me, leaning against the plastic hood of the pay phone. "They don't want you to yell your message at the other person before they've accepted the charges."

The phone line clicked, and I heard a sleepy voice say, "Bianca?"

"Vic!" I bounced up and down on my heels, and Lucas and I shared a huge smile. "Vic, you're okay!"

"Yeah, yeah. Whoa, wait a second—I'm still kinda waking up here." I could imagine Vic clutching his cell phone to his face, with bad bed-head, in the middle of an extremely messy bedroom, surrounded by his posters. Probably he had crazy sheets, plaid or polka-dotted. He yawned, then, more alertly, asked, "Am I dreaming again?"

"No dream. It's me. You weren't injured in the fire?"

"No. Nobody got hurt very badly, which was, like, crazy good luck. Lost my pith helmet, though." Vic obviously considered this a grave tragedy. "What about you? Are you okay? After they put out the fire, we were going nuts trying to find you. A couple people said they saw you on the grounds, so we knew you got out of the school, but we couldn't figure where you ran off to."

"I'm fine. I'm with Lucas."

"Lucas?" No wonder Vic sounded astonished. As far as he knew, Lucas and I had broken up months ago. We'd had to keep our relationship a secret since then. "This is getting totally surreal. If this is just a dream, I'm gonna be so mad."

"You're not dreaming," Lucas called. His hearing was sharp enough to listen in on the call, even though he was standing a foot from the receiver. "Pull it together, man. What are you doing asleep at eleven A.M.?"

"As you should recall, I am the proverbial night owl. Sleeping until noon is not only my right but my responsibility," Vic said. "Besides, as the old song goes, school's out for summer, school's out forever."

I gasped. "Forever? Does that mean Evernight Academy was destroyed?"

"Destroyed, no. Mrs. Bethany swears they'll open for business in the fall, though I don't see how. I mean, that place was *torched*."

The harder questions came next. I gripped the receiver tightly, willing my voice not to shake. "Were my parents hurt? Did you see them?"

"They're okay. I told you—everybody got out all right. Your mom and dad didn't get caught in the fire. In fact, they were helping us look for you." Vic paused. "They were pretty freaked out, Bianca."

That was as close as Vic got to a guilt trip. I couldn't really feel the impact, though; I was too elated to know that my parents had survived the Black Cross attack.

"Do you know where they are?" I didn't think they would go far from Evernight Academy. My parents would stay close to the grounds—mostly because they would be hoping I'd return. I knew I couldn't, but I hated the thought of them waiting for me there.

"They were sticking around the school last I saw," Vic said.

So much for calling them—my parents tried hard to adapt to modern life, but they hadn't quite gotten as far as having cell phones.

"What about Balthazar?"

Lucas frowned. He had some problems with Balthazar, first because Balthazar was a vampire, and second because he and I had some history. It was over between us—it hardly even got started, honestly—but that didn't mean I wasn't still worried about him.

"Balty's A-OK," Vic replied. "He was totally upset after the fire, though. I think it must've been because you were missing. The guy was crushed."

"It wasn't because of me," I said quietly. My mood darkened as the weight of everything I'd lost settled over me, and I slumped against the pay phone, suddenly tired.

"Okay, okay. Backing off."

What Vic didn't and couldn't know was that Balthazar's misery was due to his sister, Charity, who had arranged the Black Cross attack. Charity was the most important person in the world to Balthazar, and, weirdly, I thought he was just as important to her. That wouldn't stop her from trying to hurt him, or anyone who got close to him, including me.

Vic, who was becoming more alert by the minute, said, "What about Raquel? She was the only other one we couldn't find. Is she with you, maybe?"

"She is, actually. She's fine. Doing great."

"Excellent! That means we all got out okay. Total miracle."

"Where did Ranulf end up?" I asked.

"He's crashed out in our guest room right now. You want me to grab him?"

"That's okay. I'm just glad he's all right." Lucas and I shared surprised smiles. If Vic knew he'd invited a vampire to come stay in his house, he probably wouldn't be sleeping so late—if at all. Fortunately Ranulf was too mild to cause anyone harm. "Listen, we have to go. I'll be in touch, though."

"Oh, man, I cannot deal with people being cryptic first thing in the morning." Vic sighed, then said, very quietly, "Call your parents. Just—you need to, all right?"

A lump rose in my throat. "Good-bye, Vic."

After I hung up, Lucas took my hand. "Like I said, there are ways for you to get in touch if you want to."

I'd been so frightened for Mom and Dad that I hadn't stopped to consider how frightened they must've been for me.

I must have looked stricken, because Lucas gave me a quick hug. "We'll get through to them soon. You can write them or something. See, it's going to be okay."

"I know. It's just hard."

"Yeah." We kissed—a simple kiss, but the first one we'd shared in any privacy in far too long. In that moment, our exhaustion and worry didn't hold us back; we were together again, alone again, remembering everything we'd given up to be together—and reveling in it. His arms wrapped tightly around me as he leaned me backward. The whole world felt off balance except him. If I held on to him, I'd never go wrong.

Lucas is mine, I thought. *Mine. Nobody can take this away from me.*

By the time we reached New York, it was nighttime. When we first saw the Manhattan skyline in the distance, we all whooped and cheered. It looked pretty spectacular. To me, New York was almost more like a mythological place than a real one—it was where all the movies and TV shows happened, and the street names we were supposed to look for as we drove had a magical ring to them: *42nd Street. Broadway.*

Then it occurred to me that Manhattan is an island, and I shivered at the thought of having to cross a river again. But instead we drove in through a tunnel, which was fine. For some reason, going beneath the water made a difference. I wished I'd asked my parents why.

We came out of the tunnel practically right in Times Square, which glittered and shone so much that I was dazzled. The others laughed at me, but I could tell they were kind of caught up in the excitement, too.

But it turned out that after a few dozen blocks, Broadway wasn't so ritzy any longer. The bright lights dimmed, and we drove past apartment building after apartment building, stacks of them looming up around us like walls. The stores changed from posh cosmetics boutiques or family restaurants to 99-cent stores and fast-food joints.

Finally, the caravan turned into a parking garage, one that posted its incredibly expensive prices outside. The attendant waved us through, so we didn't have to pay. The garage was definitely dirty and out of the way, so its rates were far too high—and sure enough, no other cars seemed to be parked inside.

I glanced at Lucas, who said, "Welcome to New York's HQ."

Everyone climbed out of the vans and trucks sort of sluggishly; we hadn't stopped to stretch our legs on the trip, just a couple of very brief gasoline-and-bathroom breaks after lunch. We were herded into an enormous industrial elevator, which sank downward. The elevator's walls were dull, scratched steel, and the light overhead flickered fitfully.

Feeling nervous, I took Lucas's hand. He squeezed my fingers between his. "This part is going to be okay," he said. "I promise."

It's not forever, I reminded myself. *This is just until Lucas and I have a chance to make some plans. Soon we'll be off on our own, and everything will be all right again.*

The elevator doors opened to reveal a cavern, and I gasped. The high, curved ceiling was illuminated by strings of those plastic-encased lights construction guys use at worksites. Voices echoed throughout the arched space. I blinked as I made out the silhouettes of people farther away from us. They all seemed to be in a sort of trench that ran throughout the cave—

My eyes adjusted to the gloom, and I realized that this wasn't a cavern. We were in a subway tunnel.

This tunnel had to have been abandoned for a long time. Flooring of planks or slabs of concrete sat over where the tracks must have been, and I could see a few small footbridges that connected the two platforms on either side of the tunnel.

A cracked tile sign on one wall read, in old-fashioned type, *Sherman Ave.*

At first I was so amazed by our new hideout that I didn't notice how quiet the rest of the group had become. All of them were standing still, saying nothing. I wasn't the only one unsure of my welcome, apparently.

A trim Asian woman, a few years older than Kate, walked up to us with two brawny guys—I wanted to call them *guards*—on either side. Her salt-and-pepper hair was pulled tightly back into a long braid, and every muscle in her arms and legs was cut. "Kate," she said. "Eduardo. You guys made it, I see."

"Some greeting," Eduardo said. "Is everybody else too busy to say hello?"

"Everyone's too busy to hear your excuse for that ridiculous raid on Evernight," she snapped. I realized that the people milling about in the distance were deliberately ignoring us.

Eduardo's eyes blazed. "We had word that the human students were in immediate danger."

"You had one vampire's word against two centuries of experience that says the Evernight vampires don't kill while they're there. And you used that as an excuse to lead an attack that could've cost the lives of as many kids as vampires. The only reason it didn't is because you got lucky."

Kate looked like she wanted to defend her husband, but she said only, "For those who haven't met her, this is Eliza Pang. She runs this cell, and she's welcomed us for a short stay."

We're here on charity, I realized. I didn't much care—this wasn't something I'd chosen, or anything I was going to have to deal with for long—but I knew Lucas would hate that. Sure enough, he had clenched his jaw and was staring stonily at the concrete beneath his feet. I wondered if he hated it more for his or his mother's sake. We'd have to talk about it later.

No sooner had I thought that than Eliza said, "Eduardo said you had two new recruits. Who are they?"

Raquel stepped forward right away. "Raquel Vargas. I'm from Boston. Anything you guys can teach me, I want to learn."

"Good." Eliza didn't smile, exactly—already I found it hard to imagine her ever smiling—but she seemed pleased. "Who else?"

I didn't want to step forward, but there wasn't really any way around it. "Bianca Olivier. I'm from Arrowwood, Massachusetts. I—um—" What was I supposed to say? "Thanks for having us."

"You're the one Kate told us about," Eliza said. "The one who was raised by vampires."

Great. "That's me."

"I bet we can learn a lot from you." Eliza clapped her hands together. "Okay, the rest of you guys, we've set up bunks at the far end of the track. They'll do for now. Newbies, follow me."

Follow her where? I shot Lucas a worried glance, but he obviously didn't know any more about it than I did. When Eliza stalked off, Raquel went with her, and I didn't have much choice but to go along.

"Are we starting our training already?" Raquel said, as the

three of us walked farther along the subway platform.

"Eager, aren't you?" From the sound of her voice, Eliza apparently didn't think Raquel would be so eager once she saw what was in store. "Nah, you've had a big day. You can start in the morning."

We got to the end of the platform, and Eliza led us into what had obviously been a service corridor. It smelled of mud and rust, and I could hear water dripping in the distance. A small yellow sign informed me this place could serve as a nuclear fallout shelter. Good to know.

I asked, "So where are we going? Why aren't we with the others?"

"We have some permanent cabins set up in here. They're not luxurious, but they beat the hell out of the bunks the rest of your cell is taking. You'll be living with us, twenty-four/seven."

"Why do we get those?" I nearly stumbled over the broken, uneven cement beneath us, but Raquel caught my elbow. "Why aren't those for Kate and Eduardo?" I wondered if it was because Eduardo was in the doghouse and their shoddy housing was punishment. It was unfair to punish Lucas, Dana, and the others for Eduardo's mistake.

Instead, Eliza said, "You guys are new to the routine. You don't know the life, and we don't know you. Living in close quarters is a good way to make sure you learn all about us, and we learn all about you."

Finding opportunities to drink blood would be even harder

in this environment. If I didn't drink blood often enough, I'd react more strongly to sunlight, to running water, to churches— and every reaction had the potential to mark me as a vampire.

How was I supposed to keep my secret?

Chapter Four

THAT NIGHT AFTER LIGHTS OUT, RAQUEL WHIS-pered, "The more things change, the more they stay the same, huh?"

I knew what she meant. A week ago, she and I had been roommates at Evernight Academy. Now everything else in our life had been transformed, but we were still sleeping in beds that were side by side. And I guess this counted as a bed.

We'd been given a room like no other I had ever seen. Apparently, when the engineers had abandoned this subway tunnel, they'd also abandoned a few old train cars. The Black Cross cell had refitted those to serve as cabins. Our bunks sat on top of what had once been the seats, and steel poles ran from the floor to the ceiling, like we were at stripper boot camp or something. Raquel and I had about a third of a car to ourselves, with a makeshift metal wall to give us privacy on one end and the back of the car on the other.

"I miss having your collages on the walls," I said. The windows on the sides of the car had been whitewashed, but they were blank and cold. "And my telescope. And our books and our clothes—"

"That's just stuff." Raquel propped herself up on one elbow. Her short dark hair stuck out in all directions, and if I'd been feeling any less forlorn, I might've teased her about it. "What matters is that we're finally doing something important. Vampires have screwed up both our lives, and ghosts—I'm not even going there. Now we can strike back. That's worth the sacrifice."

I knew I didn't dare trust Raquel with the truth, but I wanted her to understand a little of what I was really feeling. In a small voice, I said, "My parents took good care of me."

Raquel said nothing. I'd caught her off guard, and I could tell she didn't know what to think.

"And Balthazar—he was kind to me. To both of us." I thought that might help convince her.

Instead, she sat up straight, energized by anger so immediate that it shocked me. "Listen, Bianca. I won't pretend to understand what you've been through. I thought I'd had it rough, but finding out the people you thought were your parents were really vampires—that's the worst."

I had to let her go on believing that, so I remained silent.

She continued, "They kind of brainwashed you, okay? You're going to keep making excuses for them for a long time. But the fact is, they screwed you over. Balthazar played their mind games right along with the rest of them. So wake up. Get your head straight. We aren't kids anymore. We discovered that there's a war on, and our place is here with the soldiers."

Raquel was so absolute. So sure. I could only nod mutely.

"Okay," she said. When she burrowed under her blanket, I figured our conversation was over for the night. It's not like there was anything else I could share with her anyway. Then, very softly, she added, "I'll make us a collage sometime soon."

I smiled and hugged my pillow. "Something pretty. This place could use some pretty."

"I was thinking more fearsome and wicked," she said. "We'll see."

During the next couple of weeks, every day seemed to be exactly like the one before it and the next to come.

Lights came on at some crazy early hour of the morning. I didn't know what time it was exactly, because we didn't have clocks or cell phones. But I could tell from the way my whole body protested that it was too early for me.

Everybody got ready superfast. Basically, I hardly had time to do more than rinse myself off in the showers. And these were communal showers, too—like my worst gym class nightmare— but everybody was so businesslike and quick that I didn't have much chance to feel self-conscious. Then we changed into our workout clothes and headed to their makeshift exercise area.

And stayed there. For hours.

Not everybody had to stay put, of course. The Black Cross people from New York, whose names were hardly more than a blur (*ZackElenaReneeHawkinsAnjuliNathan*), trained in the mornings, then set out on patrols after the night shift came in. They had maps of New York City up in the patrol area, with different routes marked out. Somebody was watching virtually every neighborhood of the city day and night. I knew that Lucas, Dana, and the others from our group were sometimes on those patrols, but not me and Raquel. No, we were expected to become fighters or die trying.

Me, I might've been happy to die trying. Dying seemed easier than trying to do a chin-up, much less five of them like they wanted.

"Come on, Olivier." My trainer for the day, a red-haired woman named Colleen, held my feet as I struggled through my sit-ups. "Go for sixty."

"Sixty?" My face was flushed, and I felt like I might vomit at any second. I'd just done forty. "I can't."

"You can't until you can. Push for it."

Sure enough, within a couple weeks, I could do sixty, though the last ten felt like raging hot death. Sadly I was still way short of having six-pack abs, which I felt like I was entitled to.

Other times, we were on the climbing wall, which was scary as hell—no, it wasn't a cliff, but you could fall five or six feet, and that would definitely hurt. Or we ran—not laps, because there wasn't a track—but up and down the long path they'd created on the old railway line. That I was better at, because I could get in the groove, shut down my worries, and sort of tap into the vampire side of myself—the unearthly strength and power that lurked down deep inside. I didn't run super-fast, because I didn't want them to ask themselves how I could do that, but I could go and keep going, and that was usually enough to keep my trainer off my back.

This wasn't just fitness camp. That I could've dealt with. Only mornings were for exercise. Afternoons were for something else.

Afternoons were about learning to kill vampires.

"The stake paralyzes," Eliza said. She stood in the center of the room they called the sparring chamber, but I thought of as the Murder Zone. Raquel and I sat together near the front, while about ten others gathered around us. This kind of training apparently never stopped for the hunters. "You all know that. But a lot of hunters have been killed because they thought they'd staked a vampire, when all they'd done was get that vampire really mad. Tell me, Bianca, what did those hunters do wrong?"

I shrank, as if I could somehow duck the question. It didn't work—Eliza fixed me with her stare, and I had to reply. My voice sounded strange to me as I said, "They—they didn't pierce the heart."

"Exactly. If you want to hit the heart, you have to know the right angle. Miss by a millimeter, the vampire is fine—and you're dead."

The other way, the vampire's dead, I thought.

I wasn't the naive girl I'd been a couple years ago, before Lucas entered my life. I no longer believed that all vampires refrained from killing humans, the way my parents and Balthazar did. Since meeting Charity, and seeing Mrs. Bethany in action, I'd been forced to learn that many vampires were deadly, even uncontrollable. That was part of why I'd decided never to make that first kill and become a full vampire.

But some vampires didn't cause any trouble for humans. A lot of them, actually. They just wanted to be left alone.

Lucas had learned that truth; I trusted him not to fight any vampire who didn't need to be fought. The rest of the people in this room believed that all vampires were pure evil and would kill them on sight—no questions asked.

Not that Black Cross hunters didn't know anything about vampires, because they understood a lot, so much that it shocked me. They not only knew about Evernight Academy but also about other vampire sanctuaries around the globe. They knew about our sensitivity to churches and consecrated ground of any faith. They even knew some facts that many vampires believed to be legend—for instance, that holy water burned us. (Most vampires who had been doused with holy water were just fine, but it turned out that was only because most holy men weren't committed enough to their god to transform the water. Black Cross had found true believers, who could make true holy water that seared vampire skin like acid.)

But for every fact Black Cross had, there was another bit of misinformation. They thought all vampires were evil. They believed that all vampires belonged to violent, marauding tribes; although tribes were real, only a small minority of vampires ever joined one. They thought our consciences died along with our bodies. So they had no problems with the idea of killing us. It was beyond strange to watch them practicing: stabbing the dummies with the stakes at different angles, with different holds.

What was even weirder was practicing the moves myself.

I tried imagining that my assailant was Charity—that she was attacking Lucas again, and I was the only one who could stop her—and then I could shove the stake straight into the target, earning a puff of sawdust and applause from the other hunters. That didn't make it any less creepy.

The best part of the day was the evenings right before night patrol set out, because that was when I learned about loading and repairing weapons—and was the only time I was able to spend with Lucas.

"It's like we're prisoners," I whispered as he showed me how to reload a crossbow. "Do you get out?"

"Only on patrol." Lucas handed me the crossbow, so I could try for myself. After a quick glance around the room to make sure nobody was listening, he said, "Are you okay for—well, for food?"

"I could use a big meal—seriously use one—but I'm hanging on."

"How?"

I sighed. "They let us hang out on the rooftop of the parking garage sometimes, for breaks. Most days I can grab a couple minutes alone."

Lucas didn't get it. "And?"

"All I'm going to say is that there are tons of pigeons in New York, and they're not very fast. Okay?"

He grimaced, but in a way that made a joke of his disgust, and I giggled. The laugh echoed back from the curved ceiling of the tunnel. Lucas's expression softened. "There's that smile.

God, have I missed seeing you happy."

"I just miss you." I put one hand over his, so that they were both folded over the crossbow. "I see even less of you than I did when we were forbidden to be together. How long do we have to put up with this?"

"I'm working on it, I promise. Coming by the money is hard, but I've set aside a little over the past few months. Not enough to get us started, but I'm close. Once I pay my dues and get more free time, I can pick up some work around town. Odd jobs for cash under the table."

"What does that mean, cash under the table?"

"It means they pay less than minimum wage, but in return, neither you nor the boss reports it on your taxes."

That would be hard work, then. Dirty work, like hauling boxes or garbage. I hated that Lucas had to do that—but I kind of loved that he *would* do that for us.

"This doesn't look much like practice to me," Kate said, strolling in our direction.

"Give us a break, Mom," Lucas said. "Bianca and I hardly get to talk anymore."

"I know it's hard." Her voice sounded softer than I'd heard it before. "When your father and I first met, it was in the New Orleans cell. They were such tight-asses they made this place look like a free-for-all. If I saw him five minutes a day, that was a good day."

Lucas was very still. I knew that Kate didn't talk about his real father much. With barely concealed eagerness, he asked,

"So you guys—you went on patrol together sometimes?"

"Sometimes." Kate half turned from us, stern again, and the moment seemed to have passed too soon. "Eliza says you're shaping up, Bianca. How about you join us on patrol soon?"

"Really?" Lucas looked psyched, because we'd finally have a few minutes to be alone. I wanted to be as excited as he was—I missed him so much most nights I felt crazed—but the thought of joining a vampire-hunting patrol scared me.

Kate didn't notice our reactions. She simply said, "How about tomorrow?"

"Tomorrow," Lucas repeated.

I hugged him quickly, but I didn't shut my eyes. Instead I watched the hunters around us, sharpening their knives.

It wasn't like I didn't have any way out of it. I could've claimed I had a headache or felt nauseated or something like that. But I needed fresh blood, and, even more than that, I needed to spend some time with Lucas.

So that meant I pretty much had to begin my career as the world's first-and-only vampire vampire hunter.

Eliza said our first time out should be a standard patrol, someplace all the regulars already knew by heart. Given my movie-based knowledge of New York, which owed a lot to romantic comedies, our patrol location made no sense to me. "Vampires in Central Park? The place with all the carriage rides?"

Lucas smiled a little. "It's a bigger place than you think. And the farther north you go, the wilder it gets."

We got off our transport (a repurposed tour bus) and spread out in the park. The summer night felt warm, but comfortably so, a slight breeze stirring the air like a sigh. I looked up hopefully for a glimpse of the stars, but the city lights completely obliterated them.

"I'm with Bianca," Lucas said as everyone started to scatter.

Eduardo frowned. "This is not an excuse for you two to sneak off."

For once, Eliza and Eduardo seemed to be on the same page. "Is this going to be a problem with you two?"

Lucas's temper flared, making his eyes blaze. "If you think I'd distract Bianca while we're in a known vampire hunting zone, you're crazy. I wouldn't put her in danger. Period."

Kate cut in, "Let them go. Come, we need to move—it's getting late."

Raquel gave me an excited wave as she and Dana headed south, disappearing into the park. The rest of the team mostly headed in that direction, too, but Lucas and I remained just within the park.

We stood quietly, using our enhanced hearing to judge how far away everyone else was and when we were really and truly alone. Then we looked at each other, and the rush of exhilaration hit me. These were the moments I hung on for, the ones that made all the hard work and loneliness worthwhile.

Lucas embraced me as he kissed my hair, then my forehead,

then my lips. His warm scent made me feel as if we weren't in a park but in the center of a vast forest, as alone as if we were the only people in the world. I opened my mouth beneath his, eager to deepen the kiss, but he pulled back. "Hey. What I said to Eduardo and Eliza—I wasn't kidding. We can't afford to get distracted around here."

I breathed out in frustration. "Are we *ever* going to 'get distracted' again?"

"God, I hope so."

A smile tugged at the corners of my mouth. "Because I could really, really use some distraction around now."

Lucas's hands tightened around my shoulders, and he got this incredible look on his face, like he could eat me up that second. I knew the danger was real, but that only intensified the thrill.

His voice rough, he said, "Soon." Then he let go of me, jaw clenched, like he had to force himself to do it.

Sighing, I took a few steps back. I was more elated than let down; as badly as I missed being alone with Lucas, we'd been forced to learn a lot of self-control. Seeing how much he wanted me was exhilaration enough.

Well, not quite. But close.

"So, how do we start looking for vampires?" I asked. I could hear that there were others in the park, not all that far from us, but the footsteps sounded normal. Were we waiting for a scream?

Lucas pulled out one of his stakes, but lazily, and he simply turned it around in his hand. "This is a place where new vampires come to hunt. People who come to the park long after dark—especially up here, this far from the carriage rides or the zoo or the track—usually do it for stupid reasons."

"What do you mean, stupid?"

"Drug dealers. Prostitutes. Guys getting drunk. Or people trying to rob all of the above." Lucas shrugged. "Occasionally it's more innocent than that. It might be some homeless man looking for a place to lay his head or a couple on a stroll. Or a guy who thinks he can save on cab fare by cutting through the park. Regardless, they all make pretty easy pickings for blood-suckers."

I looked up at the ring of tall buildings around the park, like a ring of light that seemed to hover above the border of trees. It was weird to think that there could be a vampire hunting ground in the middle of so much activity and noise. "So why is it only new vampires who come here?"

"Because the ones with any experience know Black Cross will be on patrol."

That made sense. "So how do we start?"

"We follow the humans." Lucas started walking along the edge of the park, his eyes scanning the horizon. "Keep 'em safe. See if anybody of the undead persuasion takes an interest."

Any vampires we find here really will be trying to attack people, I thought uncomfortably. There wouldn't be much chance for me to warn the innocent, or much reason either.

I wished I could've talked to my parents about all this. Really talked, not the half-truths we'd too often told each other. Their lies still hurt me deeply, but I couldn't be as angry with them any longer. I missed them too much.

Then an idea hit me, sudden and—in my opinion—brilliant.

At first I opened my mouth to blurt it out to Lucas; I felt certain he would approve. But I also knew that what I was about to suggest was against the rules. Better not to make Lucas break his promises. I'd take this responsibility myself. Luckily, I had a few bucks on hand, not much, but enough for what I needed to do.

Casually, I said, "I'm hungry."

"Oh. Okay." Lucas looked uncertain. "Well, I guess there's squirrels and stuff around here."

"Yeah." I honestly did need more blood than I'd been getting, and my mouth watered a bit at the thought of it. But that was secondary to what I really had on my mind. "I'll just grab something, I guess. If it's okay for me to leave you for a second—"

"We're gonna be on patrol until about two A.M.," Lucas said. "We can take quick breaks if we have to."

"Be right back."

On tiptoe, I kissed his cheek, then walked away. Once I knew I was out of sight, I left the park and walked into the city itself. The crush of traffic—honking horns and car alarms—was slightly overwhelming, but I had a mission. I'd thought I might not be able to find what I sought, but New York was a city big enough to supply any need. Sure enough, within a couple of blocks, I saw the sign I was looking for: INTERNET CAFÉ.

Once I was inside, I signed into my e-mail account. The dozens of boldface new messages at the top of the screen startled me, and the names of the senders seemed to lash me, one by one: Dad. Mom. Vic. Balthazar. Ranulf, who had apparently figured out enough about modern life to get a gmail account. Even Patrice, my sophomore-year roommate, the one I thought didn't care about anybody but herself, had reached out to check on me.

If I began reading those e-mails, I knew I'd start to cry. Instead I opened up a new message, addressing it to my parents at their Evernight Academy account, the only one they had.

Mom and Dad,
I'm sorry it took me so long to get in touch with
you. This is honestly the first chance I've had to
tell you that I'm okay. I know my running off like
that had to scare you, and I wish there had been
another way.

Had there been another way? Could I have chosen something else? I didn't know anymore.

I'm with Lucas. The people in Black Cross don't
know the truth about me, so I'm safe for now. Soon
we'll leave and set out on our own. He loves me

and will take care of me no matter what.

I know things weren't right with us before we left. For however much of that was my fault, I'm sorry. And if we could talk sometime soon— really talk, without more lies and secrets—I'd be so happy. I miss you guys more than I ever knew I could.

Now I was in danger of crying anyway. Blinking fast, I concluded:

Please let Balthazar and Patrice know that I'm all right. I'll write again sometime soon.

I love you both.

That wasn't all that needed to be said, not by a long shot, but I knew this wasn't the time to say it.

Blinking fast, I hit Send.

After I logged out and left, I wanted to run straight to Lucas's arms. Instead, I decided to grab a couple of pigeons first. In the darkness of the park, nobody would see me.

Besides, I thought, *you have one advantage. You'll be the only vampire there who knows where all the hunters are.*

It wasn't that comforting.

But the night passed without incident. Other hunters kept

coming by to check on Lucas and me, so we didn't get much privacy; that was disappointing. Still, I'd finally had plenty to eat, so I felt more reassured as we went back to HQ at three in the morning, exhausted despite not having seen another vampire the whole time. But as soon as we walked in, we learned that the Black Cross cell was on alert.

"That's not lockdown, is it?" I asked Lucas.

"No, but they'll be watching us." He clasped my hand as we walked deeper into the tunnel. Everyone seemed to be awake, and the lights remained on. The lieutenants on watch that night were talking animatedly to Eliza, who didn't look thrilled.

"What is it?" Raquel asked, nervously fiddling with the tawny leather bracelet she always wore. "Did something go wrong with our hunt?"

"Five boring hours in the park? That's not the crisis." Dana's eyes were narrow as she studied the uneasy crowd. She had a crossbow slung over one shoulder, and she rubbed Raquel's back absently, trying to settle her down. "Sure would like to know what it is."

Eliza overheard our whispers and turned toward us. Traffic overhead made the ceiling shiver a bit, and the strings of lights swayed back and forth, casting her lined face in shadow, then in light. "We might have vampires staking this place out."

Raquel brightened—like that was good news, not reason to freak. "You think they're going to try to come down here and take us on?"

"They wouldn't dare," Eliza replied, with a proud toss of her braid. "But somebody might be watching."

Mrs. Bethany, I thought with a shiver. She would get revenge for the damage to Evernight Academy if there were any way possible. "Why do you think that?"

"We keep finding dead birds near the building. Like something's killing them. At first we were making jokes about bird flu, but today Milos checked out the corpses, and sure enough, they'd been drained of blood. We've got a vamp around here, and we'll all be watching the roof and the nearby area to get a glimpse of our visitor. Then we'll ask a few questions of our own."

Lucas and I shared a glance. No vampires were watching the HQ; I had left the birds. Why hadn't I thrown them away more carefully? I had tried, but there hadn't been many options.

From this moment on, my blood supply was cut off—and that meant our time to plan our escape was running out.

Chapter Five

THAT NIGHT, AS I TRIED TO GO TO SLEEP, I KEPT telling myself, *You have five days. You were able to last that long without blood when you first left Evernight Academy. That means you can last that long again.*

Besides, Black Cross has put me on patrols. I'll be able to get out, nearly every day, and surely I'll have chances to eat then. Everything will be okay.

I couldn't have been more wrong.

First of all, my hunger for blood had grown. I'd spent only a month in Black Cross, but my body was continuing to change. The vampire inside me was growing stronger as the human grew weaker.

After I had drunk Lucas's blood for the first time, my mother had warned me: *You've turned over the hourglass.* What she meant was that my vampire nature had been awakened by the taste of living human blood. Where, before, I'd been a mostly normal teenage girl—albeit one who drank a glass of O positive with her dinner—I wasn't so normal anymore.

My hearing had become so acute that I could hear people whispering several car cabins down from mine and Raquel's. My skin had become so pale that a couple of people had remarked on it, though mostly jokingly, like Dana saying that this was what happened when white people tried to live underground. Occasionally the Black Cross patrols crossed the East River bridges to guard areas in Brooklyn or Queens; the mere thought of crossing running water made me nauseated. I felt grateful that the makeshift bathroom in Black Cross headquarters had no mirror, because I suspected my reflection was beginning to fade.

My parents had warned me what happened to vampires who didn't drink blood. Their appearances continued to change, warping until they looked like the monsters of legend: white, bony creatures whose fingernails jutted out almost like claws. Their hair fell out. Constant hunger caused their fangs to show at all times. Worst of all was the madness; when vampires truly hit the point of blood starvation, their minds went. Instead of behaving more or less like human beings, they became like wild animals, immune to conscience or restraint. Even a good vampire could become a killer if deprived of blood for that long.

Yeah, this is how your parents get you to clean your plate when you're a baby vampire. The old stories were definitely scary enough to get me to drink my whole glass of O positive back in the day. Now that childhood horror had returned as I wondered every day, *Can that happen to me, even though I'm not a full vampire yet? How am I different? How am I the same? How am I supposed to go on, not knowing?*

Even while out on the Black Cross patrols I didn't have a chance to eat. Time and again, I was partnered with people other than Lucas; night after night, we went to locations that offered me no chance to hunt for food. I was never forced to see a vampire being murdered, which was a small mercy, but by this time I was hungry enough to become selfish. I only wanted to drink, and I couldn't.

Within five days I was desperate. That was the night Lucas and I finally got to patrol together again.

"We have got to come back here once we get some free time again," Dana said as our group began patrol. The June heat radiated up from the streets, even though it was twilight; sweat beaded the small of my back. "Because this looks like a good place to party."

All around us were nightclubs and bars—some of which looked seedy to me, while the others looked sleek and expensive. There didn't seem to be much middle ground. "I think I'd get carded."

"Slap some makeup on you and Raquel, and y'all would be set," Dana insisted. "Hey, are you all right?"

"Just tired. They had me do the climbing wall twice today."

Dana thumped my shoulder. "They're making you tough."

Lucas glanced at our leader for the night—it was Milos, one of Eliza's lieutenants, a rangy guy with white-blond hair and beard. He said to Milos, "I'd like to take Bianca along the east side of our zone. Okay?"

Please say yes, please say yes. Lucas can help me get something to eat, I know he can—

"Suit yourselves," Milos said. His smile had a knowing quality—almost a smirk—but I didn't care. Let him think we were sneaking off to make out. I only wished we had that kind of luxury.

Some of the others murmured and giggled, but nobody stopped us as I took Lucas's hand and we walked together into the dark.

As soon as we were alone, Lucas said, "You look like hell."

"Maybe I ought to be mad at you for saying that, but I know you're right." He was towing me along the sidewalk, beneath a few small trees that had been planted in open squares in the pavement. From the apartments around us, I could hear snatches of salsa music at different tempos, like competing heartbeats. "I have to get something to eat. It's making me crazy."

"There's a hospital not far from the HQ. I was thinking I could break into the blood bank, almost like we did last year, remember?"

It was a good idea for the future, but I needed a faster solution. "Lucas, I can't wait any longer. I mean it. I have to have blood tonight."

He stopped, and for a few seconds we simply stared at each other on the sidewalk. Sweat marked the collar of his white T-shirt, and his bronze hair had darkened to the color of night. His thumb brushed my cheek. I was startled by how much warmer his flesh was than mine.

Haltingly, Lucas said, "I'm going to take care of you."

"I know you will." My trust in him was absolute. "But how? Is there a place around here we could hunt?"

"Come on."

Faster, driven by purpose, Lucas towed me along the sidewalk. After a couple of blocks, the neighborhood quieted down a little—we were far from any of the main streets now, closer to the water.

We reached a storefront with windows newspapered over from the inside, and signs that read FOR RENT. Lucas stopped there. "I'm guessing this is bone empty," he said, pulling a thin metal lock pick from his jeans pocket. "Which means there's probably no alarm system activated either."

"Why are we breaking in?"

"Privacy."

Lucas jimmied the lock in about four seconds flat. I remembered my own feeble attempt at burglary, almost a year ago, and envied him his sure touch.

We ducked into the store, and Lucas immediately shut the door behind us. Streetlights shone through the newsprint, casting a muted golden light. The hardwood floors beneath us were old and unpolished, and an abandoned bar lined one wall. A mottled mirror hung behind the bar, and I stood in front of it to see myself. I was only a shadow—a pale silvery outline of myself. Like a ghost.

This is how Patrice used to look when she wouldn't drink blood for a while, I thought. *I never believed this could happen to me.*

Why didn't I understand what it meant to be a vampire?

"Okay," Lucas said. He seemed nervous. "We're alone."

I smiled at him, though I felt sad. "I wish we could do something with this chance besides feed me," I said. His kisses were so far away; they were a memory almost too beautiful to belong to my real life any longer. "What are we going to do? Do you have a plan?"

"Yeah. You're going to drink from me."

At first I couldn't believe I'd heard him correctly. Of course, I had drunk Lucas's blood before—twice, so far. Both times, the experience had been intense, to say the least. Drinking blood was sensual, even sexual. I'd only ever drunk the blood of one other guy, Balthazar, and that was the closest I'd ever come to making love. But what happened between Balthazar and me was purely physical. With Lucas, the emotion made it more powerful.

So I should've leaped at the chance, right? Wrong.

Before, when this had happened between us, I'd been well fed. My loss of control with Lucas had been because of my passion for him, not because of hunger. The same love that drove me to bite him had also compelled me to stop before I hurt him. Now that I was governed by this wild craving, the one that clawed at me from within—I wasn't so sure I could stop.

"It's dangerous," I said. "We should try another way."

"There isn't any other way." Lucas slowly lifted up the edge of his T-shirt and peeled it off. I knew he did that because he didn't want to get blood on his clothes, but the nearness of his half-undressed body hit me like a blow. The golden light behind us outlined his firm, muscled form. "I trust you."

"Lucas—"

"Come on." He stepped closer to me. "This is the only way I have to take care of you. Let me take care of you."

I shook my head. "You don't understand. It's different now. I'm so much hungrier."

"You only bite me when you're not hungry?"

I remembered the two times I'd fed from him—once, after the Autumn Ball, when we'd been kissing passionately for the first time, and again when we were alone together in one of the high towers of Evernight, lying in each other's arms. "That was different."

"Doesn't have to be." He took me in his arms and kissed me.

It wasn't like any of our other kisses. This was rougher, almost demanding. Lucas opened my lips with his and pulled my body against him. I couldn't push him away; I couldn't think, couldn't move, couldn't do anything but kiss him back. I'd missed this so much—the taste of his mouth, the scent of his skin, and the feel of his broad hands.

When he moved down to my throat, kissing me along the line of my jugular, I whispered, "You're going to make me lose control."

"That's the whole idea."

"Lucas—don't—"

"If you have to get carried away to bite me, then I'm gonna make you get carried away." His hand cupped the curve of my breast. "How far do I have to go?"

My instincts took over. I pulled him to the floor, the old wooden boards creaking gently beneath our weight. Lucas lay beneath me, pressing kisses on my forehead and cheeks as I raked my hands through his hair and breathed in the scent of him. I could hear his heart beating faster. I could smell his blood. More animal than human, I arched my body against his, so that I could feel his warmth all over me.

"Come on, Bianca," he whispered into my ear. "Come on. I know you want to. I want you to."

Stop, stop, stop. I'll have to stop in time, I don't know if I can stop, I don't want him to let go of me, not ever, I don't want this to stop—"

I bit down on his shoulder, and blood rushed in.

Yes. This was what I had needed, what I had craved. I heard Lucas groan, and I didn't know if that was from pain or pleasure. My body quaked as I sucked in harder, swallowing mouthful after mouthful of his blood. It was hot and sweet, purer than anything else in the world. It was life. I could feel my body transforming, gaining strength, as Lucas's life flowed into me.

My hands pressed his against the floor, and our fingers intertwined. "Bianca," he whispered, his voice shaky.

I drank even deeper. This was perfection—hunger and satisfaction at once, inseparable. How could anyone want anything else?

"Bianca—"

Stop, stop, stop!

I pulled away just as Lucas's head lolled to one side. Shocked into sanity, I shifted off him and patted his cheek. "Lucas? Are you okay?"

"Just give me—a sec—"

"Lucas!"

He tried to prop himself up on one elbow but ended up flopping back down beside me. His breaths were coming too quickly, and his skin was now more pallid than mine. Of course, I had become rosy and flushed with the life I'd stolen from the guy I loved.

Guilt descended on me. "Oh, no. I should never have done this."

"Don't say that." His voice was slurred. "We had to—save you."

I sat up and pressed two fingers to his throat. His heartbeat was steady, if rapid. I hadn't gone too far, but I could have. I knew the danger even if he didn't.

"We can't do this again," I said, as I cradled his head in my lap. His shoulder oozed a few trickles of blood, but I resisted the urge to lick his skin. "We're going to find another solution, and soon. Right?"

"Wasn't too bad." Lucas's lopsided smile made my stomach flip-flop in the best possible way. "Kinda nice, actually."

There was a time when it would have thrilled me to hear him say that. But I knew more about Lucas now, and about his priorities, which meant that I was obligated to warn him: "Remember—if I ever go too far, I could kill you. And because you've been bitten by a vampire multiple times, you'd become a vampire yourself."

Lucas went very still. Although I, too, no longer wanted to become a full vampire, Lucas's revulsion to the idea was absolute. Death would have been preferable to him.

"Okay," he said at last. "I'll see about the hospital blood bank. Or something. But you're better, right?"

"Yeah." And now that I had drunk human blood, I felt sure I would be sustained for a while—but not forever. He had risked his life to buy me just a few days' time. Or did he have other reasons, too? Quietly, I asked, "Do you crave it now? Being bitten? Is this something you wanted for yourself?"

I wouldn't blame him if it were. Balthazar had drunk my blood a couple of months ago, and I remembered the exhilaration of it. But if Lucas was getting as hooked on my bite as I was on biting him, we were really going to have to work on the self-control.

Lucas thought over the question. "I don't know," he said at last. "Part of it—most of it—is about taking care of you. And then there's the fact that it's one hell of a turn-on."

Smiling, I brushed a last trickle of blood from his shoulder. "Yeah, there's that."

"Every time we do this, I get stronger." Lucas's eyes met mine. "I get closer to being—to being what you are. To understanding, maybe. Without having to turn into a vampire myself."

Each bite gave Lucas a little more vampire strength. His hearing had sharpened and his strength had increased—but he neither healed faster nor craved blood. The mystery of what it meant to be prepared for vampirism but not yet a vampire: That was one way in which we were truly and fully the same.

Well, not the *only* way.

I bent low and whispered, "I love you, Lucas."

"Love you, too." Tiredly he clasped my hand in his, and for a while we simply sat together, wordless, needing nobody else in the world.

Once Lucas felt reasonably steady and the bite mark on his shoulder had stopped bleeding, he put his T-shirt on again and we joined the others. We must have looked rumpled—a couple people snickered, and Dana waggled her eyebrows at us. I didn't care if they thought we'd sneaked off to have sex. What we felt for each other was too pure to be turned into anything tacky or cheap.

Besides, I felt better than I'd felt in weeks. Lucas seemed a little bleary, and his skin was definitely pale, but he could walk steadily. He put his arm around my shoulders for support initially, but kept it there all during our long ride home.

We'll be all right, I thought as he rested his head against mine. Taking a deep breath, I could smell the cedar scent of his skin, tinged slightly with the delicious saltiness of blood. *It's going to be okay soon.*

After we returned to HQ and stowed our gear, we walked in to see that someone was waiting for us—Eduardo, who leaned against one of the cement pillars. In his hands he held a coffee can. I didn't think anything of it, except that it was kind of weird to be making coffee so late at night. But the moment Lucas saw it, he stopped in his tracks. "That's mine," he said.

"You have an interesting definition of what's yours." Eduardo tossed the can upward, caught it lazily. The scars on his cheeks looked harsh in the overhead lights. "Because the way I see it, in Black Cross we have a rule. Everything we do is for the good of the group."

Eduardo then peeled back the plastic lid of the coffee can to reveal a roll of cash.

"Hoarding money," he said. "How is that for the good of the group?"

Oh, no, I thought. *Lucas's savings. The money he was going to use to get us out of here.*

"How is going through my private stuff for the good of the group?" Lucas's eyes blazed as he stalked up to Eduardo. As his voice got louder, it echoed off the concrete walls. "What, were you going to steal from me?"

Eduardo shook his head. "It's not stealing if it's not rightfully yours to begin with. And it isn't. Money like this should be used for Black Cross purposes. Not to—take your girlfriend out on Saturday nights."

"Since when do I ever get to take Bianca out? Since when do you guys let us spend more than ten minutes alone together?"

"Free time is something you don't have. You're a soldier, Lucas. Have you forgotten that?"

"Hey!" Kate came hurrying toward them, her hair wet from the shower and her blouse buttoned up wrong. Apparently somebody had come to fetch her to break it up. A small crowd had gathered—obviously interested but not taking sides. "What's going on?"

Lucas's fists were clenched at his sides. "Eduardo's stealing from me."

"Lucas is hoarding cash."

"You went through his stuff? Jesus, Eduardo." Kate snatched the coffee can of cash from him, and for the first time I saw Eduardo looking really embarrassed. "I don't expect you to be a father to Lucas, but I also don't expect you to act like his jealous kid brother."

"I'm not the one being immature here!"

"Yes, you are," Kate snapped back. "You know why? You're both acting like adolescent jackasses, but at least Lucas actually *is* an adolescent. Is it too much to ask for you to be the adult?"

"Thanks, Mom." Flushed with vindication, Lucas held out his hand to reclaim what was his.

Kate simply closed the lid. "We can't allow people to hoard money, Lucas. You know that."

"It's mine! We don't have to give up everything—we never have before—"

"I didn't say it wasn't yours." More quietly, Kate added, "If and when you need it, you come to me. If Black Cross can spare it at that time, I promise, I'll give it back to you. And I know you wouldn't want to spend it if Black Cross doesn't have cash to spare. Right?"

Lucas and I exchanged one despairing glance. There wasn't

anything else we could do or say. Already I knew that Black Cross wasn't like a job you could quit. It was more like a cult you had to flee.

And the money we needed to escape had just been stolen, which meant we were trapped.

Chapter Six

MAYBE IT WAS THE CRUSHING BLOW OF LOSING our saved money. Maybe it was the exhilaration of having been so close to Lucas after we'd been kept apart so long. Or maybe it was the rush of blood and the sweet relief of being full after weeks of hunger.

Whatever it was that distracted me so much that night kept me from remembering that drinking blood had consequences.

"Bianca?"

Raquel flipped on the small flashlight she kept beside her bed. The beam seemed almost unbearably brilliant, and I rolled away from her. "Turn that thing off, would you?"

"Were you having a bad dream or something? You kept groaning."

"It wasn't a nightmare exactly—just kind of overwhelming, you know?" Luckily, Raquel didn't pry further, and I had a moment to myself to think.

The real reason I'd been groaning was because I was in

complete sensory overload. I could hear every footstep or cough along the belt of old subway cars the Black Cross hunters slept in. I could hear water dripping farther down the tunnel and the light, quick scurrying of mice.

I'll have to remember where to find them later, if I need them—

"Bianca?"

"I wasn't having a bad dream," I mumbled, bringing my forearm over my eyes to block out the light. In the long run, drinking blood made me more able to deal with bright light or sunshine. But just after, it seemed almost blindingly bright. "These bunks are really uncomfortable, you know?" I could feel the plastic ridges of the old seats against my back, even through the pallet I lay on.

Any criticism of Black Cross was usually Raquel's cue to insist that everything was totally great. This time, she simply sighed. "It would be nice to have a real bed again. Dana and I were saying, maybe, we could save up and get a hotel room sometime—oh. That's what you and Lucas were trying to do, wasn't it?"

"Basically." That was close enough to the truth.

"I'm sorry Eduardo got up in Lucas's stuff. That was really unfair."

"Lucas worked so hard for that money."

"It sucks." Raquel sighed.

I was grateful for proof that Raquel hadn't chugged the Black Cross Kool-Aid, but mostly I longed for darkness and quiet. "I just want to go back to sleep and forget about it for a while."

"No point now." The flashlight stayed on; I could tell, just by the faint glow around the edges of my vision, even through my closed eyelids and the forearm across my face. "They'll turn the lights on soon. It's morning."

I groaned again.

If drinking blood again had affected me powerfully, that was nothing compared to what it had done to Lucas.

"Stop sulking," Kate said to him as we loaded the transport bus for our afternoon patrol later that day. "Or do you want to argue some more about hoarding cash?"

"I'm not sulking." Lucas winced as he spoke. The light in the parking garage was dim, but it hurt my eyes—and, I could tell, his, too. "I just don't feel so hot."

At first Kate looked skeptical, but then she held her palm to his forehead. The heavy men's sport watch she wore made her wrist look almost fragile. She frowned. "You feel a little clammy. Is your stomach bothering you?"

"Sorta."

I sought Lucas's eyes; when our gazes met, he gave me a small, awkward smile. Obviously we were both thinking the same thing: *We should have expected this.*

Human bodies simply weren't meant to endure the demands of vampire power.

Kate paused for a few long seconds, and I wondered if she'd tell him to go on patrol regardless. Most of the time, she acted more like his commander than his mother. But then she shrugged. "Head back to the bunks. Get some rest. Bianca, you go out with Milos's team. You and Raquel can partner up."

"Okay," Lucas said. Although I knew he would hate being stuck at headquarters for an entire day, I thought he sounded sort of happy. Maybe he didn't get much evidence that Kate really wanted to take care of him, and he liked what little he got.

We went out on patrol in one of the fancier neighborhoods in the city, where the lowest buildings were twenty stories high, and all the facades were cool steel or white stone. Doormen in uniforms stood every thirty feet or so along streets lined with the kind of expensive cars I'd seen Lucas admire in magazines. At first I thought this area seemed too secure to be a big vampire hangout—but then I realized that the elegant surroundings reminded me of the vampires of Evernight. This was the kind of existence those vampires tried to claim; maybe this was the kind of place they'd stake their turf.

"We used to have a base down here," Milos said as he strolled along the sidewalk with me and Raquel. He sounded almost friendly, which was more weird than encouraging. "Those were the days, man. We had a deal with a couple of the fancy restaurants in the area—they'd give us some of what they had left over at the end of the night. I almost got sick of shrimp bisque. I'd about kill my grandmother for rich food like that now."

"What happened?" Raquel said, squinting against the summer sunshine.

"Vampires blew our hideout." Milos's hand stole toward the

place on his belt where he'd tucked his stake. "Normally they don't come after our main cells—they don't have the troops. Tons of vampires out there, but they haven't got enough sense to work together."

That was offensive, and stupid, too. How had vampires managed to keep Evernight Academy going for more than two hundred years if we didn't have "enough sense" to cooperate toward longtime goals? The truth, I figured, probably had more to do with fighting among vampire groups. There was no one established vampire society, and that gave a tightly organized force like Black Cross an edge.

Raquel asked Milos, "What was different that time?"

"There was this one vampire—Stigand, he called himself— who got them riled up. Made them band together. That one was dangerous." A cold smile stole across Milos's face. He had a different attitude toward danger than most people. "He brought 'em in after us. Killed a lot of good fighters that day and totally ruined our old HQ. Eliza took him out, though—hit him with a spray of gasoline and the flamethrower." Chuckling, he added, "You should've heard him scream."

Nauseated, I turned my head away from Milos and Raquel. I didn't know whether I was hiding my disgust or keeping myself from seeing their pleasure in a vampire's death. At first I wasn't even looking at what was before my eyes, but then Black Cross training took over, forcing me to evaluate the scene and every person we passed.

Then quickly, I realized that I knew the man across the

street. I knew him from my dream the night before.

It came back to me now in more detail: I'd been with Lucas in a movie theater, the kind of dream that's half a memory—in this case, of our first date. But the theater wasn't rich and plush any longer. It was run-down and littered, the seat upholstery ripped and the screen empty of any image. I had been looking around wildly for Lucas, and instead I had seen this man, the one with the reddish-brown dreadlocks.

The wraith, floating next to me, had whispered, *The two of you have mutual friends.*

In the dream I hadn't known him. But I recognized him now.

"There," I whispered. "Is that—is he—?"

"You mean, a vampire?" Raquel peered at him with interest, as did Milos.

My heart sank. Had I just identified a vampire to the hunters? A vampire who was passing by without their notice? Had I just gotten him killed?

The dreadlocked vampire was in his element, though. He strolled beneath one building's dark-green canopy, nodded at the doorman, and went on in—safe at home.

I breathed out in relief, too loudly. Milos shot me a look. "You don't want to fight? You're with the wrong group."

"Give her a break," Raquel said. "It's still scary for us, okay? We'll get tough in time."

"Maybe you will at that." Milos kept staring at the apartment door. "We'll have to do a stakeout here sometime—no pun intended. For now we check the back alleys. See who else is roaming around here and not nearly ready to go home."

We continued searching the neighborhood, and to my immense relief, Raquel and I were able to split off from Milos. Raquel kept gushing on and on about how smart I was to spot a vampire like that, when he wasn't up to anything and didn't have any of the signs. It just made me feel like more of a traitor.

I cast around for something else to talk about and, almost at random, said, "Hey, where were you guys when we came back last night? You didn't respond to Eliza's call."

"Oh. Dana and I were . . ."

"Were what?"

Raquel paused. It wasn't like her to avoid a simple question. Ducking around a lady on the sidewalk who carried three big shopping bags in each hand, I repeated, "Were what?"

"We were off together on our own. Alone. So we'd have some—you know—some space."

I shrugged. What was the big deal?

Then I saw the hesitation on Raquel's face, and the hopeful light in her eyes, and I realized that I was just about the blindest person on the face of the earth. "You and Dana are—"

"Me and Dana." Raquel grinned, the brightest smile I'd ever seen on her face, just for a split second, like she couldn't hold it in any longer. But her uncertainty returned quickly. "That doesn't make you feel weird, does it?"

"Some," I confessed, "but only because you never said anything. After all the stuff we've told each other, you could've told me this."

"You never know who's going to be strange about it. Besides, you kept trying to fix me up with *guys*."

"I tried to fix you up with Vic. One guy. Not plural." My head was spinning a little. At least talking about her love life had distracted Raquel—and me. "I just never guessed."

Her lips twisted in a funny smile. "Hello? No interest in men, like, ever?"

"I didn't want to think in stereotypes."

"There's not thinking in stereotypes, and then there's just plain not thinking."

"Okay, if you wanted me to feel really stupid, mission accomplished."

We stared at each other for a second and then burst out laughing. I hugged her tightly around her shoulders and then listened to her go on for almost half an hour about how beautiful and incredible and smart and terrific Dana was. Although I completely agreed with Raquel about that, my input wasn't required. My job was to smile, nod, and be happy for her. It was easy enough to do.

Does Lucas know about this? I wondered. Probably he did, or at least suspected. He and Dana were pretty tight. This was just one of the dozens of subjects we hadn't had a chance to discuss.

We returned to Black Cross headquarters just before sundown, luckily without me betraying any other vampires to

Milos. As I changed out of my sweaty clothes, Raquel headed out, promising to get rations for both of us. I didn't really feel like eating anything, much less my seventh consecutive day of oatmeal, but I thanked her and let her go. Some alone time seemed like a good plan.

Once I'd changed clothes, I took a stroll along the tunnel. It was the first privacy I'd really had since the fall of Evernight; at every other point, I'd either had a job to do or people with me. The fathomless dark of the distant tunnel, past the strings of light Black Cross used, seemed as absolute a limit as any wall could ever be.

I saw that vampire in a dream, I thought. I had wondered before if my dreams were beginning to predict the future, but this was the surest proof I'd had yet. The vampire with the reddish dreadlocks had been revealed to me by the wraith.

After so long away from the hauntings at Evernight Academy, and after becoming used to the reassurance of the obsidian pendant around my neck, I'd managed to put aside some of my anxieties about the wraiths. But now, with the ghosts reaching into my mind and showing me the future, all that confusion and fear was coming back.

They were after me because I was, in some ways, as much the child of a ghost as of vampires. My parents had essentially bargained with the wraiths so that I could be born. Vampires on their own could never get pregnant; with the assistance of a ghost, it was possible. What my parents hadn't known at the time, and I hadn't learned until a few months ago, was that the wraiths considered themselves the rightful owners of any children born because of such bargains. I didn't know what that meant, really—though to judge by their attacks on me at Evernight, it meant they didn't want me to live as an ordinary vampire. Well, I agreed with them on that score. I'd left the school and my parents, and I remained convinced that I would never kill a human being and become a full vampire.

Apparently that wasn't enough for the wraiths. I wondered what else they would want. Would the ghosts keep intruding into my dreams? If they were still after me, why weren't they attacking me again? Were they only biding their time?

Then I realized I was worrying about something that would never happen—because I was walking alongside iron railroad tracks.

Iron! According to Balthazar, the wraiths were repelled by certain stones and metals. Obsidian, like my pendant, was one of them. The most powerful repellants of all were the metals found in the human body, like copper and iron. That meant that Black Cross headquarters was naturally, well, ghost-proofed.

Slightly relieved, I started to relax. It occurred to me that, now that I had a bit of alone time, I could maybe hunt for a few mice in the tunnels. Lucas's blood still warmed me, but I was in no hurry to be that hungry again.

That was when I heard the tapping.

Click, click, click, click.

I stared upward into the dark. Even my vampire-enhanced sight couldn't make out much more than a tangle of pipes and shadows. Once again—*click click click click*. The sound of metal on metal.

Maybe it's nothing.

Maybe it's not.

I ran back toward the subway-car cabins, looking for Raquel. Instead, I ran into Eliza, but that was even better. "Something's going on farther down the tunnel." I panted. "This weird knocking sound."

"Stuff sounds odd underground." Clearly it took a lot to rattle Eliza, and a couple of strange noises didn't come close. "Listen, I know you're freaked out right now, and no wonder. Just stay calm, okay?"

That's when I heard a tremendous roar—and the end of the tunnel caved in.

Concrete tumbled down, great blocks of it the size of rooms, and the air instantly choked thick with dust. Eliza grabbed me to tow me backward; the section of the roof above us remained solid, but how much longer would that be true? "Jesus!" she shouted. "Come on!"

We started running away from the falling debris, toward the crowd of hunters I could see hurrying to see what the problem was—when the other end of the tunnel caved in, too. That was farther away—a distant rumble—but now I recognized the sound.

"It's all coming down!" I shouted.

"This is not an accident." Eliza's face was set. She grabbed something from her belt and snapped it; instantly, it began shrieking a high metallic tone, warning everyone. "They're here."

"Who's here?"

Clouds of dust rolled past us, thick and chalky, and I coughed for air. People farther down the tunnel were screaming and shouting. Eliza ran without taking me along, and I was left to grope my way along the side of the tunnel. But I couldn't see; I could hardly breathe.

When a shape took form in the darkness, I reached out desperately—then froze.

"There you are, Miss Olivier." Mrs. Bethany stepped toward me, a sheer black shawl upon her shoulders making her part of the roiling smoke that surrounded us. "We've been looking for you."

Chapter Seven

"MRS. BETHANY!"

Her hawklike gaze froze me to the spot—I couldn't have run away from her if I'd tried. Something about her dark eyes was almost hypnotic.

She's come to take me home, I thought in my confusion. Though she terrified me more than she ever had before, the word *home* tugged at me, and for one moment I didn't know which way to turn.

"More this way!" shouted Eduardo, his voice echoing amid the clamor in the tunnels. He was running toward us, and to judge by the many shouts and curses around us, neither he nor Mrs. Bethany was alone.

I'd been in one great battle between vampires and Black Cross before; I knew what it sounded like.

Mrs. Bethany smiled radiantly. The soot and falling debris around us had no effect on her. These were her elements— darkness, violence, and blood. When Eduardo came into view, a stake in his hands, her smile only became wider.

Under his breath, he swore. "Son of a—"

"I remember you," she said. "You attacked my home. Allow me to return the favor."

Eduardo brought his stake up, calling to his team, but Mrs. Bethany was faster. She leaped at him so blindingly fast that I almost couldn't see her, and her hands clutched his head and gave it a sharp twist. I heard a sickening crack. Eduardo flopped to the ground, and Mrs. Bethany lifted her head triumphantly. Before I could see any more, the clouds of dust swirled around us, surrounding them and blinding me.

Trembling, I pushed myself against the tunnel wall, trying to put aside my horror so I could think. Mrs. Bethany had led a large group of vampires to attack Black Cross's headquarters. But how had she known to find us here?

I didn't have to ask how she dared to attack the most powerful Black Cross stronghold of them all. To get revenge for the burning of her beloved school, Mrs. Bethany would've done more than this.

Also, I knew that the vampires who had come with Mrs. Bethany wouldn't necessarily be here to help me. I was consorting with the enemy. And if any of them gave away my true nature to the Black Cross hunters—well, every fighter on *both* sides of the battle would be out to get me.

Not good.

Another slab of concrete fell from the ceiling. I screamed

and tucked myself into a ball on the floor in the instant before it smashed down onto one of the railway cars. The shock wave jolted me to the bones, and the roar and screech of twisted metal nearly deafened me. My skin was soaked in cold sweat, and I wanted to cower here until somehow it all ended.

Then I realized that Lucas was in the middle of this, right now, fighting for his life.

My head snapped up. I opened my mouth to shout for him, then thought better of it. The chances were that one of the vampires would hear me before Lucas, and calling attention to him or to me was the last thing I needed to do. No, I needed to find Lucas on my own, fast.

What about Raquel? And Dana? Fortunately, the second question answered the first. I knew now that Dana would defend Raquel to her last breath, if it came to that.

I started running through the dark, soot-filled tunnel, coughing. At first I headed in the general direction of the area where we took our meals; Lucas would've been on his way to eat dinner, so that was the most likely place for him to be.

But it was so hard to find my way. Headquarters was a murky, unwelcoming place at the best of times. Now it was like the center of a cyclone. Most of the lights had fallen during the blasts, so it was incredibly dark. Even with my vampire's sight, I could only make out shadows and blurs— the Black Cross hunters were essentially fighting blind. I kept one hand out so that I could feel the wall against my fingertips. That was the only way I could be certain I was running in a straight line. Every couple of seconds, one of the hunters set off an emergency flare, and then I could see a strobe-light flash of activity: two fighters grappling, human indistinguishable from vampire, both struggling desperately to kill the other.

Then the flare went out, and darkness fell again.

What if Lucas was one of those fighters? What if I ran past him as he was being hurt or worse?

That's when I realized that I knew I hadn't run past him. I *knew*. Something in me could tell that I wasn't close to Lucas.

It's the blood.

My parents had always told me that drinking blood created a powerful bond. I'd assumed they meant emotionally. Now I knew it was about more than feelings. Something in me could understand where Lucas was—maybe *how* he was—if only I could figure out how to harness that ability.

I'm coming, Lucas, I thought. I didn't have an actual telepathic link to him or anything, but I had to focus myself on him.

Amid all the screaming and the smoke, I closed my eyes. My fingertips against the wall were my only guides now. I reached out, searching for Lucas. When I got near him, I'd know.

There.

I stopped short and opened my eyes. It was still black as pitch, and the echoes were even stronger, making the screams and shouting more disorienting. But somehow I felt that Lucas was near. Did I dare call his name?

That's when the falling brick smashed into the back of my head.

I didn't feel myself fall. At that second I couldn't feel much of anything. I could hear the screams and the heavy thud of my body against the ground. It hurt—I knew that it hurt—but it was a very abstract sort of sensation, as though the pain were something I was remembering. Whatever connection I'd forged with Lucas was instantaneously severed. For a while there was nothing but sound. I couldn't say whether that went on for ten seconds or ten minutes.

Basically, I didn't know much of anything until I felt a strong hand clutch the top of my arm and hoist me to my feet. I couldn't stand upright, not without swaying, but the hand wouldn't let me fall.

"Open your eyes," Mrs. Bethany said.

I obeyed. The tunnel had gone completely quiet, save the rattle of small stones and dust still raining down. The blinding swirl of grit had cleared, but just slightly. Only my vampire's vision let me see Mrs. Bethany in the dark, in shadows of inky blue on black.

My throat stung from inhaling dust. I rasped, "Are you going to kill me?"

She tilted her head, as if I'd said something amusing. "You can serve a better purpose, I think."

"Did you come for revenge against Black Cross? Or just against me?"

"How important you think you are." Mrs. Bethany started,

towing me with her. Off-balance, I could only stumble along, coughing and wincing from the viselike grip she had on my arm. "My business with Black Cross began long before you were born, Miss Olivier. I suspect it will endure long after your death."

Although fear clutched at me (*Where's Lucas? What about Raquel?*), I knew Mrs. Bethany wasn't planning my death. If she were, she would've murdered me already.

Mrs. Bethany continued, "I do owe you a certain debt, however. You made this possible, after all."

"Me? What do you mean?"

"Not every vampire is a fool about technology, evidence from Mr. Yee's class notwithstanding." She was leading us over the rubble that now lined the tunnel. "When you e-mailed your parents at their Evernight account, tracking the ISP to New York was a fairly simple matter. We had recently learned where Black Cross was headquartered in this city, so you might as well have drawn us a map."

Oh, no. This attack was my fault. Lucas had explained how tightly Black Cross regulated Internet use, but I'd always thought it was just more of their stupid restrictive rules. Too late, I saw the reasons behind it.

"They said you wouldn't come here," I said, dazed. "That vampires wouldn't dare attack their headquarters—that it happened only once and they killed the leader—"

"Until very recently, that was true." The uneven stones rolled beneath my feet, and I twisted my ankle. I cried out, and to my surprise, Mrs. Bethany stopped. "But after the attack on Ever-night, many of our kind are more willing to band together and take action than they were before. We are united again. Your ill-advised romance has at least served a purpose. For me, that is. For you—well."

"You don't know anything about Lucas." Then I wondered if she did know, and for one horror-struck second, I thought she might tell me that he was dead.

Instead Mrs. Bethany said, "In recognition of the good you have so unknowingly and unwillingly done me, I offer you a far better choice than you deserve. If you like, you may come home."

"W-what?"

"As quick-witted as ever, I see. Miss Olivier, you may return to Evernight. Although the main building is unin-habitable at this time, we have set up temporary housing for the duration of the repairs, which will only take two or three months. Your parents are there, leading the rebuilding efforts. They wished to come along tonight, of course, but they were overemotional. Their recklessness would have hin-dered our efforts. How pleased they would be if you returned along with the rest of us."

She wasn't playing fair. The thought of my parents waiting back at Evernight, hoping that I would come in the door, tugged at me so hard that it felt like a sob was being torn from my body. "I won't. I can't."

Mrs. Bethany's severe, beautiful face seemed to have been

etched into the darkness in lines of steel. "Love isn't worth it, you know."

"It isn't only Lucas." And it wasn't, though I knew I could never leave him. My parents had told me too many lies. I could forgive them for that, but I needed to know the truth about what I could be—whether there was any choice for me besides becoming a full vampire. My parents wouldn't help me learn that truth. "Let me go."

I thought for sure she would fight me, and I was in no state to put up any resistance. Instead her eyes lit up, like she was glad I'd said it. Somehow making her happy seemed even more dangerous than making her mad.

"We'll meet again, Miss Olivier," she said. "By that time, I think you may have very different priorities. And so shall I."

What was that supposed to mean? I didn't get a chance to ask. In what seemed like an instant, Mrs. Bethany had vanished into the darkness, and I was alone again.

Oh, God, now what? I blinked and tried to clear my fuzzy head. The swirling dust had finally begun to settle, and I saw a small sliver of light in the distance—not much, but enough to tell me it was one of the emergency lamps hung near the exit routes. That one, at least, wasn't cut off.

They'd told us, during our Black Cross training, that if something ever did go wrong, we were all to meet at a supply shed at the far edge of the nearby park, over by the Hudson River.

But what if Lucas had been hurt or, even worse—no, I

couldn't even think it. All the same, the thought that he might be lying in the rubble around me was horrifying, and part of me wanted to remain, to turn over every last stone, if that was what it took to find him.

Yet after a few weeks of training, I understood Lucas better. I knew what he would say if he were here, so vividly that I could imagine him saying it: *You're too banged up to do any good right now. Get some help and get a game plan. That's the only way to deal with this.*

I staggered toward the light, determined to follow instructions. Maybe I was becoming a soldier, too.

This park wasn't so large or lush a green space as Central Park; it was a ridge of stone clinging to the edge of the island, steeper even than the mountains around Evernight. My body shook from exhaustion and adrenaline overload as I stumbled over the rocks. Outside it was dark—a darker night than I'd experienced before in New York, the first time we'd been away from the omnipresent electric lights. It seemed like so long since I'd had time to really look at the sky.

When I made it to the shed, a few hunters stood outside. They tensed until they recognized me, and one of them called, "Lucas? She's here."

I expected him to rush out at once, but it took a few seconds. When Lucas emerged, he walked toward me slowly, as though every step were weighed down. "Are you all right?" I said.

"I—they didn't hurt me." His expression was strange.

My hands found his. "What aren't you telling me?"

"The vampires killed seven people," he said. He seemed to want to say more, but couldn't. I realized that I already knew what was hurting him so much.

I whispered, "Eduardo. I know." Lucas's eyes met mine. I thought he would ask me how I knew, and I dreaded having to tell him I'd seen Eduardo's murder. "Your mother—how is she?"

"She's taking it hard." He stared into the distance, where the horizon would have been if we'd had any light.

Shock left me numb to the full weight of my guilt. I was sorry Eduardo had been killed, but that was about all I could feel for him. Lucas had liked Eduardo even less than I, yet he was almost bowed over from the weight of the loss. It wasn't his grief that hurt him; it was Kate's. His mother had lost the man she loved, and compared to that, what we felt about Eduardo didn't matter as much.

I hugged him tightly. "Go back to your mom," I whispered. "She needs you."

Lucas put his hands on either side of my head and kissed my hair. "Thank God you're okay. I thought they'd come for you."

It was my fault they'd attacked. I would have to confess that to him eventually, but this wasn't the time. "I'm fine."

He combed his fingers through my hair, then hugged me once more and turned back toward the shed where Kate was. As I stood there, Raquel came up to me. "You made it."

"You, too." I winced as I looked at her face. "You're getting a black eye."

"I really fought this time," Raquel said. Despite the depression of nearly everyone around us, there was a wild sort of energy in her eyes. "I struck back. It felt—amazing."

"I'm glad."

"And you don't look so pretty yourself, you know."

I must have been covered in dust from head to toe. Not that it mattered. "Dana must be okay, too, right?"

"Yeah. She's with some of the others, helping bring in the prisoner."

"Prisoner?" I didn't like the sound of that.

Just then one of the Black Cross vans came roaring up to us, headlights almost blindingly bright. Raquel and I both held up our hands to shield our eyes. I muttered, "I guess the parking garage didn't get hit."

Dana hung her head out of the back of the van. "Where are we going to take him?"

"Better ask Eliza," Raquel said, before running off to do just that.

I walked toward Dana. "You mean—you've got the prisoner?"

"Yeah, I'm the long arm of the law today." She tried to smile, but there was no spirit in it. I thought Dana felt as weird about the captive vampire as I did. "He's out cold right now, but when he wakes up, he's got a big surprise in store."

She half turned to the side, so I could look. My eyes went

wide. The crumpled figure of a man on the floor of the van, his hands bound tightly behind his back, was too familiar. I leaned closer, and horror washed over me as I recognized him.

Balthazar.

Chapter Eight

BALTHAZAR—MY DATE FOR THE AUTUMN BALL, the guy who had driven me to see Lucas countless times, my friend and very nearly my lover—lay unconscious, a captive of Black Cross. Chains bound his feet and wrists. Even his vampire's strength wouldn't allow him to escape, not wounded and exhausted as he was. I doubted Black Cross would give him any chance to recuperate. He was at their mercy.

Sometimes, over the past month, I'd thought of myself as a prisoner, but only now did I see how much worse it could get.

"Where—" My voice cracked. "Where are you taking him?"

"Milos says they've got some spaces in town they can use for backup. We'll haul him off to one of them." A crescent-shaped cut near the center of Dana's forehead testified to the fact that she'd just fought for her life. "The group's going to have to splinter up for a while—no other place for us all to stay together. The bloodsuckers didn't kill that many of us, but they made damn sure we'd be spread thin for a while."

"I'll come along," I said. I didn't know what else to do. I desperately wanted to consult Lucas, but I couldn't interrupt him and Kate now. At least if I made sure that we ended up in the same space that Balthazar would be kept, we'd have a chance to take action later.

Dana nodded. "Suit yourself. Normally I'd want stronger backup for vampire transport. No offense, Bianca, you know you're still a newbie—"

"No arguments here."

"—but pretty boy here looks like he's asleep for a while."

How could she simultaneously see how beautiful Balthazar was and not see that he was a person instead of a monster?

Maybe on some level Dana sensed how I felt, because she muttered, "I always hate this part."

As I climbed into the shotgun seat of the van—old, cracked vinyl mended with duct tape—I'd never felt so dirty. It wasn't the sweat and dust smeared thick on my skin; it was the fact that I was helping haul one of my best friends to what might be his death.

The new hideout was down by the river, on the other side of Manhattan. A loading dock was located nearby, and tugboats and barges stopped there to unload seemingly endless blue and green crates. I'd always thought of riverbanks as peaceful places, but this was all concrete and cables. The sounds of horn blasts and metal cranks drowned out the softer sounds of water.

I watched, Dana silent by my side, as Milos and a couple of

the other hunters hauled an unconscious Balthazar into what looked like an abandoned harbor station. For a second I had the powerful urge to run far away and trust Lucas to find me. But that was the coward in me trying to take over. I'd let my fear control me long enough. I'd waited passively for things to change for too long. For Balthazar's sake, and my own, it was time to be strong.

So I walked inside the building to see what we were dealing with. Dana didn't follow. She remained behind, drumming her hands against the hood of the van, staring determinedly out at the water.

The building—a harbor station—seemed to be one room, fairly small, with a raised area closer to the water and a deeper hollow in the back that had obviously been used for storage. The walls and floors were concrete—the floor so old and heavily used that it was ragged and worn to a dull brown.

As Balthazar sagged to the floor, Milos worked with the chains around his wrists, and then his arms flopped free. For one second, I felt hopeful. After all, if they were going to kill him, wouldn't they have done it already?

They could've killed Balthazar during the battle, and I'd never have known.

The terror of that thought washed over me, but it was instantly replaced by dread. Milos wasn't making Balthazar more comfortable; he was latching handcuffs around one of his wrists. While I watched, aghast, he latched the other cuff around the metal railing that surrounded the storage area. He then did the same with the other arm, so that Balthazar was bound with his hands above his head. His head lolled forward, but his body twitched slightly.

"He's waking up," said one of the hunters.

Milos walked toward a nearby bucket, one that seemed to have been placed beneath a leak in the roof. Water rippled inside. "How about we help him with that?" Then he tossed the water, hard, onto Balthazar.

The water hit him and the concrete with a loud, wet slap that made me jump. Balthazar jerked his head upright, gasping and disoriented. At his first glimpse of the hunters in front of him, he pulled backward—before realizing that he was bound. Trapped. His face shifted from surprise to anger.

"Don't like it when the odds change, do you?" Milos jeered.

Balthazar's voice was slurred as he said, "Go to hell."

"I believe that's your team's stomping grounds," Milos said, "not mine."

Balthazar was still dazed from his injuries. Vampires healed faster than humans, but it took a while to recover from something serious. Balthazar struggled to hold his head upright, and though his dark eyes were unfocused he was clearly trying to get an idea of where he was, what chances he might have to escape.

His eyes sought the door, and he saw me.

The force of his gaze hit me hard. Gripping the doorframe so I wouldn't fall, I hoped desperately that he would understand. *I'm not helping them, I'll try to get you out of this, you have to hang on, Balthazar, please—*

Balthazar's eyes drifted from me to Milos and the other hunters who surrounded him. Then he ducked his head, as if he didn't even want to meet my eyes.

For one second, I thought he was angry, but then I realized the truth. Balthazar was trying to hide the fact that we knew each other. Had the Black Cross hunters understood that—understood that I was, like him, a vampire—they would've chained me up, too. While I had completely failed to protect him, he was doing the only thing within his power to protect me.

"He's still out of it," one of the hunters said. "I say we give him a while to think over the situation he's in. Come back and talk to him later."

"Sounds about right," Milos said. "I'll stand guard."

Should I stand guard, too? Make sure that nobody lost his temper and did something stupid? No, I decided, because I didn't actually have any idea how to stop the guards from hurting Balthazar.

What I needed to do was find the one person who might know how to get us all out of this situation before it was too late: Lucas.

As I mutely followed Dana and the others around during the next hour or so, helping make up pallets for people to rest upon later, I learned two important things.

First, about twenty of the Black Cross hunters would end up staying here in a few old storage vaults that turned out to lie in the basement of the harbor station. There was actually a lot of room down there, but mostly that was used for weapons storage. I felt confident that, if I only stayed put, Lucas would find me. Since the other hunters would be in other locations all around the city, I figured that improved our chances of being able to help Balthazar. Better two against twenty than two against two hundred, right?

Second, we had to move fast. Because I soon heard their plan for Balthazar, and it was worse than I'd ever dreamed.

"Did you put him someplace where he'll be in the sun, come dawn?" Eliza said, talking about Balthazar. She had arrived here only a few minutes after the rest of us and was inspecting the new rooms, while I meekly unfolded scratchy blankets in the far corner. "That'll make it worse."

"Not if he's had blood lately," somebody said. "And how long do you think a strapping guy like that goes without blood? I'm guessing a day or two tops. Besides, it's bad enough for him tied up like that, and we can make it a whole lot worse." In the corner of the room, Dana paused in her work like she might object, but she didn't.

Eliza shrugged. "We need him able to talk. We've got to find out why they chose to attack now."

I already knew, but confessing that would have left me chained to the wall beside Balthazar.

Finally, around 3 A.M., the last hunters to remain with our group staggered in. Raquel came through the door first, and she bounded into Dana's arms like they'd been together for years instead of a couple of weeks. The smile on Raquel's face was so brilliant that I would've been happy for her, if I could've forgotten the danger Balthazar was in.

Lucas and Kate walked in last. The flickering light from the one bulb in the room painted strange shadows on their faces. Kate seemed to have aged ten years in the past day. Her dark-gold hair, usually slicked back, was disheveled, and her expression was empty. With his hand around her forearm, Lucas gently guided her to one of the pallets. His jeans and T-shirt were smeared with blood that I knew wasn't his own.

When he saw me, he gratefully pulled me into his arms. I whispered into his ear, "Outside. Now."

Though obviously exhausted, Lucas nodded. As we walked out through the separate door for the basement stairs, I expected someone to ask what we were doing, or why, but nobody did. They were too tired to care. Raquel was already stretched out on her pallet, and probably the whole group would be asleep within ten minutes.

"Okay," he said, his voice ragged from weariness, once we had stepped outside. The lights across the river provided nearly the only light. "What's up?"

"They've taken Balthazar prisoner."

Instantly, Lucas was wide awake. "Hell."

"They've got him chained up in there." I pointed to the main room. "Lucas, I think they're going to hurt him."

I hoped Lucas would tell me I was being ridiculous, but he didn't. "That happens sometimes," he said, grimly. "Most people don't like it, won't do it. Eduardo—he felt different." His gaze became distant, and I wondered what measure he was taking of Eduardo now; he'd been both Lucas's fiercest enemy and the closest thing to a father he'd known since early childhood, and now he was gone.

Swallowing hard, I said, "Lucas, you didn't—you would never—"

"I haven't ever." But Lucas didn't sound like he felt good about that answer. "If you'd asked me two years ago if it was okay—roughing up a vampire to get some information—I'd have been all for it. Only reason I never got mixed up in a situation like that was because I was too young."

"And now?"

"Now I know better, because you taught me." He put his hand on my cheek, and despite everything, I smiled.

"We have to get him out of there. Is there any way to talk to Eliza—to explain that you knew him at Evernight? We can tell them that he doesn't kill people. I could talk to her, too, and I bet Raquel would stand up for him."

Lucas shook his head. "That's not happening. Eliza's not going to let any vampire go, not ever."

"Then how do we keep them from hurting Balthazar?"

He was quiet for a few long seconds. When he spoke, his voice was almost too low to hear. "Bianca—the only way to do that might be to kill him."

"What?"

"That is *not* something I want to do," Lucas said, every word intent, "but if the choice is between a quick death or a slow one after being worked over by those guys for a week? I'd pick the quick death every time."

"There has to be another way," I insisted. The stakes were even higher than I'd feared.

"I'll try to think of something." But he didn't sound hopeful, and my worry flared into anger.

"Do you really care so little about what happens to Balthazar? Or do you want him out of the way, just because he cares about me, and he and I almost—"

I cut myself off too late. From the glare Lucas gave me, I knew he understood what I'd been referring to: One night during the spring, after Lucas and I had broken up, the attraction between me and Balthazar had flared into passion. We had drunk each other's blood and might have gone on to sleep together if we hadn't been interrupted. When Lucas and I reunited, I'd confessed everything, and so far it hadn't been an issue. Lucas knew that he was the one I truly loved.

So I shouldn't have accused Lucas of being willing to watch Balthazar die merely out of jealousy. I knew it was false, and all I'd done was hurt Lucas by reminding him of how close Balthazar and I had become.

Lucas said only, "Low blow."

"I know. I'm sorry." Tentatively, I brushed a lock of Lucas's hair away from his face.

He didn't push me away, but he didn't relax into my touch, either. "This isn't going to help us get him out, but—come on."

Lucas led me into the station, where Milos and one other

hunter stood guard. Balthazar, still sitting on the floor with his hands chained, didn't look up. When the guards turned to us, Lucas said, "Hey, you guys take a break. We'll watch him for a few."

Milos shrugged. "Why would I do that?"

"Because this bloodsucker went after my girl." Lucas pulled me against him possessively. Almost imperceptibly, Balthazar tensed. "And I'd like to . . . discuss that with him. In private."

The other guard chuckled meanly, and Milos slowly rose, nodding. I didn't like his smile. "Indulge yourself. For the next few minutes, I'm just outside getting a breath of air. Have it."

"Thanks, man." Lucas stared malevolently at the silent Balthazar until the door had shut behind them. Then he said, "Bianca, stand by the door. If they come back or somebody else walks up—"

"I'm on it."

Balthazar finally lifted his head. He looked worse than in pain; he looked sad. "Come to gloat?"

Lucas snapped, "No, dumb ass, I'm trying to figure out how to get you free. You want to help with that, or would you rather mope around for a while before your inevitable painful death? Your call."

"Wait," Balthazar said, hope dawning. "You're here to *help*?"

I went to the door, though I was unwilling to be so far from Balthazar. "Are you hurting? Did they do anything to you?"

"Bianca, what are you doing with these people? This is too

dangerous for you." How typical of Balthazar, to ignore the deep trouble he was in and worry about somebody else. "They can't know who and what you are."

"No, they don't." My voice was pitched at a whisper, so nobody downstairs might awaken and hear it. Thank goodness they were probably too tired to be roused even by an explosion. "We're sort of stuck with them right now until we can get some money and get away on our own."

Balthazar turned toward Lucas, who was testing the strength of the metal railing Balthazar was chained to. Unfortunately, it looked sturdy. "You have to get her out of this. Immediately. Don't worry about the damned money. Just go."

"Easy to say," Lucas said. "Hard to do, particularly when you've got to take care of somebody else."

"Can't you get the handcuffs off?" I pleaded. "They said it would be a while before they came back. That's plenty of time for Balthazar to get away. We could say he overpowered us."

Lucas shook his head. "There're guards set up all around here. The only place that isn't guarded is the river, and given the whole running water problem, I'm guessing Balthazar can't swim out of here."

Wincing, Balthazar said, "Absolutely not."

"I'll think of something," Lucas said. He sounded like he was trying to make himself believe it. "Why did you join this little hunting party, anyway? Didn't think you were Mrs. Bethany's errand boy."

"Hardly." Balthazar groaned. "But she said Bianca was here

and I thought—I thought she might be in trouble. The kind of trouble I'm in now."

He'd run into unimaginable danger because he was afraid for me. That made this all my fault. Touched by his devotion, but angry with myself, I leaned my head against the doorjamb and shut my eyes for a second.

I heard Balthazar say, "So why are you helping me out, Lucas? Last time I checked, you still believed in the war against vampires."

"You haven't checked lately, have you?" Lucas replied. "Besides—you'd help Bianca, no matter what. That means I help you, no matter what."

Lifting my head, I saw Lucas and Balthazar regarding each other. For the first time, there was real respect in Balthazar's eyes. "Okay."

"Doesn't change the fact that I don't have any idea what to do for you." Lucas kicked at the railing and swore. "Balthazar, I'm going to try, but I can't promise."

"I understand," Balthazar said. He was speaking to me more than to Lucas now. "Don't put yourselves in danger on my account. It's not worth it."

"Yes, it is," I whispered. Lucas's eyes darted toward me, but he said nothing. "There's no way we're leaving you here. I don't care what I have to do."

Lucas cut in, "We'll come up with something. But it might take a couple of days. Those days might be pretty rough."

With my vampire-sharp hearing, I detected Milos and the

other guards coming closer. "They're back."

Balthazar quickly said, "Whatever they do to me—I promise you, I've been through worse."

"Don't be so sure," Lucas said, "but hang on."

The door banged open, and Milos and the other guard returned. "Had your fun?"

"Just had a little chat," Lucas said. He glanced down at Balthazar, giving him a look I could see but the guards couldn't—like a warning. Then he pulled his fist back, as if to punch Balthazar, who winced. Their playacting almost convinced me. Lucas relaxed, grinning wickedly. "Let him think it over for a while, huh?"

"Sure," Milos said with a leer. "Take Bianca off to bed."

They both laughed, happy to join the taunting. Balthazar closed his eyes.

Lucas grabbed my hand and towed me outside, before I started crying. I let him even though I didn't want to go. I wasn't sure I'd ever see Balthazar again.

Chapter Nine

IF I'D THOUGHT STAYING WITH BLACK CROSS WAS claustrophobic before, I hadn't known the half of it. Now all twenty or so people staying at the harbor station were huddled in a room that wouldn't have been big enough for ten people to sleep comfortably. There was no privacy, no silence, and no chance to talk to Lucas.

At least we were near each other.

Lucas and I technically slept on separate pallets that lay side by side, but that left no space between us, not in that room. As soon as we stretched out, Lucas pulled his blanket over us and spooned behind me, his belly to my back. One arm cradled me around the waist, and I could feel his breath against the back of my neck.

I closed my eyes, luxuriating in the moment. If only we were alone. If only I weren't still so shaken from the attack and Balthazar's capture that my entire body trembled. It would have been so sweet.

Lucas softly kissed the back of my neck. I knew he was trying to tell me to have faith that we'd figure something out. But I knew as well as Lucas did how difficult that would be.

My fingertip traced along Lucas's hand and fingers. I could feel the fine hairs on his forearm, the movement of his thumb as he made little soothing circles around my navel.

For a moment, I contemplated turning around and kissing him. If the others woke up and laughed, I almost didn't care.

Yet exhaustion weighed me down, and I knew Lucas was even more wiped out than I was. Besides, tomorrow, we'd need our wits and strength.

I closed my eyes, wondering if I could possibly fall asleep with so much on my mind—and then, what seemed like a few seconds later, I realized that everyone around me was getting up. I'd slept through the night without feeling like I'd rested at all.

"Mom?" Lucas said, pushing himself up on one elbow. He was still curved behind me; we'd been tangled up in each other all night. "How are you?"

"Fine." Kate pulled her hair back tightly into a stubby ponytail. Her body was so tense that I could see every muscle in her arms working. "I'm going upstairs. We need answers."

I gasped in dismay, but Lucas put a warning hand on my shoulder. When I glanced at him over my shoulder, he said only, "Get dressed. We should be a part of this."

Robotically, I grabbed my clothes—the same stuff I'd worn yesterday—and started to pull my jeans on.

The trained hunters around us got ready and went upstairs

❖ 112 ❖

first, which left Raquel and me alone for a minute. "Looks like we're back in uniforms," Raquel said, pointing to the new white undershirt she wore; Black Cross had kept a case of them around for emergencies, which meant everyone was matching today. "We'll have to go back and look for our stuff in the tunnels. Some of it might be okay. I hope we can get your brooch at least."

I hadn't even thought about the jet brooch Lucas had given me. Though it pierced me to imagine that it was lost in the rubble forever, that wasn't exactly my top priority. "Raquel, do you know who it is they captured?"

"A vampire," she said breezily. "Wait, was it Mrs. Bethany? No, they'd have told us anything that good."

"It's Balthazar."

Raquel's head jerked around. I could tell she almost didn't believe me—as if I would've ever joked about something like that. During the school year, Balthazar and Raquel had spent a lot of time together because of me. We'd all gone into Riverton together, studied in the library, and even shared a picnic on the grounds of Evernight. She'd always liked him, at least until she learned that he was a vampire. Surely a year of friendship couldn't vanish overnight.

Each word clipped, she said, "Let's get up there. We're late."

By the time we walked into the room where Balthazar was kept, he was surrounded. The hunters, except those standing guard outside, had circled him, and Kate stood in front, only a couple of feet away. His arms were stretched above his head, still handcuffed to the railing, and I could see that the skin around his wrists had been rubbed raw.

At the sound of the door, Balthazar glanced over at me. Raquel ducked her head, perhaps ashamed. I felt like doing the same, but I saw the need in his eyes. Balthazar wanted to see one friendly face while this was happening. I'd just have to be strong enough to do that for him.

"So you say this was only a revenge thing." Kate paced the floor, her boots loud on the cement. "We hit your house, you hit ours—that's it?"

"Sounds the same to me," Balthazar said. "Except, of course, your attack endangered innocents. Ours didn't."

Kate's response was to kick him savagely in the side.

No! I braced one hand against the wall.

Kate rasped, "I'm not taking any moral lectures from a vampire. Not the night after you killed my husband."

Balthazar had the good sense to remain silent.

In the far corner, near where Lucas was, his expression grim and his arms folded, Eliza stood. I thought she meant only to oversee until she called, "You were after something. Admit it."

"I told you." Balthazar leaned his head against the wall behind him. "We were after revenge."

Eliza shook her head. "No way. That many vampires working together—that doesn't happen often. Mrs. Bethany's planning something. And you're going to tell us what it is."

"She might be planning something," he answered, surprising me. But I realized that Balthazar was looking right at Lucas as he said it; apparently he thought this information was important, something we ought to know. "I think she's traveled more in the last month than in the last century. Vampires who normally consider themselves loners have flocked to her side because of the burning of Evernight. Basically, you've given us common cause. Mrs. Bethany might be able to use that."

"Use that to do what?" Eliza demanded.

Balthazar closed his eyes wearily. "I don't know. I'd planned to leave before Mrs. Bethany said we were coming here. She doesn't take me into her confidence."

Why would Balthazar plan to leave Evernight? I wondered. Normally, I would have expected him to be the first one helping rebuild.

Then I thought of Charity—his younger sister, the psycho, who had led Black Cross to Evernight. Balthazar had been the one to turn her into a vampire, something for which he'd never forgiven himself. She'd fled after the fire, and probably Balthazar was still trying to find her, to somehow recapture the closeness they'd lost so long ago.

"So, you say you don't know." Eliza stepped a little closer. I saw that she had a gun in one hand, but it was only a neon-green plastic water gun. The toy looked incredibly silly, but I realized that it would be loaded with holy water—*real* holy water, the kind that could burn a vampire like acid. "You understand that I don't believe you."

"Yeah," Balthazar said. "I thought that was how it might go."

"You don't seem scared," Eliza said.

He shrugged as best as he could in chains. "For our kind,

death is only the beginning. Sometimes I think that second death is only one more doorway."

"Dying isn't the worst thing," Kate said, holding one hand out toward Eliza, who tossed her the water gun. Kate caught it, pointed at Balthazar, and fired.

Balthazar's flesh started to sizzle the moment the holy water made contact with it. He screamed, and the sound was so horrible I thought I would pass out. Then I smelled the burning and had to clutch at the wall for support.

"Oh, my God," muttered Raquel. She paled and ran outside. Through my tear-blurred eyes, I saw Dana move to follow her.

Kate, unmoved, stood by the smoke drifting up from Balthazar's writhing body. "You sure you don't know what she's up to?"

His voice shaky, Balthazar managed to get out the word, "N—no."

"I might believe you," Kate said. "I just don't care."

She shot more holy water at him, and he screamed again. His scream felt like acid washing over me. I slid down to the floor, huddling with my knees against my chest.

Milos said, "Hey, Lucas. Your girlfriend's losing it over here. Better take her for some fresh air."

I tried to shake my head. The only thing more horrible than seeing Balthazar hurt like this was the thought of leaving him. But Lucas was at my side in an instant, pulling me up. "Come on," he muttered. "This is enough."

"But—"

"Bianca. Please."

From his place on the floor, Balthazar shouted, "Get out! I want you gone—want you all gone—"

"You wish, bloodsucker," Kate said, her voice harder than before, and Lucas pushed me roughly out the door.

Once we were outside, I started to bawl—huge, racking sobs that made my throat and gut hurt. When I sank onto the ground, Lucas knelt beside me, his hands on my back as I wept.

"I'll think of something," he said, an edge of desperation in his words. "We've just—we've got to."

I leaned back against him, trying to stop crying. In the distance I could see Raquel sitting near the river, her head in her hands, Dana beside her. Was it possible that even Raquel saw how far over the line Black Cross had gone? Could she make Dana see it, too? If we had to do something big in order to save Balthazar, something dramatic, it would help to have them on our side.

After several more minutes that felt like an eternity, the hunters started coming out. When Kate emerged, she glanced down at Lucas and shrugged. "He passed out. We'll start on him again later."

"The guy really might not know," Lucas said. "Mrs. Bethany played favorites, and Balthazar More wasn't one of her pets."

"You two knew him?" Kate's eyes narrowed. I realized that she could now see my tears for what they were—compassion—instead of mere squeamishness. Compassion bothered her more.

Lucas quickly said, "He put the moves on Bianca last year. She told him no, and he didn't like it. Made a scene. So the guy kind of gets under her skin."

Kate shrugged. "Seems like you'd be cheering us on, Bianca."

And that was when it hit me. *Oh, absolutely, that's it, that's it!*

I dug my fingernails into my palms to keep myself from smiling. "I'm just so—tired."

"Me, too." Her posture slumped. "God, me, too."

As she walked off, I turned back to Lucas. "I know how we can save Balthazar."

At first, there was nothing to do but wait. Lucas walked with me to a nearby market, where we grabbed a couple of bottles of orange juice and some honey buns. They were the cheap kind, wrapped in cellophane and sticky like glue, but they were the first food I'd had in more than a day, so I wolfed them down.

"You need anything else?" Lucas said as we walked along the sidewalk. I knew he meant blood.

"I'll grab something if you just give me a second."

"I could—"

"No," I said firmly. "Lucas, drinking your blood has to be the last resort. It's already changed us both too much."

"It ties us together. That's not a bad thing."

I remembered how I had nearly been able to find Lucas in the middle of the battle only because of the bond created by his blood. But Lucas didn't know about that; he was talking about something else. "You're jealous of Balthazar," I said.

"Should I be?"

"I didn't mean— Lucas, you know I love you. Only you. But you know that I drank his blood, too, and I think that's freaking you out. Please understand, that was totally different."

"Totally more intense, you mean."

I shook my head. "*Different*. That's all. Trust me, there is nothing—nothing—in the world that makes me crazier than being close to you."

"He matters to you," he said quietly. "There's no hiding that."

"You matter more."

I put my arms around his neck and kissed him. His mouth was sweet with juice. At first the kiss was tender, but soon it became deeper. Lucas's hands tightened around my waist as our lips opened and I felt his tongue brush eagerly against mine. I remembered the night before, how we'd slept beside each other. Juxtaposing our closeness then with our kissing now in my mind created an image so powerful that it made me feel weak.

We kissed again, harder, but then I pulled back. "You're making me hungry."

"Like I said, I don't mind."

"And I said no. I'm going to catch something. Don't watch, okay?"

"Shy," he said, but he turned away.

Honestly, I wasn't that hungry for blood, but what we were about to attempt was risky. I needed to be able to concentrate. I needed to be strong.

Once I'd had a pigeon, and rinsed my mouth out thoroughly with another bottle of orange juice, Lucas and I returned to the harbor station. I was afraid they would already have started in on Balthazar again, but he must have been terribly hurt, because he didn't wake up for hours. It was a long time to wait.

As I did the busy work they gave me, sharpening stakes in a vacant lot nearby, Raquel sat down next to me. For a while we whittled side by side in silence, sweating in the hot sun, but finally she said, "That was rough in there."

"Yeah. It was."

"I know you used to care about him." Raquel made quick cuts with her blade. Splinters fell from the wood. "I guess it's hard to remember the lies he told you while—while something like that is happening."

"Torture." I figured we were better off calling it by its rightful name.

Raquel paused, her knife suspended above the stake for a few seconds. Then she nodded. "Yeah. It was torture."

Maybe she really was thinking sanely about this, instead of letting Black Cross do the thinking for her. I wanted to find out, but now wasn't the time. Lucas and I could do this alone, and it was better for Raquel if we didn't involve her.

Finally, around dusk, Milos called, "He's coming around."

Lucas and I glanced at each other. We waited until the others were all inside, because we'd need to make an entrance.

"I'm not much of an actress," I murmured, "but it won't be hard to act upset."

"Angry, angry, angry." Lucas was talking to himself. "Okay, let's do this. Ready?"

"Yeah. Let's go."

Together we ran toward the harbor station. When we came in, Milos turned, saw us, and scowled. "Your girlfriend going to run off crying again?"

Lucas snapped, "Bianca and I have some business to resolve."

Milos looked surprised, but he took a step back.

Lucas pushed his way toward the front of the crowd; I lagged behind. I wasn't a player in this scenario; honestly, I was more of a prop, there to look stricken and weep. Though I hated pretending to be so helpless, I'd have to take comfort in the fact that this was my plan.

Then I saw Balthazar, and there was no comfort to be had.

His flesh was striped with lines of raw skin from the streams of holy water. Both his eyes were swollen and dark, and his jaw was lumpy from repeated blows. His lips had cracked open and bled, as had his wrists. He looked worse than I knew anybody could look. Balthazar's bloodshot eyes met mine, dull and incurious, like he was past even imagining that help could come.

"Back up, Mom," Lucas said, pulling her away. "It's my turn."

"Like hell it is." Anger seemed to illuminate her from within, like a candle in a leering jack-o'-lantern. "This thing killed Eduardo. I'm going to have answers, and then I'm going to have its hide."

"He didn't just kill Eduardo." Lucas swaggered up to Balthazar, who didn't react. "He went after Bianca. You know that. What you don't know—what I didn't know until today—is how far he went. How close he came to hurting her to get his way."

My crying wasn't an act. I backed away, body shaking, as if I were somehow afraid of the bloody, broken figure chained to the railing. The hunters parted for me, respectful of what they thought I'd suffered at a vampire's hands.

Lucas grabbed Balthazar by the hair. I winced—but there was no other way to do this next part. He growled, "You tried to screw my girl."

"Well, you know." Balthazar's mutilated smirk might have been genuine. "I figured she needed somebody to show her how it was really done."

Lucas backhanded him, hard. A few of the hunters made approving noises—not cheering, but muttering "yeah" or "that's it." I hated them so much I wanted to scream.

"You listen to me." Lucas panted. His green eyes blazed, and he looked utterly wild. When he got like this, gave full rein to his hot temper, sometimes he scared even me. "You know how bad I hate you. You know I'd never get tired of hurting you. So you better tell me what it is we want to know, and you'd better do it now, or they're going to turn you over to me for the remainder of your existence. I promise you, you'd rather go fast. So what's it going to be, Balthazar?"

Under my breath, so low that nobody who wasn't a vampire could possibly have heard me, I whispered, "Make something up. We'll take care of the rest."

Balthazar hesitated, confused. Lucas kicked his leg.

Come on, Balthazar, you can think of something! Anything! Just trust us!

Lucas shouted, "Spit it out! What was Mrs. Bethany after?"

"You!" Balthazar said. "She was after you."

"Lucas?" Kate stepped forward in alarm. "Why do they want my son?"

"Mrs. Bethany blames him," Balthazar said. Could the others tell he was making this up as he went along? Apparently not. "And I think she—she thinks Lucas might have gone through her records. She's scared he knows too much. Mrs. Bethany's never gotten over the fact that you planted a spy at her school. It drives her crazy. I think the burning of Evernight pushed her over the edge."

Kate lifted her chin. "So she's scared, you're saying. Desperate. Lashing out at my son because she doesn't know what else to do."

"She knows exactly what to do," Balthazar said. "As long as Lucas Ross lives, she'll be after him. After anybody who's with him. So maybe you want to think twice about how tightly you stick to this one. From now on, anybody who's standing next to Lucas has a decent shot of ending up just as dead as he's going to be."

Coolly Kate glanced at her son. "Do you believe him?"

"Yeah," Lucas said, drawing a stake from his belt. Then he slammed it into Balthazar's chest.

I heard Raquel stifle a small cry. Balthazar gasped in pain, but he immediately slumped forward, unconscious and paralyzed.

Lucas said, "I want to burn this trash myself. Bianca can come with. I think it'll help her get over what he did, torching him."

Eliza nodded. Kate put her hands on my shoulders as I wiped my eyes. "Just remember," she said, "you're free now."

The others helped us load Balthazar's inert body into the van. I couldn't get over how, well, *dead* he looked, with the stake poking out of his chest. Milos gave Lucas a few hints about good spots for burning vampire corpses, which made me think he'd done this several times before. That gave me the shivers.

I slammed the van doors shut. Lucas started the engine and pulled onto the road. Once we were a few blocks away, I slipped into the back where Balthazar lay and said, "Now?"

Lucas nodded, never taking his eyes from the road. "Now."

With both hands, I grabbed the stake and pulled it out of Balthazar's chest.

As soon as the wood slipped free, Balthazar jerked, then writhed beneath me in pain. His bloodied hands sought the gaping wound in his chest. "What the—"

"Shhhhhh." I put one hand on his forehead. "You're okay. We had to pretend we were going to kill you. There was no other way to get you out of there."

"Bianca?"

"Yeah, it's me. You remember what happened?"

"I think so." Balthazar grimaced, but he forced his eyes open to look at me. "You and Lucas—"

"We broke you out," Lucas called. "Listen, we're on a tight schedule here. Is there a place we can drop you? Where you'll be safe while you heal up?"

Balthazar had to think a couple seconds before he nodded. "Chinatown. A shop—I know the owner—he'll hide me."

"We'll get you there," Lucas said.

"Thank you," Balthazar said. One of his hands found mine. Normally he was so strong, but now the pressure he put on my fingers was weaker than a child's. "Black Cross— They aren't—"

"They don't know about me," I said. "Lucas is taking care of me. I'm safe."

Balthazar nodded. His handsome face was twisted and swollen, and I wished I at least could've brought some bandages. Even a vampire might require weeks to recover from injuries this serious. I tried to smile for him as I wiped blood from the corner of his mouth, but it was difficult.

At last we reached Chinatown. The street Balthazar told us to turn onto was small and unbelievably crowded. Almost every single store sign was in Chinese; it really felt like we'd driven to another country altogether.

Lucas double-parked and glanced over his shoulder. "You sure you can get where you're going?"

"Maybe Bianca could walk with me."

"That's a good idea," I said. It was too easy to imagine Balthazar passing out in the gutter and being dragged to a hospital, where he'd promptly be declared dead. "I'll be right back."

"I'm going to circle the block." Lucas glanced at our passenger. "Good luck, Balthazar."

"Thanks. I mean it."

I got out first and accepted Balthazar's heavy arm across my shoulders. He could stand but just barely. Once the van doors were shut, Lucas drove away. Although several people stared at Balthazar, bloody wreck that he was, nobody said anything. That was New York for you.

As soon as we started walking, Balthazar said, "Come with me."

"I am coming with you. We're going to find the shop. I think it's right along here—"

"No, I mean—don't go back with Lucas. I can hide you here."

Shocked, I said, "Balthazar, we talked about this. You know how I feel."

"This isn't about romance." He limped beside me, and a few drops of blood trickled down from his wrist, along his hands, onto the sidewalk. "You see now what Black Cross is. What they're capable of. Bianca, if they learned the truth—if one tenth of what happened to me happened to you—"

"It won't," I said. "Lucas and I are leaving soon. I promise."

Balthazar didn't look convinced, but he nodded.

When we reached the shop, an older lady behind the counter began shouting something in Chinese. At first I wondered if she wasn't suggesting that somebody call 911. Then an even older man, almost entirely bald, emerged from the back of the store. He saw Balthazar and hurried forward; though I didn't understand a word he said—or of Balthazar's response, which was also in Chinese—I could tell he was expressing concern.

"You guys are friends," I said.

"Since 1964." Balthazar stroked my cheek with one hand. "Please be careful."

"I will. Balthazar—if I don't see you again—"

"It's okay," he said. "I know."

He leaned forward, as if to kiss me, then grimaced. His lips were too torn for that. I took his less-mangled hand in mine and kissed his palm. Then I ran into the clamor of Chinatown, back toward Lucas and the danger that awaited us when we returned to Black Cross.

Chapter Ten

"CAN I ASK YOU A PERSONAL QUESTION?" RAQUEL said.

I glanced over at her warily. We were partnered with Milos and Dana on patrol in Grand Central Terminal. Bustling crowds surrounded us, and the walls were lined with as many stores as any shopping mall. For a train station, it was incredibly beautiful—lots of white marble, a golden clock, and, my favorite part, a high cerulean ceiling painted with the constellations in gold. Despite all this, it wasn't really the place for a heart-to-heart chat, which made me wonder why Raquel had waited until now. But I said, "Sure, go ahead."

My guess about her intentions was borne out when she said, "You and Balthazar—how close did you two get?"

"I wasn't ever in love with him, if that's what you mean."

"But what Lucas said two nights ago, when he—when Balthazar—" Raquel struggled for a way to describe what she had thought had happened without the word "murder," and failed.

"He suggested that Balthazar tried to force you to have sex with him. I thought the two of you were—well, I didn't think he had to force you."

Raquel was the one person who might be able to see through the ruse Lucas and I had constructed to save Balthazar. Eventually I hoped to be able to tell her the truth about that much of it, but not now. "Lucas got angry. He took some stuff I said out of context and—blew up, I guess. You know about his temper."

"Oh. Okay." Still disquieted, Raquel shifted from one foot to the other.

A station employee nearby shot us a dirty look, assuming we were loitering teenagers. I mean, we *were* teenagers, plus we were loitering, but we were also watching out for a vampire that was rumored to be stalking prey here. In my opinion that was justification enough, but it wasn't the kind of thing we could explain. "Come on," I said. "Let's stroll for a bit."

She fell into step beside me. "So, getting seriously into the TMI zone here—did you and Balthazar ever have sex?"

"No, we didn't." When Raquel shot me a skeptical look, I added, "One time we got really close. But we were interrupted. You remember the whole thing with the ghosts, in the A/V room?"

"Yeah. Wow, that turned out to be a major save, didn't it? I mean, sex with a vampire—ewww." Raquel kept scanning the crowds in front of us, always on the lookout; she was better at this than I was. "If we didn't know better, you could almost think the ghosts were trying to help you out there."

I remembered the blue-green chill of the air that night, when the wraiths had attempted to kill me and claim me for their own. "We definitely know better, though."

We stepped out of the main rush of people into a slightly less busy corridor. Long lines of tired commuters wandered up and down, either focused on making their trains or slightly dreamy as they listened to their iPods. Everything looked pretty ordinary to me.

"It's weird that you couldn't tell," Raquel said.

"What do you mean?"

"That Balthazar was a vampire. I mean—you never noticed he didn't have a heartbeat? Or that his body was cooler than ours?"

Caught off guard, I grasped for a reply. "Well—I never—I mean, it's not the kind of thing you usually watch out for. Most girls don't have to ask themselves, 'Gosh, I wonder if the guy I'm dating is alive.' Right?"

"I guess." Raquel didn't seem convinced, but then something else caught her attention. She pointed. "Hey, check out the parka."

I knew what she meant. Vampires, who often felt cold in surroundings where humans were warm, occasionally wore winter clothing in the middle of summer. That was a clue Black Cross had told us to watch for. (My parents had always simply made sure to wear layers.) Sure enough, a guy in front of us was wearing a heavy white parka as he sauntered through the station, in the opposite direction from the usual flow of traffic at this time of day.

"Could just be a weirdo," Raquel said.

"Probably. This is New York, after all."

But I knew better. I couldn't say how I knew—maybe because of that vampire sense Balthazar had told me I'd develop in time, the sense that another was near. I knew this guy, with his white parka and his long, reddish-brown dreadlocks, was a vampire like me.

My heart sank. Ever since I'd been with Black Cross, I'd dreaded a moment like this. This was about to turn into a vampire hunt—and I had to find a way to save this guy, or else I'd become a murderer.

The most logical thing to do was talk Raquel out of her suspicions, but it was already too late. Raquel's gaze remained fixed on him, her eyes bright and avid. "Look how pale he is. And he's just got—I can't describe it, but when I try to picture him at Evernight Academy, I know he'd fit right in."

"You can't be sure," I said.

"Yes, I can." Raquel peered past me, quickening her steps to stay on the vampire's trail. "We've finally got one."

Oh, crap.

Raquel's voice was tense with anticipation. "Think we can grab Dana and Milos?"

If more experienced hunters joined us, I'd have a lot more trouble protecting this guy. "Right now I think we can handle it."

We followed the dreadlocked vampire down the white corridor that led out of Grand Central. Although it was still daytime, the rainy weather kept the sun at bay. Neither Raquel nor I had an umbrella, so we stuck close to the edge of the buildings to keep from getting soaked. Luckily, the vampire seemed to have the same idea.

Raquel pointed. "He's turning the corner."

"I see him."

We followed the vampire a few blocks north. This area was congested and busy even by New York standards; tourists in goofy T-shirts held newspapers or shopping bags over their heads as they ran, and cabs honked angrily in the streets, their wipers beating staccato thumps against the downpour. Mostly I saw office buildings, hotels, and stores. This meant the vampire might duck in any place at any second.

What am I going to do? I thought. Pretending to lose him in the crowd was no use. Raquel's sharp eyes never left him.

The dreadlocked vampire turned onto a crosstown street and went into a building whose doorway was tucked almost surreptitiously between two huge storefronts.

Raquel pulled out her cell phone. "I'm calling Dana."

"No, don't do that."

"Bianca, are you nuts? That's a vampire! This is probably a vampire lair! We need backup."

"We don't know what else is going on in there." The reasoning was weak, but I didn't know anything else to say. As she started punching in Dana's number, I hurried a few steps in front of her to inspect the door. I could see bells with names next to them in the vestibule.

Then the glass door swung open, and another resident—a human woman, scary-thin and only a few years older than me, stepped out and gave me a slightly vacant smile as she held the door open for me. She must have assumed I lived there, and her welcome apparently put the doorman off guard, because he just kept reading a magazine. Quickly, I stepped inside and let the door shut behind me.

Raquel appeared on the other side of the glass door. "What are you doing?"

"I'm checking things out, okay? You stay out here to call for help if we need to."

"Seriously, you need to wait."

Ignoring Raquel, I hurried to the elevator. Golden circles outlined the elevator's progression upward. Okay, I could work with that. Once I saw where it stopped, I could go to that floor and maybe use my sensitive vampire hearing to find where the vampire had gone.

But then I heard a whisper. "You, there."

I stared. In a small cubby at the end of the lobby, near what looked like a side door, stood the vampire. His body was tense, almost in a crouch, and his brilliant blue eyes locked with mine.

"You're one of us," he said, in an accent that I thought might be Australian. "So what are you doing with Black Cross?"

"Long, long, long story." At least he knew he was being tracked. "They're on to you. You have to get out of here for now."

"I just got this place. D'ya have any idea how hard it is to find a place on the East Side?"

"If you take off now, they won't think about coming back here even after a couple of days. They don't think we have . . . homes, or friends, or anything like that." The bitterness in my voice surprised me; I thought I'd made my peace with our situation in Black Cross, at least for now, but the pent-up tension threatened to shake loose. "All you have to do is clear out for a couple of days. Stay with someone you know."

"Summer in the Hamptons," he said, almost like he was making fun of me. But why would he do that when I was trying to save him? I decided I'd heard him wrong when he smiled. "You're one of our babies, aren't you?"

"Yeah." I smiled back. It felt nice to be recognized for what I was, to have a couple of moments where being a vampire was no big deal. For a moment, I even missed Evernight Academy.

"Name's Shepherd," he said. "Have we got ten minutes, you think? I'd like to grab a couple things before running off."

"Maybe. They won't know where you are in the building, though they have ways of tracking—"

"We'll be quick about it. Help a fellow out, would you?"

We rode the elevator to the ninth floor. The whole way up, I held my breath, sure that at any moment Raquel would call, or Black Cross hunters would be waiting for us. But we got there fine, and I hurried after Shepherd to his apartment. "You only have time to grab the basics," I said. "Some clothes, some cash, whatever ID you're using."

"Believe me," he said. "I understand the deadline."

I walked into the apartment, ready to start helping him pack up anything—until I saw Charity.

She was sitting cross-legged on a white leather sofa, intently smoking a cigarette. Shepherd said, "Is she the right one? The one you thought you saw the other day?"

"Yes," Charity said softly. "That's her.

"Don't run," she said in the last half second before I was going to flee. "We have so much to talk about. And we can't talk while we're chasing you."

As dangerous as it was to stay, I thought running might be worse. If I ran, Charity and her friend would come after me for sure; if I talked, there was every chance I'd be safe. Despite all the horrific things Charity had done, she'd never attempted to hurt me. So I stayed. "What are you doing in New York?" I demanded.

"My brother is missing. He went on one of Mrs. Bethany's foolish errands. I suppose he's trying to find you."

I turned toward Shepherd, sick at my own foolishness. "I was trying to save you."

"A word to the wise," he said. "The enemy of your enemy isn't necessarily your friend."

I took stock of my surroundings. Charity's apartment looked as though it had been very nice only a short time ago, but nobody had cleaned it in several days. The white shag rug was covered with footprints and cigarette butts and, on one corner, rusty smears of blood. A large TV hung on the wall but slightly askew, as if it had been knocked partly loose. A sickly-sweet smell hung in the air, and I realized that a human had died here not long ago. Charity had taken this apartment by force.

She wasn't in much better shape than the apartment. Her pale golden curls didn't seem to have been washed recently. Charity wore only a silky lavender slip with beige lace that might have been pretty when it was new and clean; now it was stained and threadbare, making it painfully obvious how youthful her body was. She had only been fourteen when she died.

Trying very hard to keep my voice steady, I said, "Balthazar's okay. I can promise you that."

"Are you sure? Very sure?" Charity leaped up from the sofa, her childlike face alight with hope. Even now that I knew how insane and vengeful she could be, something in me wanted to protect her—this wide-eyed, seemingly delicate girl who could look so afraid and alone.

But it was for Balthazar's sake, not hers, that I spoke. "Yes. He was injured, but he's healing. He's in a safe place now. I saw him just two days ago, and I think he'll be fine."

"Two days ago." Charity breathed out a sigh of purest relief, then held her face shockingly close to mine. At first I thought she was going to kiss me, which was weird enough, but then she inhaled so deeply that her whole body tensed. "Yes. You did. I can smell him on you still."

"Okay." Black Cross only gave us three minutes in the shower. I'd thought that was enough time to get clean, but now I felt self-conscious.

Charity's hands closed over mine—not to threaten but to soothe. "Where is he?"

I shook my head. "If Balthazar wanted you to know where he was, he'd find you. Right now, when he's weak—you need to leave him alone, Charity."

From his place on the white sofa, the dreadlocked vampire snorted with disgust. Charity tilted her head, and one oily ringlet tumbled loose across her cheek. "You won't tell me where he is?"

"Last winter you wanted him to leave you alone. Why not now?"

"I never realized how far gone he was," she said, which coming from a loony like Charity was almost unbelievably ironic. "Or what a hypocrite he's become. He used to admit he was a killer at heart. He used to remember that he killed me. So tell me where he is, Bianca. I want to remind him."

Could I run away before she caught me? I didn't think so. At least Raquel was outside; when I didn't show up after a while, she'd call for help. The best thing to do right now was stall. "I'm sorry, Charity. I won't."

"You're a vampire hunter now?" She pointed at my belt, where I wore a stake; my hand had come to rest near it, evidence of my subconscious desire to defend myself. "Black Cross, like your darling Lucas? Balthazar's not the only one who's lost."

Charity took another step forward as I shuffled back. One of her long, rail-thin arms pushed the apartment door shut, and I heard an automatic lock click. Because of her sweet, youthful face and her seemingly fragile form, it always surprised me to realize how tall she was—only a couple inches shorter than her brother. Her size was not the source of her power, but it served as a compelling reminder.

I need to distract her, I thought. *That will buy time.* "Mrs. Bethany's very angry."

"I just *bet*." She giggled girlishly. "You know how her nose gets so pinched when she gets mad? It always makes me laugh." Charity contorted her face into such a dead-on impression of Mrs. Bethany in a fury that I almost smiled despite my fear. But I didn't forget that this was how Charity worked—endearing herself to you to get you off your guard.

"Mrs. Bethany's got a lot of vampires behind her. Dozens, maybe hundreds."

That had a more powerful effect than I'd anticipated. "That must not happen," she whispered, the humor leaving her dark eyes. "The tribes must not unite behind Mrs. Bethany. It's important."

"Are you going to tell me why?"

"Yes," Charity said, surprising me. Then she smiled, too sweetly. "After you tell me where my brother is. And you *will* tell me."

Shepherd sprang toward me with blinding speed. I was able to dodge out of the way, but only barely, and I stumbled against the wall. As he came back toward me, I remembered sparring with Lucas in Black Cross training, and the moves came to me—dodge left, grab his arm, spin him around, and push. Shepherd hit the door so hard it vibrated.

I felt like a major badass—at least, for the second it took Charity to grab me from behind.

"Let me go!" I cried. "There are others coming!"

"Not in time to save you." Charity dragged me backward hard enough that I lost my footing, then she threw me onto the shag rug.

Panic seized me, threatening to rob me of the power to think or even move—until the window shattered with a crash. Glass flew everywhere, and I cried out just as Shepherd screamed in pain. He fell forward, half on top of me. Desperately I pushed him aside and glimpsed the stake protruding from his back.

A crossbow! Somebody fired through the window!

Charity swore, lunged forward, and pulled the stake out of Shepherd. I was frantically wriggling out from under him, but she seemed to have other priorities. "We'll get back to this," she said, pulling a sputtering, woozy Shepherd to his feet. "Move."

They ran out the door, and for a moment I was alone, breathing hard, almost too stunned to think. Then, outside, I heard Dana yell, "Where the hell is Bianca?"

"Dana!" I pushed myself upright. My knees felt like they were made of jelly. "Dana, I'm okay!"

But already I could hear the sounds of fighting—the dull wet thuds of body blows and shouts of pain, echoing within the hall.

I went to the doorway and looked outside. Charity had vanished. Shepherd and Dana struggled alone at the far end of the hall, near an exit door where the stairs apparently were. It was hard to tell who was winning, but I glimpsed Shepherd's face and saw that his fangs were extended, ready for the bite. "Look out!" I shouted.

Dana twisted, punched Shepherd hard with her left hand, and then pushed. He tumbled through the door, over the railing, and down the stairwell, echoing off the metal banister as he repeatedly struck it on the way down.

"Come on!" she shouted. "No time for the elevator!" I followed her, running as fast as my shaking legs would take me. But by the time we got down to the street level, Shepherd was gone. The doorman slumped over his booth, unconscious; either Dana had knocked him out, or Shepherd and Charity had.

We left the building, staggering out into the rain. I didn't care about getting wet; all I needed was never to be in that place again. Raquel lit up when we emerged. "Thank God you're both okay."

"Did you see him?" Dana said. "Wannabe Rasta boy?"

"No, nobody came out this way. Maybe Milos saw." Raquel pointed up at a rooftop across the street, where I could just make out a figure with a crossbow. Milos—one of the cruelest of the vampire hunters—was the only reason I was still alive.

"You look shaken up." Dana put her hands on my shoulders. "You okay, Bianca?"

I shook my head. She pulled me into a big hug, and Raquel embraced me from behind. I could feel their relief as powerfully as my own.

They were two of my dearest friends. They were vampire

hunters. They loved me. They stood by while Balthazar was tortured. I was so angry with them I could scream, and I loved them so much it hurt. I knew they were doing wrong to kill vampires, and yet the vampire I had just tried to save had betrayed me. None of it could be untangled; I just had to live with it.

Without a word, I hugged them back and told myself that everything past this moment didn't matter.

The next day, I was excused from patrol, which was nice enough, but Eliza went the extra mile and gave Lucas the day off, too. Well, "day off," in this instance, meant "digging through the rubble of our old headquarters instead of hunting vampires." Some others might join us later, she said, but for now the task was left up to me and Lucas, alone. As long as we were together, I'd take it.

"Are you sure you're okay?" he said for the dozenth time. We were standing near one of the old train car cabins, knee-deep in broken stone. Both of us were as dirty as we'd been the day of the attack.

"I promise, I'm fine. Charity just scared me."

"She wants to change you," Lucas said. "And it sounds like she plans to hunt you down."

"I'm safe while I have my bodyguard with me," I joked, poking at his firm biceps. Lucas was shirtless, a concession to the stifling summer heat within the tunnels. Before, fans had kept the space livable; now, it was almost a hundred degrees and so humid that walking felt like swimming.

Lucas kissed me, a sloppy, sexy sort of kiss that would've made us both desperate for each other, if our surroundings had been any less grimy. When our lips parted, he said, "We really do have to find a way to get some time together."

"It won't be long before we're alone together all the time." I rested my hands against his bare chest. Shyly, I added, "I can't wait."

His eyes sought mine, eager and questioning. Voice low and deliciously rough, Lucas said, "Whatever you're ready for—whenever you're ready—I'd never rush you, you know that—"

I kissed him again, and this time the kiss went to my head. Dizzy, I breathed, "I want to be with you. Completely."

Lucas leaned close once more, but the dizziness got to me—it was more than the kiss. I put out one hand, laughing from self-consciousness, and he took it as he lowered me into a seated position. "I said you were looking pale. Bianca, are you sure you feel all right?"

"It really is hot in here," I admitted. "Plus I'm kind of hungry."

"We can knock off any time, you know. They'll be excavating in here for months. What we get done on any one day hardly matters."

"There are some things I want to find." I brushed my sweaty bangs back from my forehead as I looked at Lucas. Once again, I found myself being far too conscious of his heartbeat and the pulse just beneath his skin. "I could do with something to eat."

"You mean blood?"

I glanced around us, though it was only force of habit; we were alone in the tunnel and could speak openly. "Yeah."

"Then I'll get you blood."

"Not yours," I said sharply. Right now I could get carried away.

Lucas shook his head. "There's a hospital not far from here. I'll make a little blood-bank run. I'll bring cold water, too."

"Sounds great."

After he went up onto the street, I sat with my back against the wall for a few long minutes. All day I'd told myself that I was only woozy because I was hungry for blood and because yesterday had been so frightening. Now that I was working so hard in the heat, wasn't it only natural for me to feel faint?

Yet the weakness I sensed seemed to go deeper than that— almost as if I were coming down with a virus or something. I so rarely got sick that I wasn't sure I'd even recognize the symptoms. Probably this was nothing more than a nasty summer cold that just happened to arrive on a bad day.

Sighing, I pushed myself up. If I was going to feel crappy no matter what, I might as well get some work done.

I went into the old subway car, then flicked on the flashlight. Gravel and glass were thick on the floor, and almost everything inside was filthy. But when I saw a scribbled line drawing still taped to one wall, I smiled. That was Raquel's work, which meant this was our old quarters.

Eagerly I began digging the rocks from beneath the bunk

that had been mine. Reaching through the filthy dust, I was able to close my fingers around a scrap of cloth and pull hard, so that my bag emerged from the rubble. The few clothes I'd had would be ruined, but maybe, just maybe—

Yes! I pulled out the jet brooch Lucas had given me when we were first dating. Although its shiny black surface was murky with dust, the fine carving appeared undamaged. Thrilled, I tried pinning it to the cheap T-shirt I wore, but the fabric was too thin; instead, I put it on the waistband of my jeans.

"Hello?" Lucas called from above. I stood on one of the bunks and pushed myself up to see Lucas making his way toward me, paper bags in both hands.

"Look what I found!" I hurried to him, trying to ignore my dizziness. "It's still perfect."

His fingers found the brooch at my waist. "I can't believe you've managed to hang onto this through everything."

"I'll never let it go."

Lucas held up one of the brown paper bags and said, "Water." Then he held up the other and said, "not water."

He could even joke about giving me blood. With a grin, I reached into that sack and pulled out a bag of blood, fresh from the hospital freezer and deliciously cool. Normally I liked my blood close to body temperature, but on a hot day like this, something cold would be perfect.

"Huh," Lucas said, furrowing his forehead. "I didn't think about getting, like, a straw."

"I can bite through with my fangs," I said, then thought

better of it. "Or just poke a hole with your knife."

"Why not fangs?"

"You really don't mind seeing me like that?" I glanced up at him through lowered eyelids.

"Considering how hot and heavy we've been every time I saw your fangs, I have to say I kinda like seeing you like that."

He was almost daring me. I enjoyed this. "Okay," I said. "Watch."

With the blood right there in my hands, it wasn't hard to give into it—the familiar ache in my jaw, then the extension of what looked like my canine teeth. When the points jutted into my mouth, I covered my lips with one hand, then let that hand drop.

"There," I said, letting him look at me. I felt so exposed, until he smiled, and then I felt—invincible.

"Go on," he said. "Eat."

I bit into the bag, welcoming the cool rush of blood into my mouth. Lucas had only been able to grab a single pint, so I went slow, making it last. Closing my eyes to savor it better, I swallowed once, twice—

"Oh, my God."

It was Raquel's voice.

My eyes flew open as Lucas and I whirled around to see Dana and Raquel, who had just come down into the tunnel. Eliza had said others might come later, but they were here early. Here now. Watching me drink blood.

Chapter Eleven

"WAIT," I SAID, HOLDING OUT MY HANDS. "HEAR us out."

Raquel and Dana didn't run, but they didn't look like they were going to listen, either. They were both frozen, shock-still, staring at me—at the friend who had just been revealed as a vampire, the creature they hated most in the world.

The bag of blood fell from my trembling hands. Red droplets spattered onto the dust and gravel. I felt like I might plunge to the ground with it at any second. My fangs slid back up into my jaw as though they were trying to hide.

Why hadn't I heard them? My vampire senses should've warned me. But I'd been feeling weak—and Lucas had distracted me—and here we were.

For what felt like eternity, we faced one another. Everyone was breathing hard. When I looked into Raquel's eyes and saw the naked hurt and terror there, I wanted to cry, but I held it together.

Lucas didn't join in the banter. "Dana, tell me what you're going to do."

"I honestly don't know," she replied. Her broad face, normally never without a smile, was gravely serious now. "I believe what you're telling me, but the fact remains that having a vampire in our organization, knowing what we know—I don't think that's a great idea. I don't care what kind of vampire she is, she shouldn't have jack to do with Black Cross."

On that point, we were in total agreement. "Lucas and I want to leave," I said. "Soon. I've always known I couldn't stay here."

"Biding your time, huh?" Dana didn't look impressed.

Lucas stepped closer to her. "We'll be gone in a few weeks," he promised. "If you don't think you can keep the secret that long—just tell us right now, and I'll get out of here with Bianca this instant. It's your call."

"You're really ready to leave us? To walk away from this work?" Dana looked disappointed—no, more like crushed. She and Lucas had been best friends almost their whole lives; losing him, and discovering that he'd kept such a major secret from her, had to hit her hard. "I thought this was your world. I thought you were committed."

"It's more complicated than I used to think. They aren't all evil, Dana." Lucas's lopsided smile nearly broke my heart. "Besides—I love her. She needs me. That means my choice is made."

"I gotta think." Dana stepped back to pace along the edge of the tunnel, at least in the small space that had been cleared of debris. That left us alone with Raquel, who had yet to say a word.

"Raquel?" I ventured. No response. "I know you're angry. I don't blame you. But if you think about it—really—can't you see why I didn't?"

She nodded slowly.

"You do?" Well, that was something, anyway. "This doesn't have to change things. Not if you don't let it."

"That's good," Raquel whispered. I started to relax. What I'd taken for horror in her reaction was probably merely shock. Maybe we'd be okay, if Dana would only come around.

Lucas's hand found mine, and I held on tightly. I wondered if we would have to run and whether I even could run, as weak and shaky as I felt.

Dana stopped pacing and said, "A few weeks, you said. What's the holdup?"

"Eduardo took the cash I'd been saving," Lucas said. "I've only been able to put away a little more since then."

"Makes sense."

"Dana, spit it out." Lucas sounded almost angry. "What are you going to tell the others?"

"Nothing."

"Don't lie to me."

"You heard me. I won't say anything." Dana's expression was flat, but she sounded sincere. "Let's go back."

"They'll ask why we aren't digging," I said, unsure whether the crisis could really be over.

"And we'll tell them it's too damn hot down here for Satan

to have a steam bath. I get the feeling we've all been through enough today already." Dana headed toward the exit, then glanced back at us. "Come on, everybody."

There didn't seem to be anything to do but follow her. None of us said one word on the way back.

Saying that night felt tense would be a massive understatement.

Throughout dinner, Lucas and I sat next to each other, trying not to stare at Dana or Raquel. We were eating plain rice for about the tenth day in a row, and every grain seemed to stick in my throat. Raquel and Dana didn't look at us. In fact, they were making such a point of not looking at us that I felt like everyone would surely notice.

Instead, the others were wrapped up in different concerns.

"For his own safety, Lucas needs to keep moving from cell to cell from now on," Eliza said, stabbing at her plate of rice with a plastic spork. "Or at least until we've taken care of Mrs. Bethany."

Easier said than done, I thought. Black Cross's best hunters had gone against Mrs. Bethany three times in the past few months, and she'd killed at least a dozen of them without taking a scratch.

Kate hadn't really been eating since Eduardo died. She simply pushed the rice around on her plate, making little grooves. "You're telling me I can't keep my son with me any longer?"

Eliza didn't flinch. "I'm saying you should dissolve your cell."

"We've been together awhile," Dana said. It was the first time she'd talked all night. Lucas and I both flinched. "Practically my whole life, and Lucas's, too."

"The cell should've been a lot more fluid long before now," Eliza said. "You know that."

"Yeah," Kate said. "I know that." She let her spork fall to her plate.

I saw the tension knotting the muscles of Lucas's shoulders. As claustrophobic and demanding as the life was, despite the zealotry Lucas had outgrown, his Black Cross cell remained the only sort of home or family he'd ever known. I knew how lost he had to feel, how alone. Sometimes, despite everything, I missed Evernight Academy—where at least I'd been warm and comfortable every night, and had as much as I wanted to eat, and knew that my parents were looking after me.

Here, I was afraid, and even my best friends could possibly turn into my enemies.

I glanced up from my rice, hoping to meet Raquel's eyes, but she was looking at Dana. Her expression was unreadable.

"Give it time," Lucas murmured, as everyone bunked down for the night. He curled behind me, as he had before; I'd never been so grateful to have him close. "I think we'll be okay."

"But Dana—" She'd been raised in Black Cross. She'd been willing to leave Balthazar to his fate. How could she accept me so quickly?

"Shhh." He said it as if he were soothing me, but I knew it was a genuine warning. The others were lying down, too, and they were close enough to hear every word.

The lights were put out, and I lay next to Lucas—both in his arms and a million miles away. He fell asleep quickly, to judge by his deep, even breathing and the relaxation of his arm around my waist.

See, Lucas thinks everything's safe. He's not worried a bit.

No, he's a hunter. He's used to resting when he can so he'll have energy to fight later if he must.

Well, then, I'll try to be a hunter, too.

As soon as I gave in to my exhaustion, sleep grabbed me quickly. I'd been more tired than I realized. My head, my eyelids, my limbs—all of it felt so heavy—

The darkness folded itself around me, as warm and comforting as a blanket.

"Get up."

The flashlight's beam blinded me, jolting me from sleep. I felt Lucas shift and heard him groan, "What's going on?"

More sternly, Eliza repeated, "Get up."

I pushed myself up on my elbows and squinted, trying to make out shapes in the room. The darkness coalesced into forms—most of the Black Cross hunters, standing around us in a semicircle, weapons on their hands.

Dana told them about me.

My stomach clenched so painfully I thought I might vomit. The rushing of blood in my ears, quickening with my pulse, deafened me to almost anything else. My whole body seemed to go cold, and I kept thinking, *Go back, go back*, like I could somehow stop time and make all of this not be happening. It seemed like there had to be some way out, but there wasn't.

Lucas's hand closed over mine. Though I knew he had to be as frightened as I was, he said, evenly, "You'd better tell us what this is about."

"You know what it's about," Eliza said. "Don't you?"

"Yeah. I expect I do." He took a deep breath as he quickly scanned the room. Dana wasn't there—coward—and she'd no doubt taken Raquel with her so Raquel wouldn't protest. But I realized that he wasn't looking for them, but for his mother. Kate was nowhere to be seen. Did she have any idea what was going on? Surely not. They had come up with some pretext for sending her away, and the one person who might still have been in a position to help us was gone. "What happens now?"

Eliza's smile was cold. "Now we go upstairs and have a little chat."

She meant the ground-level room where Balthazar had been kept.

I felt like I couldn't move, like they would have to drag me up there. But Lucas squeezed my hand and said, "Come on, Bianca. You and me. Let's go."

His strength flowed into me, and I managed to get to my feet. "Can I get dressed?" I asked. I was surprised how steady my voice sounded.

Eliza shrugged. "Throw on your jeans. But move."

In our jeans and T-shirts, we made our way up the stairs onto the harbor. It was very late—or very early—whichever way you wanted to look at it, the dead of night. No boats floated upon the river, and even the omnipresent roar of traffic was only a whisper. Briefly we were outside, a taunting taste of freedom, before they pushed us into the storage room. Blood stained the concrete floor.

I thought for sure they would handcuff us, the way they had Balthazar, but they didn't. Lucas and I stood in the center of the dark room. The others surrounded us. When the lights were flipped on, the starkness of the scene—the angry faces surrounding us and the weapons they carried—made my stomach clench even tighter.

"What is she?" Eliza demanded of Lucas.

He began, "She was born to vampires—sometimes they can—"

"Skip it." Eliza's hand rested upon a stake in her belt. "We heard your little story. What we want now are facts. How strong is she? What powers does she have?"

"You've seen her work out and fight along with the rest of us." Lucas stood partly in front of me, as if trying to shield me. "If you don't know what she can do by now, blame yourselves."

"This is a really bad time for backtalk," Eliza warned.

Lucas's eyes narrowed. "From where I'm standing, this is a really bad time, period."

"You got that right," said somebody.

I noticed that all the hunters were looking at Lucas—not at me. He was the one they talked to, the one they wanted explanations from. Although they were angry with Lucas, he was still a human being. Still a person.

I was only a monster.

Eliza's fingers tightened around the stake. Would she really use that on me? I was still alive, which meant being staked wouldn't paralyze me: it would kill me. I knew nobody in this room but Lucas would care if she did. Strong as Lucas was, he couldn't possibly defend me against twenty trained, armed hunters. My own strength and fighting skills wouldn't add much to our chances.

"How many of them are there?" somebody in the back demanded. "These—vampire spawn."

"We're rare." I blurted it out, too loudly, almost shouting. But I could at least speak for myself. "Maybe five are born in a century. That's what I've always heard."

There was a tangible sense of hesitation in the room. I could tell that they wanted to ask me further questions and learn more, but they didn't want to talk to me—to treat me as a person.

That would make it harder for them to kill me.

Fear pooled in my belly, cold and heavy. It was so hard to stand when my legs wanted to give out from under me. Only Lucas's presence at my side kept me steady. Desperately I wished for my mother and father, who would never know what had become of me. I wanted them to come save me. I wanted them to hug me one more time.

"We better find out what we can about them," said Milos. "Find out what their vulnerabilities are." I twitched as I recognized what he was holding: the neon-green water gun, no doubt loaded with holy water. They were going to start by burning my skin. *Be brave*, I thought. Would holy water burn me now? Consecrated ground and crosses had always been problems—so probably it would sear my flesh the way it did any other vampire's.

I wouldn't shrink away, wouldn't even turn my head. They wanted to see me afraid, but I could at least deny them that.

"Don't do that." Lucas held up his hands, trying in vain to reason with them. "If you guys will just listen—dammit!"

Milos sprayed holy water at me, and Lucas stepped between me and the spray. I was so grateful to him—at least, in the split second before I realized he'd made the worst mistake of his life.

The holy water hit Lucas and began to smoke. He cried out as it burned his flesh, the same way that it would burn a vampire's.

"What the hell?" Milos shouted, as people began to swear and freak out. I was nearly as shocked as they were, but only for an instant; Lucas had been gaining vampire powers and vulnerabilities ever since I first drank his blood. Now holy water was as dangerous to him as it was to me. Lucas winced in pain, but his expression soon shifted to one of horror. Our eyes met, and I could see that he knew: Now he would be only a monster to them, too.

Eliza stepped forward. There were no words to describe the depthless contempt in her voice as she said, "Lucas feeds it."

The silence that fell was deadly. I tried to think of something to say, but there was nothing. Instead I took Lucas's hand

and attempted to feel that, only that, just his fingers in mine. I wanted him to be the only thing in the world.

"Guys," Lucas began, "listen to me."

Milos held up the gun in a wordless warning to shut up. Lucas stopped talking.

Eliza said, "We need to get these two to one of the professors. Study them, figure out how they've changed and why. We need all the info we can get out of them."

Before they die went unsaid.

"Cuff 'em. Load them into one of the vans." Her eyes were cold as she finished, "Get this trash out of here."

They handcuffed our hands in front of us and walked us to one of the vans. To my shock, Dana sat in the driver's seat, and she didn't glance at me or Lucas as we were brought out. Was that guilt? Revulsion? Did she simply not care any longer?

Milos sat beside her, and he had holy water and stakes handy. Some of the others chained our handcuffs to metal bars soldered to the wall of the van; I'd always wondered why the vans had those. Well, now I knew. Dana came around briefly to double-check that we were securely bound. I stared at her with all the hatred in my heart—more hate than I'd known I could feel for a human being. She didn't seem to notice the venom in my glare as she turned to check Lucas's cuffs, too.

Then she returned to the driver's seat, and we took off. I knew there were a couple of cars following us; the headlights shone through the back windows of the van.

"Bet you cash money they didn't torch that other one," Milos said to Dana. "We're gonna have to go looking for pretty boy."

Great. Now Balthazar's doomed, too.

In despair, I glanced over at Lucas. He didn't look nearly as upset as I did. Actually, he didn't look that upset at all. He looked—*excited*.

Slowly he unfolded one of his fists to reveal handcuff keys in his palm.

How did he do that? All I knew was that we could get our handcuffs open, and maybe we had a chance.

Dana turned on the van's radio, and music flooded the space. Instantly Lucas went to work, fumbling with his own cuffs for just a second until they opened. I watched him flex his hands, testing his strength. Together we looked toward the front of the van, but neither Dana nor Milos was watching us. So he leaned forward, flash fast, and dropped the keys in my hand.

My clammy hands were slick, and I was scared I might drop the keys, but I didn't. Instead I tried to work the key into the lock; it was harder than it looked and made my fingers cramp. I wondered what we'd do once we were free. Jump out the back and run for it? With the cars right behind us, that didn't give us much hope—but it was better than nothing.

"Hey," Milos said. "Stop at the yellow."

"I can make it." Dana nonchalantly drove on.

"Dammit." Milos leaned to examine his passenger-side mirror. "The others got stuck behind the light. Cop's right there, so they can't run it."

"No big," Dana said. "They know where we're going."

Lucas lunged forward, grabbing Dana across the neck. He snarled at Milos, "Get outta the van or I slash her throat."

Dana screamed. My mind went blank with panic.

Where did Lucas get a knife? With shaking hands, I kept working with the handcuff key, and finally the metal cuffs snapped open. Milos nodded once, at Dana, and she pulled the van over with a jerk.

Milos got out, but he said, "You aren't getting far."

"Wait and see," Lucas said, leaning forward to pull the van's door shut. Instantly Dana slammed onto the gas. The van's tires squealed against the pavement. Lucas said, "You think they bought it?"

I wanted to ask what they were supposed to have bought, but it was Dana who answered. "Maybe. Maybe not. We gotta move."

"What's going on?" I demanded. The van bumped along the pavement, jarring us all.

Lucas gave me a quick hug. "Dana slipped me the handcuff keys. I knew how to play it from there. What I don't know is whether she's got any plan beyond this."

"Nope," Dana said. "This is pretty much it, plan-wise. Sorry, but I didn't have a whole lot of time."

"Why are you doing this?" I demanded. "Why turn us in and then get us out? Did your conscience finally get to you?"

There was a brief pause, during which all we heard was the

music on the radio. Dana finally said, "Bianca, I didn't turn you in."

Raquel.

Betrayal burned like fire. I should've felt angry, but I didn't. All I could think about was the picnic we had on the Evernight grounds, the one Raquel had put together to cheer me up. We'd eaten sandwiches together on the grass and pointed out the new yellow starburst blooms of dandelions. It had been springtime. She had done that for me, and then in summer she'd given me up to die.

"Don't be mad at her," Dana said. "She's new to all this. She got confused. I know she's going to regret it."

Lucas said, roughly, "Later. What are we doing now?"

"I'm dropping y'all around Grand Central," Dana said. "From there you can catch a train to anywhere."

"Not if we're broke." My voice sounded unbelievably harsh, even to me. "Did you think to bring money?"

Dana winced. "No. No time. This isn't going in the Rescue Hall of Fame, is it?"

"You're doing great," Lucas said. "Just let us out and I can take it from there."

She pulled over on a side street. Skyscrapers loomed here, their lights blazing even at this hour. It wasn't yet dawn, but the sky had begun to lighten. Nobody much was on the roads, just a few taxis. To my surprise, Dana got out of the van when we did and walked around to us. She and Lucas faced each other squarely.

"You still don't know what to think," Lucas said. "Do you?"

She shook her head. "Nope. But, Lucas, you're as close to a brother as I'm ever gonna have. I'd rather be wrong to set you free than be right to do you harm."

Lucas made this weird choking sound in his throat, and then all of a sudden, he and Dana were hugging each other tightly. I saw a tear roll down Dana's cheek.

When they let go, I wanted to say thank you, but I was still angry with her. The fact that I was wrong to be angry with Dana instead of Raquel didn't seem to have much to do with anything. I managed to say, "What will you tell the others?"

"That Lucas took me hostage."

"Will they believe that?" I said. Milos was already suspicious of Balthazar's "death."

"He will once Lucas makes it convincing," Dana said, squaring her shoulders.

I didn't get what was going on, but Lucas apparently did. He grimaced. "I really don't want to."

"Let me refresh your memory on how this works," Dana said. "I save your butt, you save mine. Do it!"

Lucas punched her in the face so hard she slammed into the back of the van. I gasped. Although Dana staggered, she managed to stay on her feet. Lucas said, "You okay?"

"Will be," she said thickly. Blood dripped from her lip onto the pavement. "Why do you have to be so good at your work?"

"Dana," I began. "Are you sure—"

"Why are you still here?" she demanded.

Lucas grabbed my hand, and the two of us began to run. My breath caught in my throat, and the sidewalk jarred my feet, but I pushed myself to go faster and faster. All I could hear was Dana's voice behind us, shouting, "Get out while you can!"

Chapter Twelve

ALTHOUGH THERE SHOULD'VE BEEN AN AGENT IN the subway booth, it was empty; maybe somebody thought 4 A.M. was as good a time as any to take a break. It gave us a chance to jump the turnstiles and wait for a train.

We sat together on one of the old wooden benches, which was layered thick with graffiti. Neither of us said anything at first. I felt like everything around me was very far away, and it was hard to remember that this wasn't some bad dream or a terrible memory. It was like my brain wanted to trick me into thinking that it couldn't be happening here or now.

The first thing that intruded into my consciousness sharply enough to goad me into speaking was the sign hanging overhead.

"'Downtown,'" I read. "That's the direction we want to go, right?"

"Don't see what difference it makes." Lucas leaned his head against the tiled wall. "As long as we're putting some distance between us and them, it's all good."

All good were not words I would've used to describe our situation. I thought I realized what he was trying to do. "I know you want to be strong for me," I said softly, "but right now I think it's more important that you be honest with me."

"Strong." Lucas closed his eyes tightly. "Is that what I'm being? Because it doesn't feel like it."

Black Cross was all he ever had in the world, I told myself. *What I went through was horrible, but for Lucas, tonight was even worse. He lost his mother, his best friend—everything but me. Maybe it's my turn to be the strong one for a while.*

"We'll be okay." I took his arm in my hands and examined the burns from the holy water. They were thin pink stripes that looked like lines of very bad sunburn. "Wait and see."

Just then a gust of wind blew through the tunnel, heralding the arrival of the train. I cast a worried glance behind us as we boarded, but nobody followed. Only one other person was on the car, a college-age guy who was asleep across the seats and smelled strongly of beer.

As the train rumbled into motion, I led Lucas toward a map of the subway system. "You know your way around New York better than I do," I said. "So you can figure out if we're going the right way."

Lucas moved slowly, like a man walking through water. He focused on the map, clearly wanting to do something useful. "Like I said before, there's no right way. Except, you know, farther from them."

"Of course there's a right way." I was surprised Lucas hadn't seen it; the answer seemed so obvious, to me. "We need money and a safe place to hide for a little while. In other words, we need to find a friend."

"Balthazar," he said.

I nodded. "So, are we headed to Chinatown or not?"

Lucas put his hands on either side of the map. "Yeah. We're going the right way."

Although Lucas remembered the name of the street Balthazar had directed us to, at first neither of us could spot the correct store. It was too early for the shops to be open, so they all looked the same: identical storefronts shuttered tightly with metal grates. We had to wait.

Waiting around in the early morning hours when you have no money, not even a few dollars for coffee? There's nothing to do, *nothing*, and time seems to stretch into infinity.

I can't say it was boring, though. We knew that at any second a Black Cross patrol might sweep through and see us. That kept the adrenaline pumping.

"We should have stayed on the train," I said wearily, after a couple hours of walking around the block. "We could've slept, like that drunk guy."

"Could you sleep right now? Honestly?"

I sighed. "Probably not."

Lucas cast a sidelong glance at me, and his mouth quirked in a half smile.

"What is it?" I asked.

"You're not allowed to get mad."

"It's my hair, isn't it?" I turned to see my reflection in the window of a nearby dry cleaners. Although my outline was a bit hazy because of the enforced diet I'd been on lately, I could see that, sure enough, my dark-red hair stuck up at weird angles. It was obvious that I'd been yanked out of bed and hadn't had a chance to take care of it. Quickly I combed through it with my fingers, trying to restore some kind of neatness. "Oh, my God."

"You look fine," Lucas said. "Just silly, kind of."

"Oh, yeah?" I gave him a mock-angry glare. "You've looked prettier, too, you know."

He rubbed his chin, clearly feeling the stubble there. Between the five o'clock shadow, the rumpled clothes, and his wild bronze hair, Lucas came across as fairly disreputable. I almost liked that nobody but me could tell what kind of person he really was.

"Maybe we should make a trip to the beauty salon," he said. "Get his and hers manicures."

I laughed. "You'd rather go back for the fall term at Evernight Academy."

That made him grin, too. "Oh, I can just see that. 'Hey, Mrs. Bethany, miss me?'"

The shared joke warmed us both and took the edge off our exhaustion and fear. We embraced, and it would've lasted a long time but for something sharp jabbing into my abdomen. "Ow. What the—"

I looked down to see my jet brooch, still pinned to the waistband of my jeans, where I'd put it the afternoon before. Tenderly

I touched the carved petals of the flowers there.

"You've still got it," Lucas said. "If we could only bring one thing with us, I'm glad it was that. Of course, if we could've brought two things with us, my coffee can of money would've been the second choice."

Although I hated to say it, I had to. "We could pawn the brooch again, like we did when we first ran away."

Lucas shook his head and said, heavily, "I couldn't get it back for you this time."

After another hour or so, the shops finally opened. It was still hard to figure out which was the right one, because most of the stores seemed to stock a lot of the same merchandise: trinkets for tourists, mostly, like paper fans and parasols or polyester kimonos and slippers. Finally, I caught a glimpse of a woman behind a counter who looked familiar.

"Excuse me," I said, as Lucas and I wove our way through the merchandise toward her. "I'm looking for Balthazar."

She froze, and for a moment I thought she was scared of us. We did look pretty frightening. Then her face relaxed as she recognized me. She hurried to the back of the store, pulled back a bead curtain, and yelled something in Chinese. The old man I'd seen before appeared from behind the bead curtain; when he looked at Lucas, his eyes narrowed, but then he recognized me. He led us through the bead curtain and up two flights of rickety steps. Rapping twice on a door, he called to Balthazar, then motioned to us, like, *take it away*.

I opened the door. Inside was a small room with a sharply

slanted ceiling—an old storage room, or maybe an attic, that had been converted into a cramped bedroom. A double bed filled almost the entire room, and crates of paper parasols and fans filled most of the rest. The one lamp had an embroidered shade in brilliant orange and pink, which made the light unexpectedly warm and almost pretty. In the center of the bed, beneath a black silk coverlet emblazoned with a dragon, propped up on some pillows, lay Balthazar.

"Bianca?" He didn't quite seem to believe his eyes. "Lucas?"

"You look better," I said. He did, but that was a matter of degrees. Scars still marked his chin and cheeks. Balthazar wore no shirt, so I could see that in the center of his chest was a dark, angry star—where Lucas had staked him. None of that seemed to matter as much as the smile that spread across his face.

"It's good of you both to come," he said, "but it's dangerous."

"You've got it the wrong way around." Lucas closed the door. "We're the ones on the run this time."

"What?"

"I slipped up," I confessed. "Raquel saw me drinking blood, and she—well, she turned me in. We only barely managed to escape."

"Raquel—that's impossible. She wouldn't." Then Balthazar thought it over, moving past his initial rejection of the idea. "I'm sorry."

"We have to talk about something else," I said quickly. "If I start crying today, I don't think I'll be able to stop."

Balthazar winced as he pushed himself completely upright.

His voice was gentle as he said, "Sit down. Both of you."

The only place to sit was the foot of his bed. As soon as I touched the mattress, I knew I wanted to lie down, so I stretched out across the end. Lucas sat next to me cross-legged and stroked my jeans-clad calves with one hand. The bed felt like the most comfortable place in the world; until that moment, I hadn't realized it had been more than six weeks since I'd slept on a real mattress. I had almost forgotten anything could be so soft.

Balthazar said, "Tell me what you need."

"Cash," Lucas said bluntly. "If you've got any."

Balthazar motioned toward the corner. "My wallet is in the pocket of those slacks. Grab it, will you?"

Lucas did so and tossed it to Balthazar. Then my eyes went wide as Balthazar pulled out seven hundred-dollar bills and slapped them into Lucas's hand. "I'd give you more if I had it on me, but I don't."

"Whoa, whoa." Lucas stared down at the money. "This is—well, it's a lot."

"You saved my life, Lucas," Balthazar said. "I guess that means I owe you one."

Shaking his head, Lucas replied, "You don't have a life to save, buddy."

"You know what I mean," Balthazar said.

"Yeah, I guess I do. " Lucas was quiet for a few moments.

I protested, "Balthazar, we don't want to take all your money."

To my surprise, he laughed. "This is hardly all my money." When I frowned in confusion, Balthazar leaned against the headboard and smiled. "I invested in sugar in the eighteenth century. Coal in the nineteenth century. In the early twentieth century, I bought some stock in Ford Motor Company. In the late twentieth century, I sold that stock and sank the proceeds into computers. Money is not one of my problems." He sighed. "If you could remain in New York another week or so, by then I'd be able to go to the bank, get some real cash for you."

"That's okay, Moneybags," Lucas said. "This will get us out of town."

"If this is about pride, please, stop and think." Balthazar looked stern. "Keeping Bianca safe matters more than scoring points."

Lucas glared at him. "This doesn't have jack to do with pride. We can't even spend one more day in New York. They'll be watching the train and bus stations by this afternoon if they aren't already."

Balthazar held up one hand. "No time even to rest, huh?"

"Guess not," I said. Regretfully I pushed myself up from the soft bed. "Will we be able to reach you here?"

"It's going to be another week or two before I'm back on my feet. I'll be staying here."

"But, later than that—could the people downstairs forward a letter to you? Or do they have a phone number we could use?" A lump had begun to form in my throat. "There has to be some way we can talk to you again someday. This can't be good-bye forever. Right?"

Balthazar and Lucas shared a look. I knew they both thought

it would be safer if this really were good-bye forever. I also could tell that Balthazar didn't want this to be the ending for us either, and that Lucas didn't exactly approve. Looking Lucas very squarely in the eye, Balthazar said, "Take one of the cards at the cash register downstairs. That phone number will work for me while I'm here, and I will check in for messages every so often after that. You might ask them about transport out of town, too—there's a way to get out of New York without coming near a bus or train station." The pause was slightly awkward, so Balthazar quickly added, "And ask them for some blood before you go. They picked some up from the hospital for me yesterday, and you could probably do with a couple of pints."

"There's something else you have to know before we go." I felt weird about discussing this with Balthazar, but I knew he'd probably find out sooner or later. He needed to be on his guard. "Charity is in New York."

"What?" Balthazar pushed himself upright in bed. "Is she trying to find me? Does she need my help?"

"She needs help," Lucas deadpanned, "but not yours."

I shot Lucas a glare. "Charity's fine. She was worried about you, that's all." I wondered whether to tell him about her attack, but I decided against it. Balthazar was injured and in no shape to deal with that kind of news.

"One more thing," Lucas interjected. At first I thought that he was going to talk about Charity's attack, but he was thinking more constructively. "Black Cross suspects we might've let you go. They'll be looking for you, too. So I wouldn't hang out in

Manhattan any longer than you've got to."

"I understand."

I crawled forward and put my arms around Balthazar's neck. Because of the wound on his chest, I couldn't really hug him, not like I wanted to, but this would do. He rested his head against my shoulder. "Thank you," I whispered.

"Thank *you*," he said. "Both of you." Now that I had stood in the center of a ring of Black Cross hunters and feared for my life, the same way Balthazar had, I could understand the depth of gratitude he felt.

Right when the embrace threatened to last too long, I let go and backed off the bed without another word. That was the end of our farewells, except for my smiling over my shoulder at Balthazar as we went out the door. He held up his hand in a wave, visible in the narrowing crack of the door as Lucas pulled it shut.

Lucas paused, the two of us standing together on the cramped stairwell, and said, his voice low, "If you want to stay here, tell me now."

I kissed him, and it was all the answer he needed.

Chapter Thirteen

BALTHAZAR'S FRIENDS DIRECTED US TO A CHINA-
town bus, a cheap mode of transportation that usually shuffled
new immigrants from Asia between different Chinese-restaurant
jobs up and down the East Coast. However, it was a mixed lot
on the next bus to Philadelphia—a few older people and a lot
of college students typing on laptops they balanced on their
knees.

The bus was late, and it ran slow. Heavy rains up north,
the driver said. Flooding on the highways. We didn't care. Our
money was rolled up in the front pocket of my jeans; though it
dug into my flesh, I found the pressure of it reassuring.

I rested my head upon Lucas's shoulder as we leaned back
in the seats. Maybe the bus was really comfortable, or maybe
we were so tired that anything would've felt good. Both of us
drifted in and out of sleep. Sometimes I felt as though dreams
and wakefulness were bleeding together like watercolors, soft-
edged and pale. All that was real was the reassuring scent of

Lucas's skin and the knowledge that, for now at least, we were safe.

At one point, while the bus rumbled down the road, Lucas reached up to stroke my hair. I realized that he thought I was asleep—really, I nearly was—and somehow that made it even sweeter.

Mostly, though, we finally got some rest.

"Isn't it beautiful?" I pulled Lucas into the great hall of Evernight, which was decorated for the Autumn Ball. Candlelight softened the room into shadows, and the dancers moved easily through the steps of the waltz the orchestra was playing.

Lucas shook his head and tugged at the tie of his evening suit. "This is so not my scene. But seeing you like this—it's worth it."

I wore a strapless white dress that flowed from the empire waist to the floor, and I could see enough of my fading reflection in a nearby mirror that I knew I wore white flowers in my hair. Never had I felt so beautiful.

But that wasn't because I'd dressed up. It was because I was finally here with Lucas.

"Do you know how to waltz?" I whispered to him.

"Not a clue. But if you want to dance, let's get out there and fake it."

Laughing, I let Lucas take me in his arms, and we spun upon the dance floor. No, he couldn't waltz, but it didn't matter that we didn't fit with the other dancers. I watched them all around us—Patrice with her hand in Balthazar's, Courtney snickering at Ranulf's clumsy footwork, Dana neatly leading Raquel through a turn—and wondered why none of them danced the way they wanted to.

Then another figure appeared amid the dancers, a translucent figure that shimmered in aquamarine. The wraith came close to us and said, "May I cut in?"

"Of course," I said, wondering how she knew Lucas and why she wanted to dance with him. But it was my hand she took, and I gave him a regretful glance as the wraith and I got lost in the crowd of dancers. I could see him watching me, but then the crowd swallowed him up.

I awoke with a start. Quickly I glanced around to remind myself where I was and rested my head on Lucas's shoulder again. He mumbled something in his sleep before drowsily turning toward me, and I smiled, reassured.

We got to Philadelphia in the late afternoon. That wasn't so much where we were heading as it was a place for us to go, a city large enough for us to get lost in. Better yet, Philly had no permanent Black Cross cell. It was less likely that they'd be able to mount a large-scale hunt for us there.

"We'll stay here a couple of days at least," Lucas said. "We can find someplace cheap. Lie low. Figure out our options."

"Buy some more clothes," I said, motioning to our bedraggled T-shirts and jeans, "so we look a little less homeless."

"We *are* homeless," Lucas pointed out.

I hadn't thought of it that way before. "Clothes," I insisted. "Not a whole new wardrobe but some clean stuff. And toothbrushes, toothpaste, deodorant—"

"Yeah, I get your point."

A trip to a big-box store took care of all that. I got a couple of cheap little sundresses, one in dark blue and one in a deep green, that looked cool and comfortable, a simple purse that would go with everything, and a pair of thong sandals that would see me through the summer. Lucas grabbed some khakis and a couple of black T-shirts. Then we went to the drugstore section to get everything we needed to be less stinky, more pretty.

We turned the corner and there, lined up in rows, were the condoms. I started to avert my eyes, the way I always did, because I'd always been slightly embarrassed just by the packaging. I'm that big a wimp. This time, though, I stopped.

"Maybe we should get some," I said. I meant to sound womanly and confident, but instead it sort of came out squeaky.

"I guess." Lucas gave me a long, hard look. "Bianca, you know there's no rush."

I played with the ends of my hair, which had become suddenly fascinating. "I know that. I do. It's just—if we want—we should have them around. Just in case. Right?"

"Yeah."

For a couple seconds, neither of us moved, but then Lucas took the closest box and dropped it into our basket. My heart turned over stealthily, surprising me with the warm glow that seemed to light me up.

I couldn't make eye contact with the lady at the checkout counter. She didn't seem to care, though.

We got a hotel room downtown, not far from the bus station.

It was nicer than I would've expected, for the price—a coffee-maker in the room, a big TV, a nice bathroom with a blow-dryer and tons of fluffy white towels, and a very large bed.

"We should get some more rest before we get anything to eat," I suggested. We were both so tired that, even with the condoms sitting there in their plastic bag, I couldn't think of the bed except as a place to sleep.

Lucas seemed to feel the same way. "Yeah, let's. There are some diners around here we can go to later on."

"You know Philadelphia?"

"Been here a couple of times. That's all."

Together Lucas and I crawled into bed. Nothing was on my mind but sleep—until the moment we were under the covers, with him next to me.

We reached for each other at the same instant. Lucas's mouth found mine, and we kissed desperately, like we hadn't been together for years. His arms pulled me close, and I wound both my legs around one of his as our kisses deepened.

Within seconds, it felt like we were still too far away. I grabbed his T-shirt and started tugging it off him; he helped me with that, then pulled mine off. We kissed again, the touch electric with the feel of his skin on mine, but it still wasn't enough. With shaky hands, I fumbled with my bra straps, pushing them down, then finally unhooking it.

I'd always thought I would feel embarrassed the first time a guy saw me undressed, but I didn't. Lucas looked at me like I was the most gorgeous thing he'd ever seen, and when he stroked me with one hand, the feeling was better than I'd imagined it could be.

I took his hand in mine and guided it down to my jeans. I wanted to show him all of me. I wanted to feel that beautiful all over.

Lucas helped me undress, then wriggled out of his own jeans and tossed them across the room. I'd never seen a naked guy before except, like, in paintings and on the Internet. Somehow I'd never thought of the sight as beautiful, not until now. I liked how Lucas looked, how he felt in my hands, the gentle way that he touched me. Whenever I had a moment that I felt nervous or didn't know what to do, he kissed me again, and all my fear went away.

Mine, I thought. It was the same kind of hunger that overtook me when I wanted his blood, but better, because this way I could drink him in again, and again, and again. The crazy need to bite him was gone, replaced by something else, something that had nothing to do with being a vampire—instead, it was part of being alive. At long last, after years of my wanting him, Lucas truly belonged to me.

Finally, when we were almost past the point of self-control, he whispered roughly, "Bianca, are you sure?"

"So sure," I said, winding my hands through his hair. "This is how it's meant to be."

"Yeah." Lucas kissed me again, and for the first time in months and months, I knew that, right now at least, everything was perfect.

The next morning, I stirred drowsily in bed, realized that I was actually in a bed, realized that Lucas was asleep next to me, that we were both naked and then memory came thundering in.

My eyes went wide. *Did I really—*

Yes, I did really.

It wasn't that I wasn't happy about it, because I was. Even though I was a little bit sore—in places I hadn't known I could be sore—I'd never felt so overjoyed or loved or *sure*.

Everything seemed so surreal, that was all. Me, in bed with a lover. I pulled the sheet around me tightly, grinning and silly, and it seemed like a shame to leave Lucas out of the joke.

I tickled his leg with my toes, and he shifted against his pillow. One eye opened groggily. Then he grabbed me so quickly it made me squeal with laughter, and towed me on top of him.

"Good morning," he murmured between kisses. "I could get used to this."

"Me, too."

For a while we simply kissed each other, silly and messy and yet more and more intense. My body felt tingly all over, and I wondered if it was too soon to give it another try.

Before things got to that point, though, Lucas pulled back from me and smiled. "I think I've figured out what we're going to do."

"Yeah, I kind of figured that out, too, seeing how we're naked in bed together."

"Not that, wanton woman." He grinned at me in amazement. "What have I gotten myself into?"

"Something good."

"That I knew." Lucas kissed my hand. "What I meant was, I know what we can do next for cash, to get ourselves settled. It means taking another loan, which I don't like, but at this point I figure we'd better deal with it. We'll have run through the cash Balthazar gave us within a week at this hotel."

I had no problems asking for help right now. We genuinely needed it. "You have a friend in Philadelphia?"

"So do you. Think about it."

And as soon as I thought, I could envision the Phillies cap on his sandy hair. My face lit up in a smile. "Vic!"

Lucas called Vic and arranged for us to meet at one of the downtown diners for lunch. We walked there hand in hand, me in my new green sundress, holding Lucas's hand. I imagined that people were looking at me differently—that somehow they *knew*—but I thought probably that was just me being silly. I felt exactly the same, only happier than I'd been in a long while. Lucas, too, seemed relaxed; I couldn't remember another time I'd seen him completely at ease.

When we went inside, Vic was already sitting in a booth, Ranulf at his side. He raised one hand in a wave. "Guys! Man, is it good to see you."

I hugged Vic tightly, then did the same for Ranulf. Although Ranulf remained rail thin, with his soft brown hair worn in a bowl cut, he was now wearing khakis and a Hawaiian shirt almost identical to the one Vic had on. I wondered if he'd borrowed it from Vic or whether he was simply buying whatever Vic bought, the better to fit in with the twenty-first century. Of course, dressing like Vic didn't really mean fitting in, but Ranulf was still catching on to the modern world.

Once Vic was done hugging Lucas, he stepped back and said, "Lucas, this is Ranulf, my roommate after you up and ditched me. Ranulf, this is Lucas. I don't know if you guys met at Evernight or what."

"We spoke once," Ranulf said helpfully, "in the library. I asked you who the saints were that some people spoke of in New Orleans, and you explained that they were not religious icons but a sporting team. It was very enlightening."

"Yeah, no way I could forget that." Lucas gave Ranulf a lop-sided smile. Although he remained suspicious of most vampires, nobody could really be afraid of Ranulf.

"So what are you guys doing in Philly?" Vic said as we all took our seats in the booth. "Is this some big elopement drama? Do Ranulf and I have to be witnesses?"

"No," I said. My cheeks felt warm, and I couldn't tell if I was blushing at the whole idea of getting married or the fact that Lucas and I had sort of already had the honeymoon. "We're just—well, we're trying to get settled. And stay hidden."

Vic looked unexpectedly stern. "Did you call your parents?"

"I e-mailed them," I answered. "They know I'm all right."

Lucas turned to me, suddenly tense. "You did? When?"

Oh, no. Too late I remembered what the consequences of

that e-mail had been. I'd meant to tell Lucas the truth, but then Balthazar's capture had distracted me. Although I hated doing this in front of our friends, I knew I couldn't wait any longer to confess. "The first night we were out on patrol. Remember when I slipped away to get something to eat?"

"Bianca—" Lucas raked his hands through his hair, a gesture I'd learned meant he was trying hard to check his temper. "You didn't know the safeguards to take. Do you realize what happened because of that?"

Black Cross had been attacked, and Eduardo had been killed. In a small, miserable voice, I said, "I realize now. I'm so sorry, Lucas."

Vic and Ranulf were both looking from me to Lucas to me during this, like spectators at a tennis match. "What happened?" Vic said. "You got spammed or something?"

"Spam is good with breakfast foods," Ranulf said, proud to have remembered something about the current world. "I shall have Spam with my eggs."

"Not Spam the meat, spam like the e-mail ads for Viagra," Vic corrected him.

"We'll talk about this later," Lucas said shortly. His face was hard and tight as he stared out the window.

"Okay." I hadn't really come to terms with my responsibility for what had happened, and I knew I'd be dealing with that for a while. Obviously, Lucas was angry—and he had a right to be—but he didn't want to hash it out in front of Vic and Ranulf. Nervous and newly guilty, I somehow managed to focus on the conversation at hand. "Vic, basically, we're kind of on the run. Not from the law, but—nobody can find us. And, um, well, we need a place to stay and food, and it gets expensive. . . ."

"My money is your money," Vic said, like that was the most obvious thing in the world. "Name it, it's yours."

"Are you sure?" I knew that Vic came from an extremely wealthy family, but still, I hated asking for handouts. "We have a little already, and we're going to get jobs."

"Seriously, anything. And, oh, wait, hey, genius idea, inbound—" Vic snapped his fingers. "The wine cellar."

"Wine cellar?" Lucas said, glancing away from that spot on the window he'd been glaring at ever since he'd found out that I'd betrayed the Black Cross cell. I wondered if he was thinking what I was thinking—that Vic was going to suggest we steal bottles for a party.

Vic drummed on the laminated menu. "We have this big wine cellar beneath the house. Enormous. It's got climate control to keep it nice and cool in summer, and it's not very crowded, because my dad doesn't collect wine the way my grandpa did. There's a bathroom on the basement level, too."

Sleeping in a basement for the summer? On the other hand, it would be free.

"I swear, it's nice down there," Vic said. Ranulf nodded encouragingly. "I'd let you guys stay in the house, but my parents are going to put on the whole security system, with the lasers." He interlaced his fingers to mimic the laser beams. "The wine cellar has a separate entrance and security system, but it's just a simple four-digit code. I can give you the code, and you guys can stay there from the night of July fifth on. How does that sound?"

"That sounds—good." Lucas nodded slowly. I could tell he was still tense and angry, but he was in control of himself. "Vic, you're the best."

"I've long suspected as much," Vic said. "Glad to know the word's getting out."

"What about Ranulf?" I asked. Although we needed a place to stay pretty badly, I thought maybe Ranulf would need it even more. "What will he do while you're gone?"

Ranulf smiled. "I am going to Tuscany as well. The Woodsons have invited me to travel with them. I have not visited Italy in many years, so I look forward to seeing what has changed."

Just then the waitress arrived to take our orders. While Ranulf ordered his eggs and Spam, Lucas and I traded a look. If Vic had any idea that his buddy was a vampire, there was no way he would've extended the invitation. On the other hand, I felt sure that Ranulf would never hurt Vic, and probably Lucas had already picked up on that, too.

So we wouldn't have said anything, if Vic hadn't come out with, "So, despite the whole char-grilled factor the place has going on right now, I think I'm going back to Evernight Academy in the fall."

Lucas and I both stared. I managed to stammer out, "W-what?"

"Yeah, I know. It's Creepy Central, and the no-cell-phones

thing gets incredibly old, but I guess I'm used to it." Vic shrugged. "Besides, I never got to take fencing. Really wanted to try that."

"Other schools teach fencing." Lucas put both hands on the table, leaning forward for emphasis. "Vic, seriously, listen to me. Do not go back there."

"Why not?" Vic looked completely bewildered, as did Ranulf, who really should've caught on.

It wasn't like I could tell him the truth. I knew he wouldn't believe me. But I didn't want him anywhere near Mrs. Bethany. "There are really good reasons, okay? The night of the fire, the weird stuff that was going on . . ." My voice trailed off. How could I explain?

Lucas tried, "What happened at Evernight was more than just a fire. Can we leave it at that?"

Vic stared at us. "Wait, are you guys freaking about the whole vampire thing?"

No way had I heard that right. "What?" I said, sort of weakly.

"About it being mostly a vampire school. Is that what you're on about?" Vic stopped and smiled easily up at the waitress as she slid our orders onto the table. Ranulf, unworried by this conversation, tucked into his Spam as though he could actually taste it. As soon as the waitress walked off, Vic continued, "I mean, come on, Bianca. You *are* a vampire, right? Or, like, half?"

I turned to Ranulf, outraged. "You *told* him?"

"I did not!" Ranulf insisted. "I mean—yes, I did tell him

about you, when he asked. But not about the school. That, Vic already knew."

"How did you know that?" Lucas said.

"I figured it out my first year. God, you two act like it was hard." Vic started counting off points on his fingers. "Half the students don't know really obvious stuff. Like, this one guy thought *Grey's Anatomy* was a medical book instead of a TV show, and another time a girl wondered why they didn't hang criminals anymore. Also, the whole thing where everybody eats in their rooms—secretive and weird—plus half the student body never showed to pick up any food orders. Dead squirrels all over the place. That creepy school motto. The facts add up."

We were speechless. Lucas finally said, "You knew you were surrounded by vampires—and that didn't bother you?"

Vic shrugged. "Judge not, man."

I was so flabbergasted that I nearly put my elbows in my waffles. Somehow I managed to lean against the table without dousing myself in syrup. "You weren't ever scared?"

"That first night after I put it all together—yeah, that seemed to go on for a really long time," Vic admitted. "But then I figured, hey, I've been here a couple months. Nobody seems to have been eaten. So what's the big deal? The vampires seemed pretty harmless, and I figured they just had a school where they could be sure people were leaving them alone. I can respect that."

"It was a relief not to have to hide my nature from him," Ranulf said.

Lucas completely ignored his corned beef hash. "You never told me about it."

"Didn't want to freak you out. Guess you learned to deal, though, huh?" Vic grinned. "Amazing how convincing a pretty lady can be."

"I can't believe you discovered the secret," I said.

"So, my duller roommate," Vic said to Lucas, "how did you find out about the fanged types?"

"I've always known about vampires," Lucas said, finally noticing that he had food in front of him.

Vic said, "No, no, I don't mean, like, in *Dracula* and stuff. When did you find out for real?"

"He's always known for real," I said. "Lucas was raised in Black Cross."

Ranulf set his fork down with a clatter. He hung onto his knife. His eyes were wide as he stared at Lucas, and I could tell that he was this close to leaping over the table—either to escape or to attack.

"I'm ex–Black Cross," Lucas said heavily. "I'm not going to hurt you. Take it easy."

As Ranulf relaxed slightly, Vic said, "Whoa, what's Black Cross?"

"A centuries-old group of vampire hunters," I said. "The Evernight vampires are harmless—well, mostly—but there are dangerous ones out there."

"They do not only attack the dangerous," Ranulf said. His eyes were dark.

"I realize that now," Lucas said. "Because when they discovered what Bianca was, they went after her, too. Now you know why we're on the run."

Vic nodded, already at ease with the new information. "You know, if this weren't so dangerous, it would be really cool."

When we finished our food, Vic suggested we drive out to his house with him. "You should see the place. I can show you where the nearest bus stop is, because you'll need to know how to get into the city for these jobs you're going to have. Hey, what can you guys do?"

"I've had to patch up cars and trucks as long as I can remember," Lucas said while we walked out the door. Bells on the handle jingled. "There's probably a garage that would take me."

I didn't answer, because I had no idea. What could I do? The only subject I knew anything special about was astronomy, and high-school dropouts didn't get jobs at NASA.

"Here we are." Vic pointed to his car, a sunshine-yellow convertible. Ranulf chivalrously motioned for me to take the front passenger seat, even though this meant he and Lucas would be sort of squeezed tight in the back. Given how tense—and angry—Lucas still was, I thought our being separated for a little while might not be the worst idea. On one hand, I felt proud that Lucas had finally mastered his temper enough to hold it in check. On the other hand, I'd never realized how ominous it could be, knowing somebody was furious with you but biding his time to speak.

Then Vic distracted me completely when he said, "Oh, and there's definitely one more thing we should do at the house."

"What's that?" I asked.

"You guys should meet the ghost."

Chapter Fourteen

"DO YOU EVEN REMEMBER LAST YEAR?" I SAID, AS we sat in the car on the long gravel driveway of Vic's house. It was an imposing brick mansion, and I would've felt intimidated, if I weren't so busy being scared out of my wits. "How the wraiths kept coming after me?"

Vic scrunched his forehead in confusion. "Wraiths?"

"That is the more common vampire term for ghosts," Ranulf said. "May I please exit the backseat? I can no longer feel my legs below the knees."

"Hold your horses," Lucas said. He leaned forward, between the two front seats, so that he could talk more directly to Vic. "There's no way this is safe."

"You weren't even there last year," Vic scoffed.

I interjected, "*I* was there, and I remember the attacks—blue-green light and cold and all that ice falling from the ceiling. So I'm not going into a house with a wraith. A ghost. Whatever."

What Vic didn't know—what very few in the world knew, even vampires—was that any child born to vampires was the result of a bargain struck between vampires and wraiths, and that the wraiths ultimately intended to claim me as their own.

During several terrifying incidents at Evernight, including one that nearly killed me, that was precisely what the wraiths had tried to do.

Vic sighed. At this point, we'd been parked in front of his house for more than five minutes, and we'd been arguing about this ever since we'd left the diner. The water sprinklers on the broad green lawn had cycled through three different speeds. He said, "We appear to be at something known as an impasse."

"I wish to make an observation," Ranulf said.

Exasperated, Lucas said, "You're not the only one cramping up in this backseat, okay?"

Ranulf replied, "That was not the observation."

"Go ahead," I said. Nobody would change my mind.

But then Ranulf said, "Are you not wearing an obsidian pendant?"

I put my hand around the antique pendant my parents had given me this past Christmas. An obsidian teardrop dangled from an ornate chain of copper that had gone green. At the time I'd thought the necklace simply a thoughtful gift, a reflection of my interest in vintage clothes. However, Mrs. Bethany had informed me later that obsidian was one of the many minerals and metals that repelled wraiths.

In other words, it could help keep me safe. Since she'd told me that, I'd never taken the pendant off, not even to bathe. I'd almost forgotten about it.

"The obsidian gives me some protection," I admitted, "but I don't know how much or for how long."

"I promise you, this ghost isn't a baddie," Vic said. "Wraith. Whatever. She's awesome. At least, I think she's a she."

Lucas asked, "Have you talked to this thing? Communicated with it somehow?"

"Not exactly, but—"

"So how do you know it's 'awesome'?"

"The same way I know I'm being mocked," Vic said, eyes narrowing. "I can just tell."

I still wanted to tell Vic to back his car out of the driveway and take me and Lucas back to our hotel. Yet I knew we could only afford a few more nights there, and that only because we'd gotten a lucky deal. Vic would loan us whatever cash we needed, but I wanted to borrow as little as possible. If we couldn't stay on his property through July and early August, we'd have to ask him for thousands. I really preferred not to do that.

My hand still clasped around the pendant, I said, "I'll go in."

"Bianca, don't." Lucas looked furious, but I put one hand on his arm to steady him.

"You and Ranulf wait out here. If you hear any screaming or the windows ice over—"

"I don't like the sound of this," Lucas said.

"I said *if*, okay?" Now that I'd made the decision, I didn't want to sit around worrying; I wanted to do it and get it over with. "If that happens, you guys come in and help. Vic and I will try it this time. We won't stay here if the wraith causes a problem."

Although Lucas still looked displeased, he nodded. Vic clambered over his driver's side door without even opening it. As I got out, I could hear Ranulf's knees crack as he straightened his legs and gave a long sigh of relief.

Vic's parents weren't home, so the house was empty. Their place was gorgeous, more like something in a magazine than any real home I'd ever been in. The foyer was tiled in green marble, and a small chandelier hung from the thirty-foot ceiling. Everything smelled like furniture polish and oranges. We walked up a central staircase that was broad, white, and flowing. I could imagine Ginger Rogers dancing down those steps in a dress of ostrich feathers; certainly a movie star would belong here more than me in my cheap little sundress.

Of course, Vic didn't quite seem to belong here either— and this was his house. I wondered if his carefree goofiness was maybe his way of rebelling against the perfect order his parents had established.

"She only shows up in the attic," he said, as we walked along the parquet hallway upstairs. The paintings on the wall looked old. "That's her special place, I think."

"You actually see her?"

"Like a figure in a sheet or something? Nah. You just know she's there. And every once in a while— Well, we'll try it. Don't want to get your hopes up."

My one hope at that moment was not to get freeze-dried by a wraith. Silently thanking my parents for the pendant, I watched as Vic opened the door to the attic stairs and started to climb. I took a couple of deep breaths before I followed him.

The Woodsons' attic was the only messy part of the house. The clutter was nicer than in most attics, I suspected. A blue-and-white Chinese vase sat on a dusty desk as wide as a bed and probably almost a hundred years old. A dressmaker's dummy wore a jacket of yellowing lace and an old Edwardian ladies' hat still jaunty with plumes. The Persian rug underfoot looked genuine, at least to my uneducated eye. Although the air smelled musty, it was a nice sort of musty, like old books.

"I like it up here," Vic said. His face was more serious than usual. "This is probably my favorite place in the whole house."

"This is where you feel comfortable."

"You get it, huh?"

I smiled at him. "Yeah, I get it."

"Okay, let's just sit down here and see if she shows."

We sat cross-legged on the Persian rug and waited. My nerves reacted to every creak of the wood, and I kept looking nervously at the one small window behind the dressmaker's dummy. The panes hadn't frosted over.

"I'm going to give you the cash, instead of Lucas," Vic said as he played with the shoelaces of his Chucks. "I've got about six hundred dollars on hand—and you're taking it all. Usually I'd have more, but I just bought a new Stratocaster." He hung his head. "I feel stupid, blowing that much money on a guitar I can hardly play. If I'd known you guys were going to need it—"

"You couldn't have known. Besides, it's your money to spend however you want. It's good of you to share it with us." I frowned, momentarily distracted from the suspense of waiting for the ghost. "Why give it to me instead of Lucas?"

"Because Lucas would probably refuse to take more than a hundred or so. Sometimes he's too proud to admit he needs help."

"We're not proud." I remembered jumping the subway turnstile with some embarrassment. "We're way too screwed for that."

"Lucas is always going to have a pride thing going on. Always. You're the reasonable one."

My lips twitched. "I wish I could tell him you said that."

"He knows," Vic said. "The two of you make a good team."

I remembered the night before and felt my cheeks turn pink. "Yeah," I said softly. "We do."

A grin spread across Vic's face, and for one horrified second I thought he'd somehow been able to tell what I was thinking. But that wasn't why he was smiling. "Do you feel it?"

The chill in the air swept around me. I hugged myself. "Yeah. I do."

No ice crystals formed. No frost carved out faces against the window. Nothing visible appeared. I simply knew that a second ago, Vic and I had been alone. Now something was with us. *Someone.*

At first, I was confused. Why wasn't this as violent and

scary as the other ghostly manifestations I'd seen? Wraiths didn't gently creep into the corners of rooms; they stabbed their way in with blades of ice. That was the way it had always happened at Evernight Academy—

Wait. The school had been specially built to repel ghosts; the iron and copper the wraiths despised were built into the school's walls and beams. Although the wraiths had been able to force their way in, that had been difficult for them. Were the bizarre manifestations of ghostly power I'd seen before—the frozen stalactites and rippling blue-green light—evidence of that struggle? Maybe in a place like this, an ordinary house, the wraiths didn't create effects so dramatic.

"Hey there," Vic said cheerfully. "This is my friend Bianca. She's going to hang out in the wine cellar for a while with Lucas, also a friend. They're fantastic; you're going to love them." He could have been introducing us at a party. "They were just kind of nervous, because Binks here has had some ghost issues before. But nothing personal, okay? I wanted to make sure you guys would be cool."

There was no reply, of course. It seemed to me that the light was a little brighter in that corner of the room, maybe a little bluer, but the difference was almost too subtle to discern.

Then I saw her.

Not with my eyes—not that kind of sight. It was more like when a memory comes back to you so powerfully that you can't even see what's in front of you any longer, because the images in your head are so vivid. The wraith was in my mind, the same one from my dreams—one of those I had seen at Evernight Academy last year. Was that Vic's ghost? Another? Her short, pale hair seemed almost white, and her face was sharp.

You might as well stay, she said. *Not like it matters.*

Then the vision was over. Startled, I blinked my eyes a few times, trying to center myself. "Whoa."

"What happened?" Vic looked around the room, like he might be able to see something. "You went all spacey for a few seconds there. Is everything okay?"

What had the wraith meant by that message? I already knew that I didn't understand her very well.

Yet I didn't feel the same kind of fright I'd known after every other encounter with a wraith. This one had shown no signs of hostility, hadn't made any demands like *stop* or *ours* or anything like that. Either she liked Vic as much as he liked her and would leave us alone for his sake, or my obsidian pendant was a definite safeguard.

As Vic carefully studied my face, he said, "Well?"

I smiled. "We can stay."

For a little while, at least, Lucas and I had a home.

Vic drove us back to our hotel. Before he and Ranulf left, Vic made a discreet trip to the ATM and gave me the six hundred dollars he'd promised, a wad of bills I stuffed inside my purse. We had the keys and code to turn off the security system in the wine cellar, and once we had jobs, Lucas and I would be able to save money. Before they left, I hugged Vic tighter than I had hugged almost anybody else in my life.

Then it was time for me to face the music.

Lucas hadn't smiled once on the way home. He talked some with Vic and Ranulf, thanking Vic for giving us a place to stay, but it was like I was invisible. He'd held on to his temper while we took care of business, but now his mood was darkening.

We rode up the hotel elevator in silence, the tension around us weighing heavier by the moment. In my mind, I kept seeing Eduardo's death at Mrs. Bethany's hands over and over again, and hearing that sickening crack.

When we entered our room, I expected Lucas to begin shouting at me right away, but he didn't. Instead he went into the bathroom and washed his face and hands, scrubbing hard, as though he felt dirty.

As he dried off with a towel, the suspense got to me. "Say something," I said. "Anything. Scream at me if you have to. Just—don't stay quiet like that."

"What do you want me to say? I told you not to use e-mail? We both know that, and we both know you ignored me."

"You didn't say why." He glared at me then, and I realized how weak I had to sound. "That's not an excuse. I realize that—"

"I told you months ago that we had to watch out for e-mail being traced! Did you think I didn't e-mail you last year just because I didn't feel like it? Why wasn't that alone enough to tell you that was a good reason?"

"You're shouting at me!"

"Oh, I'm sorry. I wouldn't want to overreact to something as insignificant as *people getting killed*."

It hit me then, the full weight of what I'd done, in a way it hadn't since the night of Mrs. Bethany's attack. I smelled the smoke and remembered the screams. In my mind's eye, I saw Mrs. Bethany viciously twist Eduardo's neck and the light fade from his eyes as he fell down dead.

I ran from the hotel room, tears stinging my eyes. I couldn't face Lucas's anger at that moment, even though I deserved it. My own guilt had come crashing down, punishing me more horribly than he or anyone else could. I had to be alone, to cry it out for myself, but where could I go?

Blindly, I pushed into the stairwell, listening to my sobs echo as I hurried upward. I wasn't running anywhere in particular, just running—as though I could outrace the knowledge of what I'd done. When I reached the rooftop and could go no farther, I walked out to the pool. A few kids splashed in the kiddie area, but for the moment I had the deep end to myself. I kicked off my sandals, dunked my feet, hung my head, and wept quietly for a long time until all the tears had run out.

At dusk, someone finally sat beside me at the pool's edge—Lucas. I couldn't quite bring myself to meet his eyes. He sat by my side, unlaced his shoes, and dunked his feet, too. I should have found that more encouraging than I did.

Lucas spoke first. "I shouldn't have shouted."

"If I'd had any idea what could happen—that Mrs. Bethany might find us from that and come after the group—there's no way I would've sent the e-mail. I promise you."

"I realize that. But you could have sent a letter. Gotten Vic to call them. There were other things you could've done. If you'd thought it through—"

"But I didn't."

"No." Lucas sighed.

My shortsightedness had cost Lucas dearly and had cost some of the Black Cross hunters their lives. Although many of them were antivampire zealots, that didn't mean they all deserved to be murdered in cold blood. Because of me, they had been. "Lucas, I'm so sorry. I'm so incredibly sorry."

"I get that. It just doesn't change anything." Then he grimaced and stared out at the city around us; Philadelphia didn't glitter the way New York did, but it was still shiny and steely, more light than darkness. "Mom's all alone. She lost Eduardo; she lost me; she lost her Black Cross cell. What's she going to do? Who's going to be there for her? I planned to leave with you, and I don't regret doing it, but when I made that decision, I thought Eduardo would be there with her. I know you think she's so tough—and she is—but this—"

I'd been so busy worrying about myself and my friends that I hadn't spared a thought for Kate. In a lot of ways, her situation was as bad as my parents—worse, even, because at least they had each other. Kate had nobody. "Surely, someday, when we're safer, you can call her or something."

"If I contact her, ever, she'll tell Black Cross. Those are the rules. She won't break them."

"Not even for you?" I didn't believe that for a second, but

obviously Lucas did.

He looked at our reflections on the surface of the pool, as if weary. Although I could see that his anger was diminishing, it was being replaced by depression. That wasn't much easier to witness. "Mom's a good soldier. Like I always tried to be."

"Like you *are*."

"Good soldiers don't sacrifice the cause for love."

"If the cause isn't love, then it isn't worth the sacrifice."

Lucas gave me a sad smile. "You're worth it. I know that. Even when you mess up. Because God knows I mess up, too."

I wanted to hug him, but somehow I sensed the moment wasn't right. The inner demons Lucas was grappling with needed to come out.

He continued, "My whole life, I've been in Black Cross. I've always known who I was, what my purpose should be. I knew I would be a hunter forever. But now that's all over."

"I know how that feels," I said. "I always thought I would turn into a vampire. Now I don't know what comes next. It's— it's scary."

Lucas took my hand. "As long as we've got each other," he said, "it's worth it."

"I know that. But I still wonder—Lucas, what will we become?"

He admitted, "I don't know."

I put my arms around his neck and held onto him tightly. We needed more than love; we needed to be strong enough for faith.

* * *

The next couple of days were quieter, even relaxing. Although Lucas obviously spent some time brooding about his mother, the argument between us had ended. We watched TV or walked around to see the sights in Philadelphia. One day we split up, so I could find out if any restaurants needed waitresses, while Lucas applied for jobs at garages. To our astonishment and relief, we both got offers to start right after the holiday.

We spent every night in our room, together.

I hadn't realized it was possible, to want someone even worse the more I was with him. All I knew was that I didn't feel shy any longer. I didn't have any doubts. Lucas knew me like no other person ever had, and I never felt safer than when I was with him, totally, completely. Afterward, I curled next to Lucas and sank into a sleep too deep for dreams.

Except, that is, for the night of the Fourth of July. Maybe it was the fireworks, or the sugar rush from cotton candy, but that night, I had the most vivid dream of all.

"I'm right here," said the wraith.

She stood in front of me, looking not like a phantasm but like any other person. I could feel the death in her, leaching heat out of my living body. That wasn't something she was doing to be mean—it was just the nature of what she was.

"Where are we?" I looked around us but couldn't see anything. It was so dark.

Her only answer was, "Look."

I looked down to see the earth far below us. We were suspended in the night sky. Like the stars, I thought, and for a moment I was happy.

Then I realized that I recognized the figures walking far beneath me. Lucas, his head bowed, walked toward a tree that swayed in the violent wind. Behind him was Balthazar.

"What are they doing?" I said.

"Shared work."

"I want to see."

"No," the wraith said. "You don't want to see. Trust me."

The wind whipped around us even more strongly. The wraith's blue-white dress rippled in the gale. "What won't you let me see?"

"Look if you want." Her smile was sad. "You'll wish you hadn't."

I have to look—I can't look—wake up, wake up!

Gasping, I pushed myself upright in the bed. My heart was pounding. Why had that dream frightened me so badly?

On July 5, after getting a call from Vic telling us that he and his family were at the airport, we checked out of our hotel. The bus ride to Vic's neighborhood took a while, and we had to walk several blocks from the nearest stop. But it hardly mattered when we walked around to the back of Vic's now-empty house and entered the security code for the wine cellar entrance.

"Wow," Lucas said as our eyes adjusted to the dim lighting. "This place is huge."

The cellar was the size of an entire floor of Vic's enormous house. It seemed to be separated into rooms, suggesting that this had been a living space long ago, even before it was a wine cellar. I remembered that Vic said his dad didn't collect the way his grandfather had, and wondered how much booze *used* to be down there. The floor was battered old oak, and obviously hadn't been refinished in a couple of generations.

As we walked farther inside to the inner rooms, we saw that a small lamp was burning—a hula-girl lamp. It illuminated a small treasure trove: sheets, quilts, and blankets, a still-in-the-sack air mattress, a simple metal folding bed frame like you see in hotels, a little wooden table and chairs, a basketful of mismatched plates and cups in blue and white, a bundle of Christmas lights, a microwave, a minifridge (already plugged in and running), some books and DVDs, an old TV set with DVD player, and even a Persian carpet, which sat rolled up in the corner.

I picked up a small piece of paper on the table and read aloud: "'Hey, guys. Ranulf and I hauled down some stuff from the attic for you to use. The TV doesn't get any reception, but you can watch the DVDs. There's sodas and some fruit in the fridge, and Ranulf left a couple pints for Bianca. Hope it helps. We'll be back in the middle of August. Don't do anything I wouldn't do. Love, Vic.'"

Lucas folded his arms. "What wouldn't Vic do?"

"Be boring." I grinned.

We settled in, making one empty corner of the wine cellar our "apartment." The table and chairs would be the dining area, and we put the hula-girl lamp on the table. The Persian rug went on the floor, and Lucas climbed on the wine racks (making me nervous) to hang up the Christmas lights, which were all white but sometimes shone soft gold where we had threaded them through the wine bottles. The air mattress was self-inflating and easy to get on the bed frame; I took pleasure in covering the mattress with snowy sheets trimmed with lace and then piling it high with quilts to help with the slight chill in the air. The walls were painted a deep green, and by the time we were done, I thought there wasn't an apartment in all Philadelphia as beautiful as ours. So what if there were bottles on the walls?

It seemed that finally everything was coming together for us. Our friends had helped us this far—but we had jobs, which meant we could pay them back eventually. We had escaped from Mrs. Bethany and from Black Cross. The only wraith anywhere around was either peaceable or wanted to steer clear of any obsidian. I couldn't believe how good everything was, how right.

Twice, though, small clouds darkened my mood.

The first time was when Lucas and I ate dinner—pizza from a little neighborhood place a few blocks away. Lucas brought it home and we ate it on the "new" dishes. While wondering how to wash them in the bathroom sink, I thought about the delicious meals my mother used to make for me. *Oh, I wonder what the recipe for that lemonade pie is? It didn't have to be baked in the stove, and it would be so good on a hot day like this.*

Then I remembered that I couldn't ask her. I also wondered how she'd managed to cook so many things so well; vampires can't really taste food, not the way humans do, so it must have been tough for Mom.

I'll write soon, I promised myself. *I'll send Vic back to Evernight with a note, maybe, and he'll claim I mailed it to him from somewhere else. That way they'll know that I'm really okay.*

The second time came later in the evening, while we were checking out the DVDs. The walls were bare, and I thought idly that it would be nice to hang something there—nothing big, because we couldn't damage anything, but maybe a drawing we could tape up.

That made me think about Raquel's collages, the crazy mishmashes of color and pictures she loved to put together. She used to show them to me with pride. Now she hated me so much that she had turned me over to people who'd tried to kill me.

I should've been furious with her. But it hurt too much to make me angry. It was a wound that I knew would never really heal.

"Hey." Lucas frowned, worried. "You upset about something?"

"Raquel."

"I swear to God, if I ever get my hands on her—"

"You won't do anything," I said. Then I bit my lip so I wouldn't cry. Let Raquel think what she wanted about me; I loved her, and despite everything, that couldn't change.

So, everything seemed pretty fabulous—until the next day. That was our first day at work. I'd never had any kind of job before, not even babysitting; Mom and Dad said children noticed things that older people missed, and vampires were better off spending as little time around them as possible.

This meant that I had no idea that work *sucks*.

"Table eight doesn't have their sodas yet!" yelled Reggie, my so-called supervisor at Hamburger Rodeo, who was only about four years older than me. He had the same mean glint in his eyes that a lot of Evernight-type vampires did, but he didn't have the power to back it up. Just a laminated name tag that said MANAGER. "What's the problem, Bianca?"

"I'm getting them!" A root beer, a cola, and what? I pulled my notepad out of my apron; both the pad and the apron were already stained with French dressing. After an hour-long training session in the morning, which was apparently not nearly enough preparation time, I'd been thrown into the lunch crowd. Quickly I scooped ice into the plastic glasses and worked the fountain machine. *Hurry, hurry, hurry.*

Table eight got their drinks, but they didn't look too happy about it. They wanted to know where their Bacon Buckaroos were. I really hoped those were the bacon burgers. Everything on the menu had a stupid cowboy name, which went with the "theme," like the posters of old Westerns on the wall and the gingham shirt and bolo tie I had to wear.

I ran back to the kitchen. "I need Bacon Buckaroos for Eight!" I cried.

"Sorry," said another, older waiter, as he walked out with a tray of the burgers for his own table. "You snooze, you lose."

"But—"

"Bianca!" Reggie yelled. "Table twelve doesn't have silverware yet. Silverware! That goes out with the menus, remember?"

"Okay, okay."

I went back and forth, back and forth, over and over. My feet ached, and I could feel the grease sinking into my skin. Reggie kept yelling at me, and customers kept scowling, because I didn't get them their really awful food fast enough. It was like hell, if hell served cheese fries.

Excuse me. "Cheesy Wranglers." That was what we had to call the cheese fries.

As the lunch rush began to die down, I hurried to the salad bar to do my "side work," which meant this whole other job we each had to do in addition to waiting tables. Mine, for today, was making sure the salad bar was fully stocked. I grimaced as I saw that nearly everything was running low: salad dressings, croutons, tomatoes, etc. This would take me almost ten minutes to fix.

"This is not a good first day," Reggie muttered into my ear, like I needed that news flash. Ignoring him, I hurried back to the kitchen to chop some tomatoes.

I grabbed the first tomato, picked up the knife, and quickly started chopping—too quickly. "Ow," I whined as I shook my cut finger.

"Don't bleed on the food!" said another waitress. She led me to the sink and started running cold water on my hand. "That's a health code violation."

"I'm no good at this," I said.

"Everybody's first day blows," she said kindly. "Once you've been doing this a couple years, like me, you'll have it down pat."

The thought of spending two years at Hamburger Rodeo

made me dizzy. I had to think of something else to do with my life.

Then I realized, that wasn't what was making me dizzy. I felt bad. *Really* bad.

"I think I'm going to faint," I said.

"Don't be silly. The cut's not that deep."

"It's not the cut."

"Bianca, are you—"

Everything went black for what seemed like only a second, as if I'd simply blinked my eyes. But when I opened them again, I was lying on the rubber mat on the floor. My back hurt, and I realized that was because I'd fallen down hard.

"Are you okay?" the waitress said. She held a dish towel to my cut hand. Several of the other waiters and cooks were circled around, all tables forgotten in light of the drama.

"I don't know."

"You're not going to throw up, are you?" Reggie demanded. When I shook my head, he said, "Have you sustained a work-place injury that requires us to fill out paperwork?"

I sighed. "I just need to go home."

Reggie's lips pressed into a line, but I guess he figured I might sue if he fired me for being sick. He let me leave.

The dizziness stayed with me as I waited at the bus stop, and throughout the long ride home. My pitiful few singles in tips were crammed in my pocket. If I hadn't felt so awful, I would've been depressed about having to return to Hamburger Rodeo tomorrow.

Instead, I just tried to hold on—and not to think.

I tried not to think that I'd felt the same way the day Lucas and I were clearing out the destroyed Black Cross tunnel, and on a couple of days since.

Or that, lately, my appetite for blood—which had been growing sharper and sharper from the day I'd first bitten Lucas—had suddenly almost vanished.

Don't freak, I told myself. *It's not like I'm pregnant or anything.* We'd been careful, and, besides, this had begun before Lucas and I first made love. No, pregnancy wasn't what I was scared of.

All the same, I knew something was happening to me. A change was coming.

Chapter Fifteen

"IT'S NOT FUNNY," I REPEATED FOR THE FOURTH time, but I couldn't keep from smiling as I said it.

"I know it's not funny. We need the money." Lucas was able to keep a straight face until he continued, "And Hamburger Rodeo is the challenging kind of job most people couldn't keep for even four days."

"Shut *up*." I thumped his shoulder soundly, but I was laughing as hard as he was. Although it was embarrassing to drop an entire tray of glasses of water in front of the whole restaurant, at least I'd managed to soak Reggie in the process. I'd lost my job a couple of days after I'd come back from my sick leave, which would have worried me if it hadn't been so hilarious.

Lucas was peeling back the cellophane on a couple of microwave pizzas, which was what we had for dinner most nights. Although we were free to shop for what we wanted now, instead of scraping by on the bleak rations Black Cross provided, we didn't have cash for much. Also, neither of us knew how to cook.

I didn't mind, though. I wasn't that hungry these days.

"How was your day?" I asked. Lucas didn't talk about his job at the garage much; he just came home gasoline scented. I didn't mind that, though. He always took a shower first thing and emerged warm, damp, and smelling just great.

"Same old," he said shortly. "Listen, don't worry about that hamburger place anymore, all right? You'll find something better. You ought to fill out some applications at the bookstores in town. You love to read."

"That's a good idea." Which would I rather recommend: Jane Austen or Bacon Buckaroos? No contest.

I thought happily about my potential new career in book sales as I finished setting the table, reaching down to the basket to grab a couple of glasses—until the dizziness crashed over me.

Everything went sort of grayish, and I could see spots in front of my eyes. A weird chill swept through my body. I hung onto the wall for a moment, trying to get my breath.

"You all right?" Lucas turned toward me, concerned.

I gave him a quick smile. "Yeah, just turned around too fast. That's all."

He didn't look like he believed me, but then the microwave dinged, and he turned to collect our dinners.

Not for the first time, I wondered if I shouldn't have told Lucas about the weak spells I kept having. I hadn't even spoken to him about fainting at work. But saying something to Lucas would mean admitting something was wrong—really wrong— and I wasn't ready to admit that yet.

We sat down to dinner, splitting between us the newspaper Lucas had brought from his job at the garage. It smelled a little like motor oil, the same way Lucas did when he got home. Weirdly, the smell of motor oil had become slightly sexy to me. I grabbed the want ads (just in case any bookstores were listing openings), the front page, and the entertainment section. Lucas took the sports pages, but he never read those first. Every evening, he went through the local news—scoured it really, paying close attention to each story. I figured he was trying to learn more about our new city, but I was wrong.

Lucas straightened up and pushed a page toward me. "Look at this."

I looked. A woman had been found dead in a Dumpster downtown. "That's sad."

"Keep reading."

I didn't see how it was going to get any less sad. Then my eyes widened.

Sources say the victim's throat had been slashed. The lack of blood at the scene has led police to conclude that she was killed elsewhere and dumped in the alleyway later. Anyone who saw a suspicious person or vehicle in the area between 10 P.M. and 6 A.M. is encouraged to contact the authorities.

My mouth was dry as I whispered, "A vampire."

"A vampire who's let us know where he's working." Lucas

smiled grimly. "Which means a vampire who's just made a big mistake."

"You don't mean you want to—to hunt this vampire?"

"He's killing people."

"But what are you going to do? Just—kill him first?"

Lucas was very still. "I've done it before. You know that."

He'd killed a vampire to save Raquel during his year at Evernight Academy. Although I believed that he'd truly had no choice, and that Raquel might easily have been killed otherwise, the thought of hunting down a vampire and killing him in cold blood made me feel sick inside. "It seems like there should be another way."

"Well, there's not." Lucas pushed back from the table, energized by the thought of action. "It's not like there's a vampire jail or anything." Then he paused. "Is there?"

"Not that I know of."

My unease must have showed clearly on my face, because Lucas covered my hand with his. "Once the vampire knows we're after him, he might take off. Leave town. That happens a lot. The second they find out a hunt is on, they split."

"Here's hoping," I said. "For his sake."

Lucas gave me a lopsided grin. "That's the spirit."

"You really need this, don't you? A mission. A reason for—" *For being,* I wanted to say, but the look on Lucas's face stopped me.

"Hey. You're my reason. Having a normal life—well, as normal as hiding out in a wine cellar gets—I've waited a long time for that. The fact that I get to live that life with you just makes it more perfect."

"Okay, you don't need a mission." I folded my arms. I wasn't actually annoyed with him, but I felt Lucas needed to know I had his number. "But you really like having one."

Sheepishly, Lucas nodded. If the situation had been any less grave, I might have laughed. He looked so boyish when he got called out. It was cute, really.

I hadn't become a master hunter during my six weeks with Black Cross, but I had learned a few key things, including the first rule: Never go out for a hunt unarmed. Lucas and I didn't have the Black Cross arsenal to turn to. We searched around in the Woodsons' garage to see if there was anything we could use; it worked on the same security code as the wine cellar, and was happily laser free. Obviously Vic's parents weren't going to have gallons of holy water stored near the riding mower, but whatever they had on hand would beat going on patrol with nothing but good intentions. Luckily, Lucas found some gear—including several wooden gardening stakes, which could serve if needed.

The garage was closed on Sundays, which meant that Lucas and I had the next day free. I'd come up with all sorts of plans for us earlier in the week, like maybe taking a carriage ride through the historical section of Philadelphia or maybe just staying in bed for hours.

Instead, we set out for the downtown neighborhood where that woman had died.

As the sun set, Lucas and I arrived in the alleyway. We

couldn't walk all the way down to the site of the murder; part of the alley had been sealed off with strips of yellow tape that read CRIME SCENE.

"We could duck under it," I suggested. "Even if the police did see us back there, they'd just think we were going to see it because it was gross or something. On a dare, maybe."

"Not worth the hassle. We know how things ended here. What we have to figure out is where it started."

Lucas and I began making our way through the neighborhood, looking for a place where a vampire might scope out potential prey. Neon beer signs in the window of a nearby bar served as a pretty good guide.

"I'm going to go in," he said. "Get a look at the crowd in there."

"Don't you mean *we're* going in?"

"No." When I gave him a dirty look, Lucas sighed. "Listen, we're both too young to be in a bar legally. But I'm twenty and can pass for older. You're seventeen—"

"Only for two more weeks!"

"—and you look seventeen. If I go in, chances are nobody's going to throw me out. If you go in, it's fifty-fifty at best that the bartender's going to let us stay. Besides, dressed like that"— Lucas gave my blue sundress an appraising glance that made a slow smile spread across my face—"you'd definitely draw too much attention."

"Well. When you put it that way."

Lucas kissed me softly, and I rested my hands against his

chest. I liked feeling the rise and fall of his breath. He murmured, "Get yourself something to eat, okay? We ran out of Ranulf's stash a couple days ago. You've got to be starving."

I hadn't even noticed that I'd gone without blood. "I've had a few things," I lied. "Don't worry."

He gave me an odd look, and I thought that I'd betrayed my concern. But Lucas kissed my forehead and headed toward the bar without another word.

You know, I really should eat. I began looking around for any sign of life. Probably it didn't matter that I hadn't wanted blood. Humans lost their appetite when they were sick, after all. Probably I had a touch of the flu or something, and instead of having human symptoms, I had vampire symptoms. I should make sure I had plenty of blood so I could get well.

Alleyways are good places to prowl for food, both for vermin and the creatures who hunt them. Within a couple of minutes, I heard some scurrying behind a garbage pail. I wrinkled my nose from the odor as I darted behind the can and grabbed—a rat, a small one, twisting in my grasp. It smelled no better than its surroundings, and I didn't like the thought of where it had been.

This never bothered you before, I told myself. *Remember the pigeons in New York? Flying rats, basically.* Before, my craving for blood had driven me past the gross-out factor. Without any appetite, this was a lot harder to do.

As the rat squirmed, I said, "Sorry about this." Then, before I could chicken out, I bit down, hard.

The blood flowed into my mouth, but the taste was—flat.

Empty. Like a bad imitation of the real thing. I forced myself to take all four swallows the rat offered, but it did nothing for me. In fact, it tasted sort of disgusting. I recalled the one time Lucas had tasted blood, and the face he'd made as he spit it out. Finally I knew how he felt.

I tossed the rat's corpse into the garbage can and hurriedly fished some mints out of my bag. The last thing I wanted was rat breath.

Yet the mints seemed flavorless, too. Maybe I hadn't really noticed, because Lucas and I had mostly eaten bland microwaved food these days, but human food didn't taste right either.

What's wrong with me?

"What's wrong with you?"

I jerked back to attention. The voice I'd heard—a woman's voice—came from perhaps a block over. With my vampire hearing, every word was as clear as if I stood only a few feet away.

"Nothing's wrong with me," said a man's silky voice. "Nothing's wrong with you either, so far as I can smell."

"I don't smell bad," she retorted. "And it's—your teeth—"

"What, you're not going to be shallow, are you? Judge on appearances?"

I grabbed a stake from my purse and hurried toward the voices. Hopefully Lucas was also on this guy's trail; if not, I wasn't going to have any chance to reach him. My thong sandals slapped against the pavement, and I wished that I'd had the sense to choose something quieter and more practical for my only pair of shoes. But I also suspected the vampire was distracted.

❖ 219 ❖

When I reached the corner, I stopped and glanced around. They were silhouetted sharply against a nearby streetlight. Dusk had only just turned into night. The vampire was short but stocky and powerful, and the woman was tiny, hardly up to his shoulder.

"You're making me nervous," she said, trying to make it sound like she was flirting, though I could tell she meant it. She didn't want to admit how scared she was. That was the number-one thing vampires used to their advantage—people's refusal to believe that the worst-case scenario could really be happening to them.

The vampire leaned closer to her, his arms on either side, almost pinning her to the brick wall of the nearby building. "I'm trying to make you excited. Get that pulse rate going."

"Yeah?" She smiled feebly.

"Oh, yeah."

I'd had enough. Although I had no illusions about being able to scare the guy, I thought I could surprise him. That might do the trick.

Quickly I held the stake up in a fighting position, spun around the corner and said, "Back off."

He glanced at me—and smirked. So much for the element of surprise. "Or what, little girl?"

"Or I'll paralyze you with this. After that, you'll be out of luck."

The vampire's eyes widened slightly; because I'd accurately described what staking did to a vampire, he'd realized I knew what I was talking about. That was the general idea. But it wasn't nearly as intimidating as I'd hoped. "You might *try*."

"Excuse me," the woman said, "but do you two know each other?"

"We're about to get real well acquainted." The vampire took his arms from around the woman, and she wisely took off running. Her footsteps clattered against the sidewalk into the distance. He swaggered toward me. Though he was a short guy, his shadow from the streetlamp was tall and thin, stretching over me.

Lucas, I thought, *this would be a really good time to step outside the bar and check on me.*

The vampire stopped. "You don't smell human."

I raised an eyebrow. Finally I had his attention. Every other vampire I'd ever met was impressed by the fact that I was a born vampire, a rarity.

This one simply shrugged. "Hey. Blood is blood. Who cares where it comes from?"

Oh, crap.

Then a voice rang out, "You're gonna care when it comes from you."

"Lucas!" I cried.

The moment I saw him at the other end of the alley, Lucas started running straight for the vampire. I was forgotten. The vampire turned and sprang at Lucas, who dodged him and slammed his joined fists into the vampire's back, sending him sprawling.

Well, if the guys had forgotten me, that didn't mean I had to forget them. I grabbed a broken brick from the alleyway and threw it at the vampire as hard as I could. My aim had improved, thanks to my training with Black Cross; the brick caught him square in the gut. He turned to me, eyes reflecting eerily in the streetlamp, just like a cat's.

"Get out," I pleaded. "Get out of town for good. That way we don't have to kill you."

The vampire snarled, "What makes you think you could?"

Lucas tackled him, and they fell to the pavement. Those were bad odds for Lucas; short-range fighting always worked to a vampire's advantage, because a vampire's best weapons were his fangs. I ran forward, determined to help.

"You're stronger"—the vampire gasped—"than a human."

Lucas said, "I'm human enough."

The vampire grinned at me, a smile that had nothing to do with the desperate situation he was in and was therefore even scarier. "I heard somebody was looking for one of our babies," he crooned to Lucas. "One of the powerful ones in my tribe. Lady named Charity. Heard of her?"

Charity's tribe. A jolt of panic shivered through me.

"Yeah, I heard of Charity. In fact, I staked her," Lucas said as he tried to twist the vampire's hand around his back. He left out the part where Charity got away and was still after us. "Think I can't stake you, too? You're about to learn different." Yet Lucas couldn't gain the advantage. They were too evenly matched. He wasn't even going to have a chance to go for his stakes. The vampire could turn the tables on him at any second.

That meant it was up to me.

Can I really do this? Can I actually stake another vampire? It seemed so impossible, so savage. But if that was the only way to save Lucas, I would have to find the courage.

My hand shook as I came closer to them. Sweat had slicked my palm and made my grasp on the stake more tenuous. If I could just get a clear mark, a way to strike the blow—

Fear and nervousness added to my earlier nausea, and the world tilted strangely. I didn't pass out, but I stumbled and had to brace myself against the wall to keep from falling. The stake clattered down; I couldn't keep my grip.

"Bianca?" Lucas's eyes went wide with fear.

The vampire seized the opportunity and pushed Lucas away, so that he fell. Horrified, I lurched toward them; if the vampire was about to attack Lucas again, I'd find the strength to pull him away no matter what. But the vampire was smarter than that; he ran, leaving us alone in the alley.

Lucas crawled to my side. I was on my hands and knees, down there in the garbage, and all of it stank so badly I thought I might vomit. My head felt too heavy for me to lift. The ends of my hair trailed into a puddle of some liquid I really didn't want to identify. "I'm okay," I said weakly.

"Like hell you are." Lucas pulled me toward him, so that I could lean against his shoulder. We were on our knees beneath the streetlamp. My heart seemed to flutter in my chest, like a trapped bird, scrabbling to free itself. "Bianca, what's wrong?"

"I don't know." The harsh light of the streetlamp had turned everything into shades of gray, like we were in a black-and-white movie. "Do you think—do you think the vampire will leave the city?"

"Don't worry about that right now. I'm going to take care of you."

Lucas folded me against his chest. A cool spatter of rain on my cheek, then another on my calf, told me a summer storm had come. Neither of us moved as the rain quickened, wetting us both and plastering my hair to my head. It didn't seem to matter to Lucas, and as for me—

I didn't have the strength to move.

Chapter Sixteen

LUCAS FLUFFED THE PILLOWS BEHIND MY HEAD and drew the covers over me. "You sure you're okay?" he said for about the eightieth time in the past two hours.

"I need to rest. That's all." I wanted him to stop worrying; he'd been half crazy with concern the whole way home, cradling me in his arms and stroking my hair as we took the bumpy bus ride back through the rain. Now the storm raged outside, rattling the wine bottles with thunder. "That vampire—he knows Charity. He's going to tell her about us."

"That's why we're never going on patrol in this city again." He half turned as a lightning bolt crashed down nearby, and I could imagine him counting silently: *one Mississippi.* The storm was close.

I put one hand to my forehead; either it was warm or my hand was cold. My hair was still damp, which probably wouldn't help.

"Did you not eat enough today?" He started rubbing my hands between his, trying to warm them up. It was like he couldn't rest, couldn't even think straight, until he'd fixed what-ever was wrong. "Or—oh, my God."

Lucas's face went as pale as a sheet. I knew exactly what he was thinking, and it was so incredibly obvious that I had to laugh despite everything. "I'm *not* having a baby."

"Are you positive?" When I nodded, he sighed in relief. "Well, that's something, anyway."

I didn't have the strength to admit to myself that this might be something serious, much less to admit it to Lucas. "I'll be fine after I get some sleep. Wait and see."

"Do you need blood?" He squeezed my hands, sort of happy, like he was talking about surprising me with a box of chocolates. We'd come a long way from the time when my being a vampire used to freak him out.

"I ate earlier." I couldn't even think about blood right now. The idea of eating anything, especially blood, was sickening.

Lucas paused, and I knew he remained worried. He wanted to ask me more questions, and I didn't want him to ask. I wanted to pretend that none of it had ever happened. I needed to pretend that, for just a little while.

I was relieved when he said only, "Okay," and leaned forward to kiss me on the cheek. Closing my eyes, I made believe that I was well, that this wine cellar was a real house, and that we could stay here happily forever and ever.

Lucas didn't keep worrying about my fainting spell the next day, but he insisted that I wait before filling out any more job applications. "You're exhausted," he said. Something in his voice suggested that he'd made up his mind what was going on, and I thought I'd try to believe in it, too. "After the fire at Evernight and Black Cross—you've hardly had a chance to catch your breath."

"You haven't either," I pointed out, "and you work hard at the garage."

"Your life changed more than mine, and we both know it." Lucas shrugged. "Seriously, you need a break. Take a break. I'll take care of us for a couple weeks."

The money he brought in from the garage wasn't that great; Lucas worked hard, and for lots of hours on the days they called him in, but it was under the table, which meant they could pay him less than minimum wage. So far it was enough to buy our food and pay our bus fares, with a teeny bit extra, but we'd barely begun scraping together the money to repay Balthazar and Vic. I'd started looking in the newspapers for places we might rent after Vic's family returned from Tuscany, but I couldn't believe how expensive even the smallest apartments seemed to be. Even if Vic let us have the stuff from the attic, we'd need to buy extra furniture and more clothes and maybe a car someday. I didn't know how we would ever manage.

But I saw the determination on Lucas's face. He was so committed to making this work, to looking after us, that I loved him even more.

"Just a week," I said. That would be enough time to get well, surely.

"Make it a week and a half. You wouldn't want to start work next Monday, would you?"

That would be my eighteenth birthday. I couldn't believe I'd forgotten, but Lucas had remembered for us both.

So, for the next week, I was a lady of leisure. I mean, there was work to handle: dishes to clean, dirty clothes to bundle up, so we could haul them to the Laundromat on the weekend. But most of the days, while Lucas was at the garage, I was basically alone without anything much to do. This was the first time it had felt like summer vacation. I took it easy, just as Lucas and I had agreed. Although I sometimes went for a walk or something like that, I watched a bunch of the DVDs, read the eclectic group of books Vic had chosen for us, and took a lot of naps. By the time I'd gone four days without a dizzy spell, I felt like there was no more reason to worry.

But one day, during an afternoon catnap, a dream intruded.

"Do these dreams mean something?" I asked.

The wraith smiled. "You're finally figuring that out, huh?"

We stood on the roof of Evernight Academy. It was an early morning, foggy and cool, and somehow I knew we weren't alone, although she was the only one I could see. The sky above looked milky and gray, like the fog below; the only substantial thing in the world seemed to be the school's stones jutting up dark and real. The gargoyles' silhouettes snarled around us.

"So you're really speaking to me," I said, "through my dreams."

She shook her head. "We'll meet again soon. I don't know anything about it yet, though."

"How is that possible?"

"I'm not telling you our future," the wraith replied. "You're the one who sees it. Not me."

I could tell the future? That didn't seem very likely, given how many times I'd received nasty surprises. "I think these are only dreams. I don't have to pay any attention to them."

She floated upward, and at first I thought it was because she was trying to leave me behind. Then I realized that I was floating up with her. The roof was no longer beneath my feet, but it didn't matter.

The wraith looked down at me, her face almost inexpressibly sad. "You'll have to face the truth soon enough, Bianca. The lies can't protect you much longer."

She rose faster than I could, though I reached upward in a vain effort to speed my ascent. "Wait!" I cried. "Wait!"

I awoke on the sofa. For the first time, after one of the dreams of the wraith, I wasn't frightened. If anything, I felt calmer than before.

Seeing the future—well, I clearly wasn't psychic or anything like that. But some of the dreams I'd had before had sort of come to pass: the black flowers that later turned up on the brooch Lucas bought for me, or Charity helping to set Evernight Academy on fire. I'd have to think about that in-depth later, really ask myself what my dreams might be telling me about days to come.

But what I thought of most was the last thing the wraith had said to me: *The lies can't protect you much longer.*

"I feel stupid wearing this blindfold," I said. "Is everyone on the bus looking at us like we're crazy people?"

As I tried to pull the scarf away from my eyes, Lucas playfully caught my hands to prevent me. "Mostly they're laughing, because they can tell I'm trying to surprise you."

"I don't need a surprise!" I protested only to make him insist. Really, I loved the fact that Lucas had thought up something special for my birthday.

"We're almost there," he insisted. "Hang tight."

Finally, we reached our stop, and Lucas guided me off the bus and down the steps. Bright sunlight made the scarf slightly translucent, a soft turquoise shade that I thought I would always love because it would remind me of this day.

"Ready?" Lucas began untying the knot at the back of my head. I bounced on my heels in excitement as the scarf dropped. We were standing in front of a museum but not just any museum.

"The Franklin Institute," I said. "The *planetarium*."

He gave me a lopsided smile. "Thought you'd like that."

"I love it!"

I'd lost my telescope when the school burned. Shuttling from city to city since then, I hadn't had a chance to go stargazing in months, and I missed it desperately. This would be the next best thing. I loved that Lucas had thought of it; this really was the best present imaginable.

We went in and goofed around for a while before the next

show, climbing through an enormous model of a human heart that thump-thumped so loudly it made us laugh. But the best part was when we finally got to enter the planetarium itself.

I loved planetariums. They were big and cool and quiet, with high-domed ceilings; they reminded me of the presence of something really infinite, really beautiful. I always wondered if maybe that was what a cathedral felt like, for people who could enter churches.

Lucas and I took our seats. I was about to point out a funny T-shirt someone else in the crowd was wearing when Lucas said, "Better do this before it gets dark in here."

"Do what?"

From his pocket he pulled out a beautiful bracelet of red coral. As I stared at it, he said, "You like it, right? I didn't know what kind of thing you might want, so I figured this was kind of like the brooch."

"It's—*amazing*." The carving on this bracelet was even more delicate than on the jet brooch. Chinese dragons rippled across the silver links that held together the ovals of coral. Although I desperately wanted to slip my hand into it, I had to say, "Lucas, I love it, so much, but—"

"I don't want to hear anything about the money," Lucas said. His face was set. "I'll pay the guys back every cent, and I don't care how long it takes me. But you're my girl. You're going to have a birthday present. Something you deserve."

That was his pride at work again, but not only that. I couldn't argue with him any longer. Instead I hugged him tightly.

He slid the bracelet around my wrist. "There you go," he said, his voice rough. "Happy birthday."

"I love you."

"Love you, too."

The lights dimmed around us, and the "sky" above blazed into a thousand glittering stars. Lucas and I settled back in our seats, his hand clasping mine, as the narrator began telling us about supernovas. The coral and silver of the bracelet laced around my wrist, cool and heavy. Already, it didn't feel like some other possession I owned; it felt like a part of me. A talisman. A link between me and Lucas, just like the brooch.

He wants to take care of me, I thought. *He wants to protect me, no matter what it costs.*

The lies can't protect you any longer.

It was wrong of me to keep looking for protection—to keep relying on Lucas to face so much of our hardships alone, or to depend on him to get my blood supply. And it was wrong for me to hide behind lies. Lucas deserved an equal partner in our fight to be together. That meant he deserved the truth.

Above us, the image zoomed closer to one star, a sluggish giant near the end of its life. It glowed red, darker than blood, and its gaseous surface rippled feverishly like the sea during a storm.

"Lucas," I whispered, carefully pitching my voice so low that I wouldn't disturb anyone nearby. "I have to tell you something."

He half turned toward me. The dying star above silhouetted his face in crimson. "What?"

"When I fainted—on the hunt—it wasn't the first time."

The star went supernova, crashing outward into a spectacular blaze of white light. For a moment it was as bright as day, and I could see the confusion and worry on Lucas's face as the crowd oohed and aahed around us. "Bianca, what are you telling me?"

"It started weeks ago. I've been having dizzy spells since shortly after I joined your Black Cross cell. They're happening more frequently, and they're getting worse, and I don't really want to eat anymore. Or, well, drink. I know I should've told you before. I just—I didn't want you to worry."

Lucas opened his mouth to speak, but then he shut it again. I could see that he was balancing between being frightened and being angry. I didn't blame him for either feeling, but that didn't make it much easier to see.

Finally, he said only, "We'll get through it."

I nodded and leaned my head on his shoulder and looked up at the newborn nebula, which was opening above us like a pale blue flower. Although I knew I hadn't solved the problem by sharing it, at least I didn't have to carry the secret around any longer. Now I could celebrate my birthday the way Lucas had meant for me to, looking up at my stars.

When the show ended, and the lights came on, I led Lucas out of the planetarium as we both blinked. "That was really gorgeous," I said. "Thanks for bringing me here."

"Yeah." Lucas looked distracted.

"You can't really think about that right now, can you?" When he shook his head no, I sighed. "Come on. Let's talk."

We headed out into the early evening. Instead of going straight to the bus stop, we walked along the street. The neighborhood was a nice one, with lots of museums and big houses, and tall old trees with broad branches that swayed slowly in the breeze. Our path took us by the side of a park, where a few others strolled or walked their dogs.

The first thing Lucas said was, "Are you *sure* you're not pregnant?"

"Positive." He gave me a worried look, and I shook my head. "Honestly, Lucas, I already told you that."

"You cannot tell a guy you're not pregnant too many times."

"I'm not, I'm not, I'm not."

"Thanks." Lucas put his arm around my shoulders. "So, what do you think it is? Do you know?"

"I don't know anything for sure, but—" I hesitated. It was hard to put this into words. "I keep remembering something my mother said to me once. The night after I bit you for the first time, actually."

"What did she say?"

I glanced around to make sure nobody was standing too close to us. There were a few people walking a couple of steps behind, slightly wild in garish clothes and heavy makeup, but they were talking loudly among themselves and wouldn't overhear. "She said that, once I'd first tasted human blood, I'd turned over the hourglass. That I couldn't keep going forever as what I was—part human and part vampire. She said the vampire in me would grow stronger and that eventually, I'd have to—" I wasn't going to say *kill* out loud in public. "I'd have to complete the transition."

Lucas said, "And they never told you what would happen if you didn't?"

I shook my head. "I asked them tons of times, but they just acted like that wasn't an option. They didn't say how long I had, either. Now I'm starting to wonder."

"You think how you're feeling is your body trying to tell you to kill somebody?"

"Shhhhh." There was another group of people, maybe a little older but with equally wild appearance, coming near us from a side street. Our paths would intersect soon. "Do you have to say that so loudly?"

Lucas's steps slowed. "How do you feel right now?"

"This second? I'm fine, I guess, but—"

"Good. Get ready to run."

"What are you talking about?" But then I saw what Lucas had seen: a third group of people, all dressed in similar rags, were approaching from across the street. This wasn't random. We were surrounded.

Then I recognized a man in the third group, a guy with an aquiline profile, skin as pale as mine, and long, reddish-brown dreadlocks. *Shepherd.*

"That guy," I said. "He hunts for Charity."

Lucas grabbed my hand and squeezed. "The bus stop. Go."

We started to run. As soon as we'd taken two steps, the vampires around us gave up any pretense of just hanging out. They swirled around as fast as a flock of birds, right on our heels. And they weren't laughing any longer.

Lucas sped up, calling on his enhanced speed to propel us forward. I clasped his hand as tightly as I could, once again cursing my stupid sandals, but I couldn't quite move as fast as Lucas. Before, I usually outran him. Not anymore.

The footsteps behind us pounded closer and louder. I could hear their belts and bracelets jangling. Lucas kept trying to tow me after him. By now we both knew we weren't going to get back to the bus stop in time, not with me running so slowly. So I wrenched my hand from Lucas's and took off running to the right. "Bianca!" he shouted, but I didn't turn back.

I had thought the vampires would split up, half chasing Lucas and half chasing me. Lucas would be able to escape from his pursuers, and as for me—well, maybe I had a chance if I only had to fight half. Instead, from the sound of it, they'd all followed me.

Lucas, please get away, please get out of here! I didn't dare look back to see if that was what he was doing. They were too close, so close, getting closer—

A hand grabbed my arm and pulled me around. I stumbled and nearly fell, but Shepherd caught me.

"Smile for the people," he whispered. "They want to think we're just kids playing around. So you smile and make them think that. Or else we'll make you scream."

There were ten of them and one of me. I smiled. Nearby, in the park, I saw a young couple with a stroller shrug and keep going, satisfied that nothing was really wrong.

"Let her go!"

Lucas pushed his way through the vampires, like they were any other crowd of punks. Nobody fought him, but the vampire didn't let go. Shepherd said, "We're taking her for a ride, or we're taking her out, here and now. You know we can do it. It won't be any trouble to take you out, too."

We didn't have stakes or holy water or any other weapons. We'd come out for my birthday, not for a fight. Lucas's eyes met mine, and I could see him recognizing the hard odds we faced.

Shepherd continued, "So you have two choices, hunter. You can come for a ride with us, or you can turn around and go home like a good boy."

"Lucas, please," I pleaded. "They're only after me."

But he shook his head. "Where you go, I go."

They walked us around the corner to a slightly less busy street and pushed us into the back of a truck. I thought for a moment of our escape from Black Cross, but that hope died instantly. We didn't have Dana to help us this time, and the cab of the truck was completely separate from the metal box we had to stay in. When they slammed the doors shut behind us, blackness fell, save for a few lines of light around the corners of the doors.

Once I'd had nearly perfect night vision. That was starting to fade.

"Hang on, Bianca." Lucas put his arms around me as the

truck rumbled into motion. "We're gonna have to think fast when they open those doors back up."

"They'll still outnumber us," I said. "And they're taking us to a place where they'll be more in control than they were here."

"I know. But we had zero chance out there. We have to hope the next situation is going to work more to our advantage."

I didn't see how that was even possible, but I tried to follow Lucas's example and think like a fighter.

It seemed to take an incredibly long time before we reached our destination—a large, one-story building that had evidently been abandoned for a long time but had been either a health club or a gymnasium. Several of the windows were broken, and graffiti striped the walls. This building was waiting to be torn down, and apparently some vampires had decided to take advantage of the delay. They tugged us out of the back of the truck—four vampires flanking each of us.

"Let's head to the pool," Shepherd said. Lucas and I shared a look; I knew he was telling me to look out for anything we might be able to use for weapons or an escape. I wasn't sure how we were supposed to take out that many vampires at once, but we had to remain focused.

The pool area looked even more torn up than the rest. As we walked inside, I could see that was where the vampires had chosen to stay. Beer bottles littered the floor and windowsills, and every corner had become a trash heap. It smelled like cigarettes. In the center of the room was the swimming pool itself, long emptied of water; the abandoned high-dive board stood above, lonely, with a cobweb dangling from the end.

At first I thought nobody else was inside. But then a solitary figure in the corner moved. Somebody in rags had been sleeping in a huddle on the floor, and I'd taken her for another trash heap.

She pushed frowsy pale hair back from her face and looked at us steadily. Even from across the room, I recognized her immediately. Ever since our capture, we'd known who we would be taken to—but that didn't make her any easier to face.

Lucas whispered, "Charity."

Chapter Seventeen

CHARITY WALKED CLOSER TO US. HER FAIR CURLS hung loose, making her look even younger than usual. She wore a lacy sleeveless cotton dress that probably used to be white instead of bloodstained and gray. Her feet were bare, her red toenail polish badly chipped. I thought of a small child awoken from its nap, confused and cranky.

"You brought them here," she said to Shepherd. "You brought them to our home."

"You wanted to find the girl, right? Well, we got her." Shepherd grinned. He clearly considered this a job well done, and Charity's displeasure didn't even register.

She tugged at her hair and frowned. "You brought the boy, too."

"That's right," Lucas said. "Miss me?"

Charity pulled down the front of her dress far enough for us to see the pink, star-shaped scar above her heart left from when Lucas had staked her during the burning of Evernight. Stakings

were the only wounds vampires could receive that left permanent marks. She traced the edge of the star with her little finger.
"I think of you every day."

Great, I thought. *She's obsessed with us both.* I stepped between
them, so that she and I were only a few feet apart. "What do you
want, Charity? Balthazar's probably left New York by now, so it's
not like I can tell you anything."

"I've been thinking," she said. "The best way to find Balthazar is . . . not to find him. To make him come to me. And
how better to do that than by taking something he wants?"

A chill shivered through my body as I realized she was talking about me.

"I don't want to join your tribe." I said. My voice sounded
clear and didn't shake—the opposite of how I truly felt.

"If wishes were horses, beggars would ride," she said.

This was it. There was no way to escape. Lucas and I were
outnumbered and surrounded. Charity would turn me into a
vampire. Tonight, I would die.

I tried to tell myself it wasn't the worst thing that could happen. I'd spent most of my life expecting to become a vampire
someday. Maybe I'd feel some weird bond to Charity. That often
took place between a new vampire and the older one who had
brought her over. But I'd still be me. Lucas had already accepted
what I was, so we would still love each other. It wouldn't be so
bad, would it?

But I had wanted to *choose*. I had wanted to have some say in
what I would become, what existence I would lead. I'd wanted

to be free—and now I never would be.

"Fine," I said. I blinked quickly, hoping she wouldn't see my tears. "I can't stop you. Just let Lucas go."

"Bianca," Lucas pleaded. I couldn't turn to look at him.

Instead I remained focused on Charity, whose dark eyes widened with disappointment. It was like she wanted me to be happy about becoming a vampire. How could she expect me to feel any other way? How could she not know that I hated her? "You want to force me to do this? That'll make you feel strong, convince you that you took something away from Balthazar? Then do it."

"She isn't Balthazar's girl," Lucas said loudly. "She's mine."

That was the worst possible thing he could've said.

"Yours?" Charity clasped her hands together. A jelly cord with only a few beads left dangled from one wrist, the cheap, ruined reflection of the coral bracelet I wore. "Bianca is yours. That makes you hers."

I got even closer to her, so she would stop looking at him. "Leave Lucas out of this."

"How can I leave him out of it, when you belong to each other? What I do to you affects him. And—what I do to him affects you."

She flicked her hand. Shepherd and another vampire grabbed Lucas and began dragging him backward. Lucas struggled, elbowing Shepherd so hard in the ribs that he doubled over, and for a moment Lucas pulled free. I saw his hand go to his waist, where he had for so many years worn a stake—a useless reflex, a remnant of the life he'd abandoned.

Shepherd recovered himself, and a third vampire joined in. Lucas fought against them with all his strength, but he was outnumbered.

"What are you doing?" I cried, struggling against the hands that held me fast. "Leave him alone!"

"You will determine his fate," Charity promised. "Only you."

"Balthazar always said vampires could never change, that it was the tragedy of what—of what we are." It was bitter to again include myself with Charity, to admit that soon there would be no difference between us. "That's the only reason he still cared about you, Charity. He thought you hadn't changed, but you have. You've become a monster."

Charity shook her head. "My poor brother never did understand. I haven't changed. This is what I always was, even in life." Her gaze was distant, focused on the past, on people no longer here. "But now I have the courage to act."

"This one is strong," Shepherd called as he continued struggling with Lucas. "Too strong."

Charity's face lit up in a giddy smile. "He has vampire strength? You've drunk his blood, Bianca. Was he sweet? He looks sweet. I wouldn't mind a taste."

"Don't you bite him," I said, and my voice shook now. "Don't."

"If I bit him, and drank all his blood, and he died," she singsonged, "Lucas would become a vampire. Would you drink willingly then? To join your lover?"

I slapped her. Her head jerked sharply to the side, and most of the vampires froze in their tracks, like they couldn't believe anyone had dared strike Charity. She pressed her own delicate hand to her cheek, which was flushed red from my blow. Otherwise, she acted as though it had never happened. "You will ask me to join my tribe," she said. "You will beg me."

"Why would you think I would *ever*—" The words choked in my mouth as I realized why she thought that, what she was planning to do.

She whispered, "You'll beg me for it, and you'll open your throat to me. If you don't, I'll kill your boy."

Lucas tried harder to free himself, but they had him fast, and another of the vampires was duct taping his wrists and then his ankles together. Then Shepherd threw Lucas over his shoulders, like he wasn't even a person, just a bag or a thing.

"Climb the ladder," Charity called, and Shepherd began ascending to the diving board, Lucas still in his grasp. She walked to the edge of the empty pool, and I followed, unable to understand what was going on. But when I looked in the pool, my stomach turned over. The pale-blue surface was horribly stained with blood, splash after splash of it, dark brown with age. Glimpsing the terror on my face, Charity whispered, "Sometimes, the ones that bore us, we give them a chance to get away. If they can survive the fall, we tell them, we'll let them go. It's so much fun to watch them on the diving board. They cry and they scream and they beg, but eventually they all decide to jump. They all fool themselves that they have a chance. Then they fall. So messy. All that wasted blood."

"You're disgusting," I said.

"Sometimes it takes them hours to die. Days. One poor fool kept whining down there for nearly a week. How long do you think Lucas would suffer?" Charity's dark eyes glinted with pleasure at the memory of others' pain. "Beg."

"It wouldn't work anyway. I can't become a vampire unless I take a life."

"If I drink your blood—if I drain you far enough—you'll become so desperate for blood that you'll attack the first human you see. I promise to keep you away from your darling boy, though it wouldn't make any difference to you, not in that state."

I thought about how crazed I'd been for blood at times, especially during my captivity with Black Cross. Even then there had been times I'd been in danger of losing control with Lucas. I didn't doubt that Charity was telling the truth.

"Don't do it," Lucas said. "She'll kill me anyway."

"I won't. Cross my heart. You did me a favor once—I do remember, you know." The small hesitant smile on her face was as girlish and trusting as ever. "You really can choose. You can walk out of here right now, safe and sound, and live out your life as a—well, as whatever you are. We'll let you get far away before we drop him, so you don't have to hear."

I closed my eyes tightly, willing myself to be somewhere else. Anywhere else.

Charity continued, "Or you can be a good girl and beg me nicely, and we'll let your boy go. He'll have to watch you die, of course. Otherwise he wouldn't believe us. But we'll let him live. On my word."

The crazy thing was, I believed her. Charity believed in bargains and debts. Also, she was a sadist. If she were simply going to turn me into a vampire and then kill Lucas anyway, or have *me* kill Lucas anyway, she'd say so and take pleasure in watching me scream. No, I had a real chance to save Lucas's life. That meant I had to take it.

Slowly, I forced myself to say, "Please."

"Bianca, no!" Lucas thrashed in Shepherd's grip, but there was nothing he could do.

Charity gave me the most tender smile, like I was a prodigal child who had come home. "Please?"

"Please—make me part of your tribe." Was that enough? No. I hated every word. Every single heartbeat felt precious, because I knew I wouldn't feel that much longer. Brokenly, I thought that I would die on my birthday—just like Shakespeare, I remembered. My life was being stolen from me, and I had to beg. For Lucas, I would beg. "Please turn me into a vampire."

"Do you want to stay with me forever?" Charity's hands framed my face. "Will we be sisters? Then Balthazar will see that you're mine instead of his. We'll show him. Please say yes. Oh, please say that's what you want."

That was why she wanted me to beg; so she could convince herself it was true and that she was building a family again. She didn't want me to get back at Balthazar; she wanted me to replace him.

I'd begun shaking so hard I felt like I couldn't stand up, but I managed to say, "Yes. That's what I want. Please."

She stuck out her bottom lip, a spoiled little girl. "If you really wanted, you would plead. You would go down on your knees."

It was impossible for me to hate anyone more than I hated her at that second. I thought of Lucas and sank to my knees. The broken tile floor scraped my skin, and I put one hand over my coral bracelet, the last token of love Lucas had given me. "Please, Charity. Please take my life."

"There," Charity said. "That wasn't so hard, was it?" She smiled at me sweetly, and her fangs were out. It wouldn't be long now.

"No!" Lucas shouted. "Don't! Bianca, you can fight, forget about me!"

I tilted my head backward, looking up at the metal rafters. Cobwebs drifted lazily, like wicked clouds. My throat was bared to Charity, and I knew this was the end of my life.

I'll be a vampire now, I thought. *Please let my parents be right. Please let it not be so bad.*

As Charity cupped her hand around the side of my throat, I saw a strange flickering in the rafters. Like light reflecting on water in a pool—though there was no water in the pool—

My eyes opened wide.

"It won't hurt much," Charity promised. "Really it won't."

The blue-green light brightened and spread, covering the entire ceiling as it coalesced into something that looked like clouds. A cool breeze flowed around us, making a summer night into winter, and I shivered.

"Charity!" Shepherd cried. "What is this?" All the vampires were staring upward now, and even Lucas had stilled his struggling.

Charity gasped. "Oh, they wouldn't dare. They wouldn't *dare*."

Sleet began to fall. Sharp pinpricks of ice rained down, jabbing my skin and crackling against the floor. Charity skittered back from me, and I got to my feet, wishing I could run. Maybe I could escape, but I couldn't leave Lucas behind, not even now— not even during an attack by the wraith.

The sleet thickened, silvery curtains that blurred our vision and made Charity cry out in pain. Ice fell so hard that it hurt. I winced, and then gaped in astonishment as one of the silvery curtains grew more solid, more distinct, and a face formed in the sleet. Though the ice kept falling, the face and form remained.

Even more shocking: I recognized him. He was the first wraith who had ever spoken to me. His long, dark hair flowed loose, and he had a beard. Although his clothing was indistinct, it looked old-fashioned to me—like something from a couple of centuries back, with a long cloak and high boots. *The frost man*, I thought. It was the only name I'd ever had for him.

In a voice made of the sound of breaking ice, he said, "This one is not yours."

"She *is* mine! She is!" Charity stamped her foot. "You heard her! She said she wanted to join us!"

He tilted his head, curious and disdainful, then punched forward. His fist went through Charity's gut.

She opened her mouth as if to scream, but no sound came out. Her entire body shifted color, turning the same pale blue as the wraith. I realized he was freezing her—and apparently, even vampires could be frozen to death.

Charity jerked her head upright and shrieked, "No!" She pulled back, which seemed to take all her strength, but she staggered away from the frost man's fist. There wasn't any blood. Stumbling, she cried, "Get out of here! Everyone, out!"

With that, Shepherd threw Lucas from the board.

I screamed, reaching out for him in vain as he tumbled downward. But then the blue-green light appeared in the pool—more like water than ever—and it slowed his fall. Lucas still hit the bottom, but not that hard, and I could see him struggling to get free of his bonds. Obviously he was okay.

The wraith saved him, I realized. *The wraith saved* me.

There was no time to wonder about it now. I had to get Lucas.

I hurried to the ladder and descended, through the blue-green light. It was cold—even colder than ice—and yet somehow it didn't hurt. Instead it felt like waves of energy, or maybe electricity, dangerous to be near. I ran through it, or tried to run; it slowed my steps. My long hair trailed behind me, almost as though I were swimming instead of running. "Lucas!" I cried.

Lucas tore his hands free of the tape just as I got to him. Together we pulled at the bonds on his ankles. "Is this what

I think it is?" he asked.

"Yes." The tape came off at last. "We have to go!"

We pushed through the blue-green energy toward the ladder. Lucas shoved me upward so that I could get out first. As I clambered out, I saw the frost man staring at me.

Not knowing what else to do, I said, "Thank you."

"You are not hers," he said. "You are ours."

So, they could kill me but nobody else could? That wasn't so comforting.

Lucas climbed out of the pool. "Bianca, run! Come on!"

We ran through the silvery-gray sleet, now pounding down so hard I knew I'd have bruises tomorrow. The wraiths didn't try to stop us, or if they tried, they failed. Lucas hit the nearest door and pulled me through into a long hallway that connected the pool area to the rest of the building. Although it was cold here, there was no sleet and no unearthly light.

"You!" Shepherd appeared at the far end of the corridor, and we both skidded to a halt. "You brought this down on us!"

Lucas dragged me to the left. "Side door. Move."

I didn't see any side door. "Where is it?"

"I was more hoping one would be here," Lucas admitted.

"Oh, crap." I could hear Shepherd's boots pounding as he ran after us. He appeared to be separated from the other vampires, but that didn't mean I wanted to be cornered by the guy.

Lucas shoved a chair underneath the doorknob, and then glanced around the room. Mostly it looked like the pool area had—heaped high with trash, rags, bits of old paper, half-empty bottles of booze, cigarettes, and lighters. That didn't look promising to me. However, Lucas grabbed a bottle of vodka and a stained bandanna. "Find me a lighter," he said.

I grabbed a plastic lighter from a nearby windowsill. "Lucas, what are you doing?"

"You didn't get to this part of the training, huh?" He knotted the bandanna around the neck of the bottle and dipped the long end of the cloth into the vodka.

Shepherd slammed into the door. The chair rocked, and it clearly wouldn't hold the door shut much longer. "Lucas, he's here!"

"Good." Lucas flicked the lighter. As Shepherd burst into the room, smiling evilly at us, Lucas set the rag on fire and tossed the bottle at Shepherd.

Alcohol is flammable—when the fire gets to the liquid—

Lucas tackled me to the ground just as the fireball exploded outward. I heard Shepherd scream, and possibly he was dying; fire was one of the few things that could kill a vampire. Before I could see what was happening, Lucas yelled, "Cover your head!"

I did. He got up and threw a chair through the window. Glass sprayed everywhere, and I could feel shards of it prickling into my scalp. Lucas then grabbed my hand.

"Let's get out of here," he cried. The fire behind us was blazing brightly now. Shepherd's screaming had stopped. Either he had escaped or he was dead.

I leaped through the window, avoiding the jagged glass that

still jutted out from the edges. To my relief, I saw the car the vampires had used to bring us here. It was parked only a couple dozen feet away, and nobody was inside. They'd come for it soon, which meant we had to take it first. It would speed our escape and slow their pursuit. We could actually get away.

The door wasn't locked. I slid behind the driver's seat as Lucas jumped in the passenger side. Breathing hard, he said, "Tell me they left the keys in this thing."

"They didn't," I said as I fumbled with the wires beneath the dashboard. "Good thing I got through some parts of the training."

Black Cross taught everyone how to hot-wire an old-fashioned car. They said you'd never know when you needed to get away in a hurry. Well, they were right about that.

The wires sparked, and the engine rumbled to life. I put the car in drive and stamped down on the gas. We spun out of the parking lot, back into safety and freedom.

Thanks to Black Cross, I thought. *And thanks to the wraith. My life couldn't get any stranger.*

When I started to laugh, Lucas glanced at me in concern. Probably I sounded a little hysterical. "Bianca, take it easy, okay? We made it. Don't freak out."

I simply focused on the road and muttered, "Happy birthday to me."

Chapter Eighteen

"WE SHOULD DUMP THE CAR," I SAID.

"Slow down, okay?" Lucas kept his hands braced against the dashboard, like he was scared I was going to steer us into a ditch at any second. He might not have been wrong. I'd gotten an A in driver's ed, but between not knowing where I was going and shaking from adrenaline, I wasn't really in control of the vehicle. "I don't think the vampires can track this thing. We'll park it in back where it can't be seen from the street. For now we need to get home as fast as possible."

"This isn't the vampires' car! You know they stole this. Which means if we're found with it, the police will think *we* stole it."

"We won't be found with it if you just slow down and stop driving like a crazy person." Lucas put a hand on my shoulder. "Deep breaths. Come on. Oh, hey—turn left here."

I turned left and realized I recognized this street from one of the bus routes; we were getting closer to Vic's neighborhood and our temporary home. That helped me calm myself a little bit. We'd have to get rid of the car eventually, but for now, we were all right.

We drove to the end of Vic's driveway and across that perfect lawn. I hoped the tires wouldn't gouge too deeply into the soil. Once the car was more or less hidden behind the house, we stopped.

Somehow it felt strange, walking back inside the dark, quiet wine cellar. It hadn't changed in any way, but I felt that I had. I stepped out of my sandals and unfastened my hair with trembling hands.

Lucas put his hands against the wall and bowed his head, as if he lacked the strength to go any farther. His wrists were still red from the duct tape that had bound them. The silhouette of his broad shoulders made me shiver.

I looked down at my own wrists, at the delicate bracelet Lucas had given me. A present for my birthday—a happy symbol of a day that seemed to have taken place a lifetime ago, not only a few hours in the past.

"Charity's not going to stop looking for you," he said. "She's obsessed now. She's decided you're the barrier between her and Balthazar."

"It doesn't matter," I whispered.

"Bianca, we can't stay in Philadelphia. We'll have to go farther away. Where, I don't know—"

"It doesn't matter tonight," I repeated.

Lucas turned to argue with me, but then our eyes met and

he fell silent. I lay one hand on his chest, so that I could feel the rise and fall of his breath and the beating of his heart.

We're alive, I thought. *This is what it means to be alive.*

"Bianca—"

"Shhh."

I traced his lips, the strong column of his neck, the swell of his Adam's apple. I could feel his breath against my fingers, coming faster as I touched him. Still he was too far away. My hands shook as I pulled his T-shirt over his head. Then I could wrap my arms around his waist and lay my head against his chest. I could hear his pulse rushing against my ear, the way the sea does in a shell. It wasn't enough.

"Closer," I whispered, pulling him down for a kiss. Lucas's mouth captured mine, and his hands began tearing at my dress the way I'd torn at his clothes. I helped him push away the straps of my sundress, without ever breaking the kiss, because I didn't want to stop touching him.

My clothes crumpled to the floor. His skin was against my skin, the cedary scent of him the only air I could breathe. All I wore now was the red coral bracelet, and it shone against his bare skin as he pulled me toward our bed.

In the morning, I felt terrible. Probably that was because I'd been chased by vampires and pounded by sleet, not to mention chilled to the bone, but Lucas freaked out about it.

"You said you've been really sick." He pressed his palm to my forehead, which was silly, because his body temperature was almost always warmer than mine. "Any more dizzy spells?"

"You haven't even let me get out of bed yet. How would I know if I'm dizzy?" I gestured at the quilt that covered me and the pillows beneath my head. "Usually you have to stand up to tell."

"I'm just concerned."

"Well, that makes two of us. But I don't want you to have to worry."

Lucas sat heavily on the corner of the bed and rested his forehead in his hand. "I love you, Bianca. That means I have to worry. Something's wrong with you that neither one of us understands. We need to talk to some vampires—and not the kind we dealt with last night."

I confessed, "I've thought about talking to Mom and Dad. Not because I wanted to—though I do, so much—"

He took my hand, to show that he understood.

"—but I don't think they'd hear us out." As much as I hated this knowledge, I felt that it was true. My parents would respond to my call in only one way: They'd come get me. They would do whatever it took to separate me from Lucas, and they'd probably try to force me to become a vampire like them.

Lucas considered that for a second. He seemed to have some trouble getting the next words out. "Well, what about Balthazar?"

It had cost him a lot to admit that Balthazar might be the one to help me, I knew. But that, too, was a dead end. "I already asked him, at school last year. He doesn't know what happens to born vampires if they don't complete the transition."

"Damn." Rising from the bed, Lucas paced. I watched him from my tangle of covers. *Forget about it,* I wanted to say. *Maybe it's nothing. We got away from Charity; we should be celebrating!*

That was me trying to pretend that nothing was wrong. I'd told Lucas the truth in part so that I couldn't pretend any longer. It was time to face this.

Lucas stopped in his tracks. "We're assuming that this has something to do with your vampire side. But what if it isn't? I mean, you could just be sick. With walking pneumonia or something like that."

"It's possible. I've thought about it." Full vampires never caught viruses or got appendicitis or anything like that, but growing up, I'd had the sniffles and stomachaches like any other child. In the past few years, I'd been very healthy, and my parents had said that was my vampire strength buoying my immune system. But maybe it was still possible for me to get sick like anybody else.

"Dana had walking pneumonia a couple of years ago. It messed with her appetite, her strength, that kind of stuff. That might be all this is."

"Maybe so." I liked the idea a lot. Too much, really—nobody should *want* to have walking pneumonia—but it beat the alternative.

Lucas sat back down on the bed, more cheerful than he'd been since the planetarium. "So, we'll get you to the doctor. He can check you out, figure out what's wrong."

It sounded like a good idea, save one thing. Hesitantly, I said, "Can we pay for the doctor?"

"We've got enough money for a visit to the clinic. It sets us back, but—we can manage."

"If I need antibiotics—Lucas, that stuff can be really expensive—"

"If you need antibiotics, we'll sell the car."

"The stolen car?"

"What other car would I be talking about?" Lucas wouldn't meet my eyes.

"Lucas, that would be wrong! That belongs to somebody who probably wants it back." I couldn't believe he'd said such a thing. "Besides, how would you even do it? The car is stolen. It's not so easy to sell a stolen car. I've seen it on TV; there are serial numbers and all kinds of things to track it down."

He sighed heavily. "Bianca, I work at a chop shop."

I was confused. What was a chop shop? The first thing that made me think about was chop suey, and I imagined a Chinese restaurant. But Lucas worked at a garage. "I don't understand."

"A chop shop is a garage that deals in stolen cars." Lucas stared down at his hands as he said this, rubbing absently at the raw skin on his wrists. "We scrape off the VINs, break 'em down for parts, repaint them, doctor license plates, whatever people need. I'm not proud of it. But I can do it."

"Why would you work at a place like that?"

"Bianca, get real. I'm shy of my twenty-first birthday, and I don't even have a high school diploma, much less any certifications as a mechanic. Who else do you think would hire me? I hate working with crooks. I hate it so much, some mornings it makes me sick. But I have to do something so we can survive, and a place like this—that's pretty much the only place that would hire me."

My cheeks burned. I felt so stupid, for not having realized the situation we were in. Lucas's pride must have tormented him every single day; he believed strongly in right and wrong. He did this job only because he thought he had to for us.

Gently I laid my hand on his. "I understand."

"Wish I did, sometimes." Lucas shook it off. "Listen, I know the rightful owner of that car deserves to have it back. But I'd bet a million bucks that he doesn't need it back because he needs the cash to get medicine for someone he loves. If he knew that— if he knew how badly you need it—you think he might not be so angry?"

I nodded, blinking fast. I had become a burden, and we were becoming criminals. It hurt, but I had to face the consequences of our choices—and of my nature.

It turned out there was a free clinic at one of the local hospitals, so Lucas took a day off and went with me. The minute we walked in, we could see why it was free. Every chair in the waiting room was filled, some with old people who looked lonely and lost, others by entire families who seemed to have come together. Coughing echoed from every corner. Yellowed posters on the wall warned against various health risks and seemed way too focused on STDs.

I put my name at the end of a really long list, just some Xeroxed sheets on a battered old clipboard. The whole place smelled like Lysol.

"Sit down," Lucas said. "Let's get you off your feet."

Although I would've liked to tell him not to be such a mother hen, I really did need to sit down. I felt weak, and my body kept flushing hot and cold at odd moments. Sometimes I wanted a blanket; other times, even my sundress seemed stifling.

Lucas sat next to me, and we leafed through some of the magazines lying around in the waiting room. They were mostly about being parents of little kids. The covers showed happy, healthy, beaming children who didn't bear much resemblance to the wailing infants I saw around us. All the magazines were faded and dog-eared; the first one I picked up was nearly two years old.

"This place is creepy," I whispered to Lucas.

"Doesn't seem too bad," he said with a shrug. I realized that Lucas probably had never been taken anywhere else for medical care; Black Cross wouldn't pay for much, and they would never have been in one place long enough for him to have a regular doctor.

I remembered my pediatrician back in Arrowwood, Dr. Diamond. He'd been a kindly man with glasses who always let me pick out Band-Aids with my favorite cartoon characters on them before he gave me a shot. Mom said they'd taken me to him from the time I was a tiny baby, and I'd only just become too old for his practice when we moved to Evernight. In all that time, giving me vaccinations and checking my reflexes, he'd never noticed anything especially odd about me—though he did mention, once, how my mother seemed ageless.

My experiences with Dr. Diamond had convinced me that, if I were only sick with some normal virus, a physician would be able to help. If the problem was something vampiristic, well, I'd be out of luck—but the doctor would be none the wiser.

It took forever for them to call my name, but they finally did. Lucas gave me a wave as I headed inside.

A heavyset nurse whose nametag read SELMA walked into the exam room after me. "What seems to be the problem?"

"I'm having dizzy spells." The paper atop the table crinkled as I sat upon it. "And I never want to eat anymore."

Selma shot me a look. "Any chance you could be pregnant?"

"No!" My cheeks flamed. I knew doctors might ask you questions like that, but I wasn't quite prepared for it. "I mean— I have—I do—I'm sexually active, I guess you'd say, but we're careful. And I know I'm not pregnant. For sure. Really."

"We'll get you checked out." Selma popped a thermometer in my mouth, and I obediently held it under my tongue as she reached for the blood pressure cuff. "How are you feeling today?"

I waggled my hand back and forth. *So-so.*

Selma nodded and began to put the cuff around my arm— but then she stopped. I glanced sideways and saw that she was staring at the readout screen for the thermometer. It read 91 degrees.

I'd always run a little cool—Dr. Diamond used to joke about my being 97 degrees—but that wasn't so very unusual. Apparently 91 degrees was unusual.

"Give me that." Selma took the thermometer out of my mouth and reset it, then popped it back in. She fastened the Velcro cuff around my upper arm and started inflating it; a tight band of pressure squeezed my bicep.

My eyes remained fixed on the temperature screen. *Come on*, I thought. *Move up. At least to 97 degrees. She won't think that's too weird.*

The temperature readout changed, slipping down to 90 degrees.

Selma's eyes went wide. At first I thought she'd seen the readout, but then I realized that my blood pressure must be wrong, too. She ripped the cuff off my arm. "Lie down," she ordered. "I'm getting the doctor in here this second."

"It's not an emergency," I said weakly. "Really, I just feel sort of dizzy."

"Lie down before you fall down." Selma pushed my shoulders backward onto the table. Despite her forcefulness, there was something kindly in her manner; she must have been a good nurse. She hurried out, and I lay there, hands folded across my belly, trying to convince myself this wasn't a huge problem.

Unfortunately, I knew better.

My temperature wouldn't be that low if I had walking pneumonia, I thought. *Or any kind of flu or other virus. People run fevers when they get illnesses like that. I don't think it does much to blood pressure, either.*

In other words, whatever was wrong with me was no human illness.

Down the hallway, I could hear the nurse talking animatedly to someone, probably one of the doctors. Did they consider this an emergency? Were they about to take me into the hospital? If they did, could I get out again?

Quickly I pushed myself upright—too quickly. My head swam with the sudden movement, and for a second, I thought I might fall. But I steadied myself against the table and took a couple of deep breaths. Soon I felt I could walk again.

I peeked into the hallway. Selma was only a few doors down, but she was deeply engrossed in conversation with the doctor. Her words were only barely loud enough for me to overhear: "I'm sure that thermometer is working correctly. It was only ten minutes ago. I'm telling you—"

Time to hurry. I tiptoed halfway down the hall, then took off running toward the waiting room. Another nurse appeared in the corridor, and she looked startled as I pushed past her.

Don't look back. Without slowing down, I ran through the doors and into the waiting room. "Lucas!" I called over my shoulder. "Let's go!"

He stared at me, startled, but was on his feet in an instant. We were going to get away. We'd make it. Then we were outside, sizzling July sun enveloping me in an instant. Waves of heat rippled up from the steps and the sidewalk. It was too much, and

I slumped against the guardrail. The stairs seemed to stretch and tilt beneath me.

"Bianca!" Lucas caught up with me and scooped my arm around his shoulders. Staggering against him, I was able to get down the steps and around the corner.

"Keep walking." I panted. "They'll come out and look for me, I know it."

"We're walking. What happened in there?"

"My readings were coming back weird. The nurse freaked out."

Lucas took me down a side street, keeping our pace quick. I felt a little steadier but knew I needed to lean on him. "What do you mean, weird?"

The truth hit me then. I'd spent my whole life preparing for this moment, in one way or another, and yet it was strange and terrible to face.

"I'm not yet a vampire," I whispered. "But—I'm no longer human."

Chapter Nineteen

WE RETURNED HOME FROM THE CLINIC AT SUNSET. Lucas poured me back into bed, and we worried about what to do. I told him everything that had happened at the clinic and the weird readings that had made the nurse panic.

"Never happened before?" he said. I shook my head. "Then—you're changing. Whether you like it or not. You're becoming a vampire. A full vampire, I mean."

"I can't be a full vampire unless I kill. That's the only way it works."

"How do you know?" Lucas demanded. He lay on the bed with me, though I was beneath the covers and he was on top of them. "Nobody really understands what happens with kids like you, right?"

"Almost nobody. But my parents understood. They never would explain most of it, but this part, they were really clear on." I stared up at the white ceiling, studying the whorls of plaster. "There are only two ways a person becomes a vampire. Either you're a regular person who gets bitten repeatedly by a vampire and then is killed by the final bite, or you're a born vampire—like me—who makes a kill. That's it."

"Then what's happening to you?" He cupped my cheek with his hand. His dark-green eyes were anguished. "I can't stand this. Not knowing. And I realize it's got to be worse for you."

I held his hand to my face and tried to smile. I couldn't bear to tell him what I was starting to believe.

With my body weakening, I had begun to experience the strangest sensation—a kind of sinking, a wearing away, as though I were somehow *less* each day. Something inside me was fighting against the force of life, and that something was winning.

My parents had always refused to tell me what would happen if a born vampire refused to make that first kill and complete the transformation. Now I thought I knew what had frightened them so badly that they wouldn't even speak of it.

I was beginning to wonder if the only alternative was to die.

Lucas's fingers threaded through my long hair as he combed it to soothe me. At last I said, "If I wrote my parents a letter, would you promise to send it if—"

"If what?"

I closed my eyes. "If anything bad were to happen."

"Bianca—"

"I don't want to talk about it anymore right now. But if you would promise—it would mean a lot to me."

Lucas was quiet for a while before he whispered, "I promise."

* * *

The next morning, as soon as I woke up, I knew something inside me had changed for the worse.

Before, even on my worst days, I'd been able to get around a little bit. Now I was so weak I couldn't get out of bed without Lucas's help. To my embarrassment, he had to walk me to the bathroom. He brought me breakfast in bed, but I couldn't eat more than a wedge of toast. Even that, I had to force down.

"Do you want me to get you blood?" he asked. His hands gripped the back of the chair so tightly that his knuckles were white. "I could catch something, or I could bust into a hospital, hit the blood bank."

"I don't want any blood. I don't want anything. Just—some water, maybe."

Really, I didn't even want the water, but at least that way Lucas could feel like he'd done something for me.

The passage of time meant nothing to me; I didn't go outside at all. Lucas called in sick to work; I was scared he'd get fired, but then again, maybe a chop shop didn't expect every single employee to show up every day. When I asked him about it, Lucas nodded. "Places that break the law don't usually get too excited about enforcing the rules. Don't worry about me, okay, Bianca? Just take care of yourself."

But how was I supposed to do that?

That night, Lucas went out to fetch some more groceries, returning in record time with paper bags he tossed on the table and seemed to forget about. "Hey," he said. "Were you able to look at your book?"

"A little." He'd found a paperback copy of *Jane Eyre* earlier that day and brought it to me, but I felt too dizzy and weary even to read. The black type against the white pages seemed to burn my eyes.

Lucas nodded and sat in the chair. I wondered if he sat there now because he wanted more distance from me than he could get if he sat on the side of the bed, or because he wanted a better look at my face. He sat staring at the floor, his forearms on his knees. One foot scuffed against the floor, back and forth, revealing the agitation he had otherwise fought so hard to hide.

"Whatever you want to say," I whispered, "just say it."

"I sent a letter to Balthazar today," Lucas said. "I e-mailed Vic, too, and asked him if there was any way possible he could come home, or maybe Ranulf, even. Maybe one of them will show up soon and know something to do."

Vic wouldn't be able to help, and I suspected that Balthazar had already given us all the answers he could. As for Ranulf— well, he'd been around awhile, so who knew what he'd learned? But I doubted there was any way out of this situation. Whether he knew it or not, Lucas had summoned them because he needed support. "That's good," I said.

Lucas shook his head. "I never should've taken you away from Evernight."

"How can you say that?" I tried to sit up, but dizziness overtook me. Instead I settled for propping up on one arm. "I wanted to leave. I was the one who asked you!"

"Wouldn't have mattered if you'd begged me. I still shouldn't have done it." He raked his fingers through his bronze hair, like he wanted to tear at it. "Your parents knew what was going on. So what if they lied about it? At least they would've known what to do. At least they could've taken care of you. And I can't. The only thing I want in the world is to make you well, and I can't."

"Stop it. Lucas—what's happening to me—it's part of who I am. Part of what I was born to be. Our running away didn't make this happen."

"But your parents could've made it stop."

"We don't know that. The only thing we do know is that they would've tried to convince me to become a full vampire, and I don't want that. Not even now."

Lucas wouldn't be consoled that easily. "You've been on the run. In danger. You haven't had enough money to do what you wanted to do, even eat what you wanted to eat—I told you I'd take care of you. And I let you down."

"You *never* let me down." I had to make him understand. This was one of the only things in the world that I knew to be true. "These past two months with you have been the best of my whole life. Even with Charity after us, even when we were stuck with Black Cross—it was worth it, because we were together."

He hid his face in his hands. "I'd give it up to make you well."

"I wouldn't. And it was always my decision, not yours. I

didn't make a mistake." When Lucas finally lifted his face to look at me, I smiled at him. "I would do it again. A hundred times over, I'd do it all again to be with you."

Lucas came to me and held me close. For that moment, that was the only courage I needed.

When I awakened in the middle of that night, though, it became harder to be brave.

"Hold on, okay?" Lucas braced me against his chest, rubbing my back. "Just hold on."

"I can't!" My body shook uncontrollably. It wasn't a seizure, because I still knew who and where I was, and I could move; I just couldn't stop shaking. It had begun in my sleep, waking Lucas before it woke me. He'd had to shout my name a few times before I fully regained consciousness.

"Please, Bianca. Please."

"I can't stop, I can't stop—"

"You don't have to stop. Don't beat yourself up. Just ride it out. I'm here with you. Okay?"

"Okay," I gasped. But the shaking didn't end for almost an hour, and by the time it did, I was so exhausted that I felt like I'd never move again.

One thing was for sure: After that, Lucas and I were both much too fried to even think about sleeping.

Once we could no longer deny that it was morning, I asked Lucas to find a pen and paper for me, which he did. Dark shadows circled his eyes, and his skin was ashen. I wanted so badly to be able to take care of him, instead of lying here helpless.

I let Lucas prop me up on a couple of pillows. Then, despite my trembling hands, I managed to write a short note.

Mom and Dad,

If you get this letter, it means that—

I had to pause there. I knew what I should write, but I wasn't strong enough to do it. Imagining my parents reading those words was too much for me.

—I can't come home to you anymore. Lucas has promised that he would send it, if anything happened to me.

I realize you thought you were doing the right thing, telling Mrs. Bethany about my last e-mail. I don't blame you for trying to find me again, especially now that I understand how scared you must have been. But that was why I couldn't reach out to you afterward. It would have put Lucas in danger, and I couldn't do that.

Please don't be angry with Lucas about this. He has been wonderful to me, and given me everything he could. I've been so happy with him this summer. I think if you could have seen us together, and known what it was like for me, you would understand. This is the first time I've realized what it's really like for you two, the way that you love each other no matter what. Lucas and I had that, even if it was only for a few months. I know someday you'll be thankful to know I had that, too.

I love you both so much. Thank you for all the things you did for me. Even through all the arguments we had, and the separation between us now, I've always known I had the best parents in the whole world.

Love,

Bianca

That day passed in a haze for me. I drifted in and out of sleep—at least, sometimes it was sleep. Sometimes it was unconsciousness. I couldn't tell them apart any longer.

Although I felt feverish, I knew that actually my body had become very cold; I could tell from the way Lucas's touch seared like fire every time he mopped my forehead or held my hand. My sweaty limbs tangled in the sheets, and I pawed restlessly at the strands of my hair that stuck to my neck and back. Nothing seemed entirely real for a very long while.

Instead I wandered through memories, all of them disjointed and unconnected to any of the others. Most of the memories were happy, so I was content to let my mind drift. One moment, I was walking down the streets of New York with Raquel, laughing about how our muscles ached from the morning's workout. The next, I was back at Arrowwood, and Mom was proudly putting the finishing touching on my fairy princess costume for Halloween. Then I was at Evernight, letting Patrice give me a manicure that matched hers, so both of our nails shone in soft lilac. Or in the fencing hall, facing Balthazar, who was letting me off so easy that he laughed even as he wielded his sword.

Or in the diner with Vic and Ranulf as they sat side by side in their Hawaiian shirts. Or in the van with Dana as she cranked up the radio and sang along.

In the woods with my father, listening to hooting owls and talking about why I needed to stay at Evernight Academy.

In Riverton with Lucas, cradling the jet brooch he'd given me, and looking up at him with all the gratitude and love in the world.

Why would I ever want to come back from that?

When my mind finally cleared, I realized it was nighttime. I had no idea whether it was just past dusk or two in the morning. Groggily, I turned my head, seeking Lucas. He stood by my bedside, his face pale. When our eyes met, I smiled, but he did not.

"Hey," I whispered. "How long was I out?"

"Too long." Lucas slowly knelt down. His face was more or less even with mine. "Bianca, I don't want to scare you, but— what's happening to you—"

"I know. I can feel it."

Our eyes met, and the pain in his eyes almost outweighed the fear and sadness I felt for myself. He closed his eyes and lifted his face toward the ceiling; if I hadn't known better, I would have thought he was praying.

Then he said, "I want you to drink from me."

"I'm not hungry for blood," I whispered.

"You don't understand." Lucas took an uneven breath. "Bianca, I want you to drink from me until I'm dead. I want you to change. I want you to become a vampire."

The shock left me powerless to speak for a moment. I could only gape at him in astonishment.

"You turned away from being a vampire a long time ago, I know," Lucas said. He clasped one of my hands in his. "But this looks like your only choice. If that's what it takes to save you, it's not so bad, is it? You could go back to your parents. Be young and beautiful forever."

It wasn't as simple as that, and we both knew it. But if Lucas was really ready to take this step with me, I could consider it. "You would become a vampire, too," I said. "We'd make the change together. Can you do that?"

Lucas shook his head. "No."

"What?"

"Bianca, you have to promise me—you have to swear on everything that means anything to you—when I'm dead, before I come to, you have to destroy me. Don't let me rise again as a vampire. I'm willing to die."

So he could accept my transformation, but not his own. The fragile hope I'd felt for a few seconds shattered.

Lucas tugged at the neck of his shirt, exposing his neck. Quietly, he repeated, "Drink from me."

"You want me to kill you," I whispered. "You'd give up your life to save me."

He gave me this look like that was so *obvious*, so *necessary*, and tears welled in my eyes.

"I know what I'm doing," he said. The shadows in the room framed his face; it seemed as if the light in the room was drawn only to him. "I'm ready. The last thing I'll ever know is that you're going to be okay. That's all I need."

I shook my head. "No."

"Yes," he insisted. But I still had enough strength to push back.

"How could I go on, knowing you'd died to save me? The guilt— I can't live like that, Lucas. I can't. Don't ask me to."

"You don't have to feel guilty! I want you to do it!"

"Could you?" I asked him. "Could you kill me, even to save your own life?"

Lucas stared at me, trying and failing to contemplate the horror of doing that.

I said, "You have to promise me to lead a good life. Not to sit around mourning me."

"Oh, Christ." Lucas grimaced, and I knew he wasn't far from tears. He buried his face in the blankets on my bed, and I rested my hand on his hair. "Bianca, please. Please do this. Save yourself." I could see in his eyes that he was wavering in his conviction—that if I pushed harder, he would let me turn him into a vampire. But I knew that to him it would be a sacrifice even greater than dying. I realized then that I couldn't ask him to do it, not to save myself, not for anything.

"No," I said, and this time I knew he would understand my answer was final. "Promise me, Lucas."

"What kind of a life am I supposed to have without you? You were the one good thing, the only good thing I ever found."

I started crying then, and he gripped my hand tightly. Soon he laid his head on my shoulder, and that was comforting, knowing that at least he was near.

After a while, I couldn't hold onto his hand as tightly. The shadows in the room seemed to darken. Lucas became very worried, but I couldn't quite pay attention to what he was saying. Certainly I couldn't find the strength to respond.

He got me water, but I wasn't able to drink much. I fell asleep—maybe it was sleep—and came to after what seemed like a very long time.

Lucas stood against the wall, his hands braced against it like he needed that to keep from falling down. His eyes were wild.

When he saw that I was awake, he said, "I nearly called an ambulance. It wouldn't do any good, but standing here—I can't do a damn thing."

"Just stay close," I whispered. My chest felt so heavy. Speaking was such hard work.

A tremor passed through me, wringing me out. My whole body had become too leaden and feverish to bear. I wanted to push myself away from it. I wanted to be free.

Something in my face must have told Lucas how I was feeling, because his eyes went wide. He came to my side and put his hand to my cheek. For a second, he struggled for words, but then he gasped out, "I love you."

"Love." I couldn't say anything else. Lucas's face dimmed as the light in the room went away. It would be so easy to let go.

I gave in to the tide pulling me downward.

And then I died.

Chapter Twenty

NOTHING WAS CONNECTED ANY LONGER—THAT'S the only way I know how to describe it. For instance, I still understood that gravity was at work—I could feel the difference between earth and sky—but it didn't seem to apply to me. I could drift upward or downward, and sometimes it felt like I was doing both at the same time.

After days of feeling my body ache worse, until at the end it had seemed as though nothing existed but weight and pain, I was now feather light and free. Yet it was an empty sort of sensation. I felt hollowed out. Lost.

I tried to open my eyes, but I realized that I could already see. What I saw made no sense, though. The entire world had blurred into a milky blue gray, through which shapes wafted without ever taking recognizable form. I tried to move, but although I was entirely unencumbered, my limbs didn't seem to respond.

How long has this been going on? I thought. I had no sense of how quickly time was passing. I could've been like this for ten seconds or a year, and I couldn't remember how to tell the difference. *Silly, start by counting your breaths. Or your heartbeat. Either one will tell you.*

But then I realized I had no heartbeat. Where my pulse should've been—the steady, unceasing warmth and rhythm right at the center of me—there was nothing.

The shock slammed into me, a blow that was somehow even stronger for having no body to strike. My terror slashed through the mist that surrounded me, and for a moment the scene cleared and I could see.

I remained in the wine cellar, although I no longer lay in bed. Instead, I seemed to be floating just beneath the ceiling. Below me, I could see myself, lying beneath the covers. My face was as pale as the sheets, and my eyes stared blankly.

Next to the bed, Lucas knelt, his forehead on the mattress next to my motionless hand. He'd covered his head with his arms, like he was trying to shield himself from something, although I didn't know what. His shoulders shook, and I realized he was crying.

The sight of him in so much pain made me want to comfort him. Why didn't I sit up and comfort him? I was lying right there.

Wait, that's not me. I'm me. How could there be a difference between the person I saw lying in bed and the one who was seeing all this? None of it made any sense.

Lucas, I called. *Lucas, I'm right here. Look up. Just look up.*

But I had no voice to speak with, no tongue or lips to shape my words.

To my astonishment, he lifted his head. Yet Lucas didn't turn his face up toward me, and he didn't even seem to have heard anything. His eyes were bloodshot and dull. Roughly he wiped at his cheeks with the back of his hand, then reached toward me—the me that lay on the bed. As I watched, both horrified and fascinated, he passed his fingers over my eyelids to shut them. That seemed to take the last of his strength, because as soon as he was done, Lucas slumped forward to lean against the metal bed frame, as motionless as the body in the bed. My body.

No. That couldn't be right. I wasn't going to think like that. Whatever was happening right now was a mistake, just a big mistake, and we could fix it once we finally figured out how.

I'd gotten through to him just now, hadn't I? When I'd called Lucas, he'd heard me, even if he didn't realize it. I had to call him again. *Lucas, I'm right here. Right here. All you have to do is look at me.*

He didn't budge.

Maybe it would help if I got closer to him, I thought. But how was I supposed to do that? I didn't quite understand how— or if—I could still move, since my body and I seemed to have become separated.

Then I looked at Lucas again and saw the sheer anguish on his face. He looked so desperately lost and alone. I wanted to hold him, to comfort him somehow—

And that wanting was like a tow line, pulling me from the ceiling down to his side. Suddenly I could feel the warmth of his body all around me, comforting as a blanket and I sensed that I'd broken through. "Lucas!"

He jerked backward. His eyes went wide, and Lucas pushed himself away from the bed, crawling back toward the corner.

Why was he scared? *Lucas, I'm right here.*

But already I could tell that he hadn't heard the last thing I'd said, and I didn't think he could see me. Lucas blinked a couple of times, then sagged back against the wall. No doubt he thought he'd imagined it.

Then all of a sudden, I couldn't really see him either. The blue-gray mist closed in again, and once again I felt myself drifting, unanchored. Was I traveling up or down? Was I traveling at all? There wasn't any way to tell.

I have to find my body again, I told myself. *If I find my body, I can simply climb back inside.* In my imagination, I saw it working a lot like getting into a sleeping bag and zipping it up. Seemed easy enough. So why couldn't I find my body?

It's not yours any longer.

Startled, I tried to look around to see who had said that. But I couldn't really look anywhere, much less see anything besides the billowing mist. Nor had I *heard* another voice, exactly, so much as I had perceived one.

I'm going back to the wine cellar, I decided. *I want to be with Lucas. So I'm going to be with him—right now.*

Just like that, I was with Lucas once more—but not in the

wine cellar. He stood in the driveway of the Woodsons' house; I seemed to be right behind him, as if I were peeking over his shoulder. Apparently it was nearly dawn; the sky had begun to go gray and stark. A car had just pulled into the driveway, and as we watched, a tall figure stepped out.

Balthazar strode across the grounds toward Lucas, his face drawn and tense. Bruises still showed on his skin, and he walked more slowly than he normally would, but obviously he had mostly recovered from his injures. "How is she?" he said. Then he got a good look at Lucas's face and stopped in his tracks. "Oh, no."

"She—" Lucas couldn't get the words out. I could see the muscles in his jaw working, like he was struggling even to speak. "She's gone."

"No." Balthazar shook his head. His expression was flat, almost panicked. "No, you're wrong."

Lucas said, "Bianca is dead."

His saying it made it real. I wanted to scream, but I couldn't. I wanted to run, but that was impossible, too. There was no more hiding from what had happened.

Balthazar said, "Let me see her." Lucas answered by stepping aside. As Balthazar rushed past him, he seemed to run through me—oh, that felt weird, but sort of amazing, because for one second, all Balthazar's strength and desperation and love echoed inside me. It wasn't like being alive, but it was something real, more real than I was.

As Balthazar ran into the wine cellar, he seemed to tow me

after him. Maybe that was because of the way he'd run through me; I wasn't sure. All I knew was that I felt myself flowing past the long corridors of wine bottles, toward Balthazar's silhouette—and then past him, so that I was in the room, looking back at him, as he looked down at me.

My body lay exactly where I'd seen it last, when Lucas had shut my eyes. Balthazar stood there, staring down at me for a few long seconds like he couldn't believe any of it. Then he slumped against the wall and just—fell. He slid down until he was on the floor, and he clenched his fists in his curly hair.

I tried to hover over my body; it looked fine to me. A little sick, maybe, but it didn't really look any different from the way I guessed I did when I was sleeping. The only change was that I wasn't breathing. And I could fix that, couldn't I? All I had to do was hop back in.

Well, that sounded easy, but it wasn't. I kept looking down at myself, trying to feel the same magnetic pull that both Lucas and Balthazar had on me now. If I could tap into that same energy, I reasoned, I'd be drawn back into my body and would be alive again.

But the pull never came.

After a while—several minutes, I thought, but I couldn't be sure—Balthazar pushed himself to his feet. Behind him, I heard Lucas's footsteps. Soon they stood together at the end of the bed, looking at me.

Balthazar's voice was hoarse as he asked, "What happened?"

"It was like I said in the letter." Lucas sounded so tired. I wondered how long it had been since he'd slept. "She just kept getting weaker and weaker. We knew there was nothing a doctor could do, so I just had to watch—"

Lucas swallowed hard. Balthazar hesitated, and I thought for a moment he might pat Lucas on the shoulder or something, but he didn't.

"I tried to get her to change over," Lucas continued. "I offered to let her use me to turn into a vampire. But she wouldn't do it unless I came over, too. I said no." He thumped his fist against the wall. "Dammit, why didn't I just let her do it?"

Balthazar shook his head. "Bianca made the right decision. Not only for you but for her, too. There are worse things than death."

"You're gonna have to forgive me if I can't agree with you right now."

"I understand."

They stood together like sentinels watching over me. I kept wanting to shout at them that this was all a mistake, that there was something we could do to fix this, but that had begun to feel like a lie.

I'm dead. This is the out-of-body experience that I always read about, and any second there's going to be some kind of bright light, and I'll have to go into it.

I wanted to cry, but crying required a body. Even that release was lost to me. All that sorrow and terror was bottled inside me with nowhere to go.

At last, Lucas said, "I can't call the police or an ambulance.

There's too much about this I can't explain."

"No, you can't do that," Balthazar said. "You'll have to bury her here, and before the sun comes up, so nobody will see. I'll help."

Lucas took a deep, shuddering breath. "Thank you." It was the first time I'd ever seen him drop his guard around Balthazar. They looked at each other without any rancor; the jealousy and defensiveness between them had vanished.

Balthazar walked around the side of the bed and brushed my hair back from my face. He bent over and kissed my forehead; as he did, he shuddered, and I could tell he was struggling against tears. In an instant, that had passed, and he was once again purposeful and solemn. Balthazar pulled back the quilt and bundled the sheet more tightly around me before picking me up in his arms.

They're going to bury me. If they bury me, I can't ever return! I didn't let myself admit that I might not be able to go back no matter what. All I could think was that I had to prevent them somehow from doing this. *Please, Balthazar, Lucas, stop. You have to stop!*

Instead, Balthazar took me a few steps from the bed. His eyes were troubled, and he couldn't quite look down at what he was doing. He whispered, "Cover her face." Lucas, his face drawn, pulled the sheet up over my head. Once that was done, Balthazar seemed more focused. "Is there anything you want to—is there anything you want Bianca to have with her?"

Lucas took a deep, shuddering breath. "Yeah."

He walked to the cardboard dresser where I kept my few things. As he opened the top drawer, I saw two of my only three pieces of jewelry: the jet brooch he'd given me in Riverton when we were first falling in love and the red coral bracelet I'd received as a present on my last birthday. Lucas's hand closed around them both, and I knew he meant to put them in my hands so I'd have something of him with me for eternity.

Don't let him do that. You have to keep those with you!

Startled, I looked around again for the source of that other voice. Not only could I not see it, but the world around me also faded again, threatening to disintegrate into the bluish mist that clouded my vision.

Who *was* that? The only person who was supposed to speak to anybody after they died was God, and I felt completely positive that God's first message to me from the Great Beyond wouldn't be telling me to hang on to my jewelry.

Still, that was the only guidance I'd received so far. I figured I had better listen.

As Lucas picked up the jewelry, I tried to say, *Don't. Leave them behind.* He hesitated, but I couldn't be sure if that was my influence or not. What else could I do?

Then I remembered how it had felt when Balthazar walked through me downstairs. For a moment, I had felt every emotion within him as intimately as I felt my own. I didn't know if Balthazar had sensed anything in return—as upset as he'd been, he might not have noticed. It seemed worth a try.

I focused tightly on Lucas, told myself how badly I wanted

to be with him, and then—it was like I zoomed forward, almost too fast to see, and then I was with Lucas, all around him, *within* him. His grief welled inside me, so powerful that it blackened my vision and made me feel as though I were sinking. The yearning I felt—the sense of isolation and futility—was almost too over-powering to bear.

He shivered, as if from the cold. "It's like she's still here," he whispered. "When I look at the things I gave her—Bianca's so close." Lucas simply put the bracelet and brooch back in the drawer. "I can't give them up."

"Okay."

My focus shifted, returning to Balthazar. What I saw then burned its way into my spirit, a dark mark I'd never be able to forget: Balthazar, standing in his black T-shirt and slacks as though he were part of the night, cradling my dead body in his arms. The white sheet shrouded me almost completely, save one hand that dangled downward and the fall of my long red hair.

This is real. This is absolutely real.

I'm dead.

Balthazar said, "Do you have the tools we'll need?"

"In the garage." Lucas hunched over, like he was trying to protect himself. "They—they have shovels."

Shovels? Shovels. I don't want to see this. I want to be somewhere else—

Then I *was* someplace else—nowhere else, sort of. The world once again held nothing more than blue-gray mist. Amid this fog, I was lost and alone. Although I despised that feeling,

I could endure it more easily than I could endure the sight of Lucas and Balthazar digging my grave.

In the mist, a face began to take shape. A girl, perhaps my age, with short, fair hair—whom I'd seen many times before.

"The wraith." My words sounded real to me now, although I didn't think any living person could hear me. "You're the wraith. I didn't recognize you before."

"I'm hardly the only wraith," she said. Her smile was thin and sort of smug; right now, I wanted nothing more than to slap it off her face. "And, yeah, we sound different on the other side, don't we? Like ourselves."

"What's happening to me?" I demanded. "Am I really dead? If so, are you keeping me from—from going to heaven or into the light or just going to sleep, whatever it is people are supposed to do after they die?"

She stroked the mist around us with a wide sweep of her arms, clearing the swirling fog. "There are plenty of choices, you know. And I'm not holding you back from any of them."

Now that the fog had cleared, I realized I could see beneath us. We seemed to be suspended above the trees outside the house. Movement below caught my attention—Lucas and Balthazar, driving their shovels into the earth, hard at work digging my grave.

"This was my dream." If only I could have wept. I needed to cry so badly. "One of the dreams I had about you— Do you remember them?"

"Of course not." She looked almost offended. "They were

your dreams. Your visions of the future. I wouldn't have anything to do with them. If you saw me, it's the same way you saw them—as part of what's to come."

"You said I didn't want to know what they were doing. Because if I'd looked that hard—I would have foreseen my own death."

The wraith cocked her head, and her fair hair ruffled in some unseen breeze. "It's time for you to forget about the life you lost. It's time to embrace your future."

"Forget? You think I could forget Lucas? And what kind of future am I supposed to have when I'm *dead*?" The mist thickened around us, blotting her out. "Leave me alone."

Then I thought of Lucas and willed myself to his side. *I'm coming back to you, I promise. I'm here!*

The mist vanished. I found myself in the clearing behind the Woodsons' property, looking down at a small mound of earth. Balthazar patted the surface of the dirt down with the back of his shovel while Lucas knelt by the grave. I could smell the sweat from their skin, the loamy scents of the soil and summer grass. The sky had lightened to a soft pink. A new day had started, without me.

Lucas bowed his head, weighed down by misery. Witnessing him like that was more than I could endure.

Please see me, I thought. I concentrated on all the sights and smells around me, on everything that was real and solid. I made myself part of the world. *Lucas, please see me, please, please*—

"Lucas!"

Both of them jumped backward. Lucas said, "Did you hear that?"

Balthazar nodded. "It—it sounded like— It can't be."

Yes! I had it. Focusing even harder on the here and now, I put every ounce of my will into the memory of how my body had felt. How I had looked. For a moment, I could feel myself again—phantom limbs, phantom hair—and both Lucas and Balthazar gasped. They'd seen me!

But my elation distracted me, and I knew I'd faded from their sight almost instantly. Could I do it again? I wasn't entirely sure how I'd managed it the first time. Being dead was *hard*.

"Balthazar," Lucas said, "have I gone crazy?"

"I don't think so."

"So you saw her, too?"

"Yeah." Comprehension swept over Balthazar's face, but whatever revelation he'd had didn't look like a good one. "Oh, my God."

"What? What do you know?" Lucas said.

Balthazar started pacing beside the grave "If Bianca was born because some wraith helped out two vampires—"

"Right," Lucas said.

"And one of the options for her future was becoming a full vampire—"

"Yeah," Lucas said. His eyes widened.

"Then the other option must have been for her—not simply to die but to become a wraith. That's why the Oliviers were so frantic for her to change. The alternative to being a vampire was never for Bianca to live as a human being. It was always for her to become a wraith." Balthazar blinked at the spot where they'd briefly glimpsed me. "And now she has."

I really wanted Balthazar to be wrong, but unfortunately, every word he'd said made sense.

"See?" The wraith—the other wraith, I should say—seemed to drift beside me. "It's like we always tried to tell you."

I said, "What do you mean, 'always tried to tell me'?"

"You remember." She smiled triumphantly, and in that smile I saw the message I'd been given at Evernight Academy, in letters engraved in frost. *"Ours."*

Chapter Twenty-one

SO, THE WRAITHS THOUGHT THEY COULD CLAIM me for their own? Well, they were wrong, and I intended to prove it.

"I'm not yours," I said to the wraith who floated in front of me. She wore a white, filmy sort of dress, maybe an old-fashioned nightgown; I wondered if it was what she'd died in. If so, I was stuck in a white camisole and blue cotton pajama bottoms with little clouds on them for all eternity. I looked down and saw the pajama bottoms, slightly translucent like the rest of me but definitely the same. Great. "I belong to myself. That's it."

"But you're one of us now." Her aqua-green face shone in the soft dawn light. "Don't you see how much better this is?"

Lucas turned to Balthazar. "If she's a ghost—a wraith—then how do we contact her?"

"I'm right here!" I called. But they didn't hear.

Balthazar looked entirely lost for words. "I don't—vampires

and wraiths—we learn how to avoid them, not how to talk to them."

"Who would know?" Lucas's eyes were desperate. "Is there a way? Any way? I don't know of one—maybe there isn't one—Dammit, there's got to be one. Gotta be." He glanced down at the grave, and then shut his eyes tightly.

"I'm thinking, okay?" Balthazar didn't look much more encouraged than Lucas. "Do you know anybody in Black Cross who could tell us something?"

Lucas groaned. "Plenty of people. None of whom I can ever speak to again. Except—maybe—"

He was considering it—seriously considering reaching out to Black Cross, although the hunters might well be under orders to kill him on sight. *Oh, no*, I thought. *Lucas can't do that. He's upset, he's confused, it's a terrible idea—*

The world dissolved into bluish fog again, and I lost any sense of a corporeal body. Although in some ways that sensation was liberating—kind of like flying in dreams—I didn't enjoy not having a body. Bodies were good. Bodies told you where you were and what you could do. Already I seriously missed having one I could rely on.

As I attempted to pull myself into some kind of shape, the wraith coalesced beside me in the mist. "You'll actually learn to have fun with this in time. But it takes some getting used to."

"I'm not getting used to it today." When I spoke only to her, the words had begun to feel like talking—even if nothing was actually said aloud. "We have to discuss what's happened to me."

"So, talk."

"Not while we're—floaty and lost and whatever! Take me someplace real. Someplace we can both be real."

"Fine, be that way."

In the blink of an eye, the mist vanished. She and I stood in the attic of Vic's house, not far from the dressmaker's dummy, which still wore its jaunty plumed hat. I could smell the musty old books and see the clutter piled high—although a little less, since he'd provisioned our wine-cellar home. The wooden slats of the floor showed vividly through our translucent feet.

She smiled at me, still smirking a bit. The wraith could have been pretty, if it hadn't been for the expressions on her face. Her fair hair was stick straight and cut short in a bob. She had a narrow chin, a strong nose, and sharp, knowing eyes. It startled me to realize that she was probably a year or two younger than I was.

Well, that she'd been a year or two younger when she died. For the first time, I realized I would never get any older. That somehow felt more final than all the rest.

The wraith said, "I'm Maxie O'Connor. I died here almost ninety years ago. I've haunted this house ever since. You'll feel drawn to this place, too, since you died here and everything, but I'm telling you right now, this house is mine. I let you guys camp in the basement as a favor to Vic, but that's all. Visit, don't stay."

Like I'd even want to visit. Her name sounded vaguely familiar, but I couldn't place it and didn't much care. "You're a wraith."

The next part was hard to say, but I managed it: "Like me."

Maxie nodded.

Ugh—a wraith. I'd learned to hate and fear the wraiths during my last year at Evernight Academy. As far as I could tell, all they did was frighten and torment people. The one in Raquel's house had been a true monster. Now I was one of them. The revulsion I felt cut me deeply; it was like it would've been better to be nothing at all. For the first time, I truly understood Lucas's resistance to becoming a vampire. Turning into something I'd never meant to be—never wanted to be—meant losing something important about myself, maybe losing myself entirely. He'd seen that all along.

Despite my dying hopes, I had to ask: "And there's—there's no way back? To being alive, I mean."

"Oh, yeah, it's easy as pie." Maxie smirked. "You just snap your fingers. That's how come I didn't change back to being human years ago."

"You don't have to be sarcastic."

"True. I don't have to. I threw that in at no extra charge."

Maxie had been the wraith who had attempted to kill me at school. I now realized that might have been the high point of our relationship. Then I thought about that for a second. "Wait—I saw you at Evernight Academy. Repeatedly. How could you be there when you were haunting this house?"

Like it was the most obvious thing in the world, Maxie said, "Vic, of course. I'm connected to him, and he traveled to Evernight. From there, I was able to contact you."

"You're Vic's ghost." I remembered how fond he'd been of Maxie. Obviously he hadn't interacted with her very much. "Why don't you just appear to him outright?"

"It's difficult to appear to the living. Those two guys downstairs—"

"Lucas and Balthazar."

"Lucas I knew, but not the vampire. They're hot, by the way. And you had them both on the string? Nice job."

I ignored that comment. "You don't talk like somebody who lived ninety years ago."

"I've spent the past seventeen years hanging out with Vic."

"That would explain it," I muttered.

She continued, "Well, the guys downstairs—you can appear to them because you seem to be powerfully emotionally connected to them both. That usually helps. Even then, it's usually not a sure thing. With Vic—" Maxie hesitated, and I realized that this subject was delicate for her, though she evidently didn't want me to see it. "I didn't meet him until years and years after I died. He grew up in this house."

"And he used to read stories to you, when he was little," I said.

"He told you that?" She didn't quite know how to keep talking, after that. If ghosts could blush, I suspected she'd be brilliant pink. "Well. Yeah. So, maybe I could materialize for him now. But at this point, I think it would scare Vic." More quietly, she added, "I don't want him scared of me."

"You didn't worry about scaring me," I said angrily. "You

appeared to me at Evernight—a lot of you did—and you fright-ened me out of my wits every time. You nearly killed me twice, and one of those times was definitely on purpose. So forgive me if I don't think you're actually that softhearted."

She looked angry. "But you were ours! You were always ours!"

"Stop saying that!" I wished I could've hit her, but I sus-pected my hand would whoosh right through her incorporeal body, which would both be unsatisfying and deeply creepy.

"It's true!" Her blue eyes blazed. Maxie was obviously some-body who could not be pushed. "You were born to be a wraith! And not just any wraith but one of the pure ones. Okay? You've got it good. You're strong. Your power can help the others. The wraiths need you, and your parents wanted to go back on their word and steal you from us."

"First of all, giving a person another choice isn't stealing."

Maxie cocked her head. "But your parents didn't give you that choice, did they?"

"Neither did you, so stop acting high and mighty about it." My mind whirled from all the new facts I had to process. "One of the—pure ones? You mean, one of the children born to vam-pires, one the wraiths created, right?"

"About time you caught on."

Maxie could tell me a lot, I realized; she offered the answers I'd waited for my whole life. But she wasn't ever going to be a friend. For her, I suspected, I was a means to an end.

To what end?

"Other ghosts need—ghosts like me," I said. When Maxie nodded, I continued, "To help them do what exactly?"

"You make us stronger. You help us materialize, so we can connect with the world again." Maxie drifted along the length of the attic. Her feet didn't touch the floor, which startled me, although I couldn't have said why. "Stop with the self-pity and imagine what it would be like, months and years and centuries of only that blue mist. That's how it is for some of us. The ones who get lost like that—they'll do anything, anything to take form again. Sometimes they can only do it by attaching themselves to people's fear and making it worse. But most wraiths want another choice. Another way. You can give them that."

I remembered the ghost who had tormented Raquel for so much of her life. Had hurting her been his only way to escape from a prison of mist? Was he one of the wraiths who had made the wrong choice?

Maxie added, "When we're around you, a lot of us, we can do many things we wouldn't be able to do alone. Like, all of us were able to appear to you at Evernight, even though we had to push through the barriers. You weren't a full wraith yet, but that power was still inside you."

"So, basically, I was born and died so you guys could have some extra batteries." How was that news supposed to make me feel better? "I don't have to help any of you. I'm going back to Lucas."

"Will you just wait? Please?"

Maxie faded almost to transparency, and in the few shadows of her face that I could still discern, I could see how hurt she looked. After almost a century in Vic's attic, she was probably lonely. And maybe she'd been dead so long that she'd forgotten how terrible it was. My pity didn't outweigh my caution, though.

"If you need a friend," I said slowly, "you have to act like one."

The attic, and Maxie, disappeared. This time, the fog hardly seemed to close around me before I found myself back where I wanted to be—with Lucas.

In the blink of an eye, I had returned to the wine cellar, where Lucas and Balthazar sat at the small table. They looked even more exhausted than they had before. Lucas leaned against the green wall, stubble shading his angled jaw. The dark circles beneath his eyes made it look as if he'd been beaten up. Next to him, Balthazar leaned his forearms on the table, and his head drooped forward.

Neither of them could see me, apparently. I was so happy to see them that I couldn't even be upset about my invisibility.

My hearing kicked in mid-sentence, as Balthazar said, "—phone call, maybe, or a letter. That might be a smarter move."

Lucas shook his head. "The cells move around too much to be sure of a letter, and she lost her cell phone during Mrs. Bethany's attack. Four hundred years old, and you never bothered learning anything about the guys who hunt you?"

He was baiting Balthazar, like he always did, but the sting in the words was gone. Their old rivalry had become no more than a reflex for them.

Balthazar ran his finger along the wall of the wine cellar, tracing an irregular shape—movement without purpose. "You said Black Cross tracked e-mail, too."

"Yeah, but I can at least be sure Mom will get the e-mail. If she knows something—maybe even if she doesn't—she'll come."

Then Lucas shivered, and his eyes narrowed. "You feel that?"

He knows me! Lucas knows I'm here!

"Yes." Balthazar turned to search the room, and I hoped against hope that he'd catch a glimpse of me. But his gaze traveled past the spot where I felt myself to be. "I think she's back."

"It's definitely Bianca," Lucas said, after a pause.

"I agree. It—it *feels* like Bianca. And that perfume she used to wear sometimes, the stuff with the gardenias—"

"Yeah." Lucas glanced over at Balthazar, obviously not thrilled that somebody else could recognize the scent I'd worn. But he seemed more relieved than angry. Maybe the most important thing for Lucas now was having someone who could convince him that the haunting was real, and not evidence that he was going crazy.

"Is it any consolation?" Balthazar asked quietly. "Knowing that something of her lives on?"

"What do you think?"

Balthazar sighed. "No, of course not."

"I want her *here*." Lucas slumped forward onto the table. "I keep thinking, if I want it bad enough, if I just figure out how, I can undo everything that's happened and go back to when she's safe. Like this can't possibly be for real."

"I remember that feeling." Balthazar lifted his head and stretched his shoulders, grimacing as though it hurt. "After Charity—after what I did to her—I wanted it not to have happened so badly that it seemed impossible I couldn't make it right. I couldn't make myself believe that the universe could work so differently from the way it should work. Obviously, I know better now."

Lucas frowned. I realized what he was going to say. *No, no, Lucas, don't, you remember what this does to him, don't!*

"Charity's in town," Lucas said.

So much for telepathy.

Balthazar straightened in his chair. "You've heard rumors, found evidence of the tribe—"

"No, we got kidnapped by the tribe about a week before Bianca—about a week ago." Lucas swallowed hard, then kept going. "Charity was hot to turn Bianca into a vampire. She had some stupid idea that it would make you and her and Bianca one big happy undead family."

"She was going to kill Bianca?" Balthazar looked so wounded, so disappointed in her. Despite the ample evidence that Charity was a psychopath, he still believed in his sister and loved her as much as ever. His faith would have been touching,

I decided, if it hadn't been so willfully blind. "You rescued her, though."

Lucas shook his head. "The ghosts did that."

"The wraiths *saved* you?"

"That's what it seemed like at the time." Lucas's gaze became more distant. "Now I see it, though. What they were really doing was making sure Bianca would die when they wanted, the way they wanted. So they'd get their prize. If Charity had done it, she'd have been doing us a big favor."

"I told you before, being a vampire isn't the same as being alive."

"It beats being a ghost, though, doesn't it?" Lucas pushed back from the table, too angry with himself to sit still. "If Bianca were a vampire, she'd still be here. She'd have her friends back, and she could go see her parents, and—nothing would have changed."

Balthazar's expression darkened, nearly to anger. "Everything would have changed for *her*. And you know that."

"I could touch her," Lucas whispered. "She would be here. I'm never going to touch Bianca again."

Never? Really never? The sorrow of it overwhelmed me. Then the kitchen suddenly looked very misty, became very far away. *No, not again!*

The blue foggy nothingness swallowed me once more. I struggled against it, but I had no fists to fight with, no feet to plant firmly upon the ground. All my will seemed to count for nothing. In my misery and desperation, I felt as frightened and bewildered as a lost child crying for her parents.

And then I wasn't in the mist any longer.

Instead, I had appeared at Evernight.

I glanced around, trying to understand what this could be. I knew it wasn't a memory because I was sitting on top of the gargoyle outside my bedroom window—not something I'd ever done before. It didn't feel like a dream, either, though I couldn't guess what wraiths' dreams felt like, if they even had them.

No, weird though it was, the most logical guess was that I'd somehow just transported myself back to Evernight Academy. Maybe my afterlife assignment was to haunt Mrs. Bethany or something.

Peering downward, I saw the gargoyle's scowl. Had I bruised his dignity by perching on top of his head?

For the first time since Vic's attic, I had a definite sense of physical form. I could even see my feet dangling past the gargoyle's claws. So I pressed my hands against the window glass, mostly just to do something with my hands, but also in hopes of peering inside.

When my fingertips touched the glass, frost flickered across the surface. I watched the tendrils spread in featherlike patterns, completely covering the pane. So much for snooping about what was going on in my old bedroom, but the effect was kind of cool.

Noise from the ground below made me look down. To my surprise, several trucks were parked on the driveway, and at least a dozen people seemed to be milling around. The other summers

I'd spent at Evernight Academy had been almost unbearably quiet. Nobody came to visit, save a few deliveries and the laundry service. So who were these people?

I realized the truth as soon as I recognized that they were all wearing coveralls. These were the workmen rebuilding Evernight.

Before that moment, I hadn't heard much of anything—mostly, I thought, because I hadn't been listening. How weird, to have to *choose* to hear. Now I could make out the growling of buzz saws and the thumping of hammers. Most of that seemed to be coming from the roof, but probably people were hard at work on the inside, too. Despite the fact that I loathed Evernight Academy, I hated Black Cross even more, so it gave me grim satisfaction to think that the damage done by Black Cross's fire was being undone. Mrs. Bethany wouldn't stand for anything else.

Then I heard a voice from inside my bedroom. "Adrian?"

That was Mom, calling my father.

I turned back to the window, eager to catch a glimpse of her, but frost still covered the pane of glass. That had to be what Mom was looking at. *Rub the glass!* I thought. *If you clear the glass, you can see me!*

Footsteps echoed inside the apartment, coming closer. Then I heard Dad say, "Oh, my God."

I pressed my hands against the glass eagerly. Too eagerly—the frost thickened. Now it would be even harder for them to see me. But they would, wouldn't they?

"We knew the wraith would return." Dad's words were hard, even cold. "Mrs. Bethany warned us."

"But here—in Bianca's room—" Mom sounded like she was crying.

"I know," Dad said quietly. "They're still looking for her. At least we know they haven't found her yet—that she's still alive."

Oh, Dad. I covered my mouth with my hand, as though I could still cry and had to hold back the tears.

"And this time we can cast them out," my mother said, voice shaking but determined.

What does she mean by that? I tried to imagine what she could be referring to—some trick Mrs. Bethany had figured out, perhaps—

It hit me like a wall: a terrible rush of force pushed me away from the window, the gargoyle, Evernight Academy, and anything else that was real. The physical form I'd inhabited dissolved like a sand castle beneath a wave. I was too overwhelmed to know anything save that I was lost in the mist again, nothing and no one, a dead thing.

"Why did you go there?" Maxie demanded. Her presence, annoying though it was, served as my only touchstone in the swirling unreality of it all. "Do you want to be destroyed?"

"I've already been destroyed."

"That's what you think." I could hear a sort of smug smile in her words. "It can be much, much worse than this."

"How, exactly, does it get worse than *dead*? I can't be with my parents ever again. I can't be with Lucas ever again."

"True. Well, mostly true."

"What do you mean, *mostly* true?"

"There's one way you can say hello to your precious Lucas. It's going to hurt both of you more than if you just did the decent thing and moved on—but you never know when to leave well enough alone, do you? Here—try *this*."

I felt as though I were being thrown forward, and then I saw Lucas. He was still in the wine cellar, but now he was alone, lying on the floor, fully clothed but with a pillow beneath his head and a sheet pulled over him. I had the sense that it hadn't been too long since I'd last seen him—it was probably afternoon at the latest—but I realized exhaustion must have demanded that he get some sleep. Balthazar was nowhere to be seen.

Lucas stirred fitfully beneath the sheet. For a moment, I wondered why he was asleep on the floor—before I remembered that I'd died in our bed. Probably Lucas didn't even want to lie down on that bed alone.

"You said you wanted to be with him, right?" Maxie said. "So, *do it*."

Just like that, Lucas and I were in the bookstore in Amherst, alone in the basement room where the textbooks were kept. He was kneeling on the floor, holding an astronomy textbook in his hands. A comet trailed fire on the page.

"Lucas?" I said.

He looked up, and his eyes were instantly alight with relief and wonder. "Bianca? You're here?"

"Yeah, but—where's here?"

Lucas dropped the book and clutched me in his embrace. The shock of feeling his arms around my back, of the welcome pressure of his body against mine, made me cry out in surprise and delight.

"You're alive," he whispered into my ear. "I thought you were dead. I was so sure you were dead."

But I am dead. "Lucas, where are we?"

"I was going to find you in the stars. See?" Instead of gesturing at the astronomy book he'd dropped on the floor, Lucas pointed upward. To my bewilderment, I saw not the ceiling of the bookstore but the night sky, sparkling and bright. Lucas said, "I knew I could find you there. Remember the part of *Romeo and Juliet* you quoted to me that time, when you were trying to convince me Juliet was an astronomer, too?"

I whispered, "'Give me my Romeo; and, when he shall die, take him and cut him out in little stars. And he will make the face of heaven so fine that all the world will be in love with night, and pay no worship to the garish sun.'"

"Yeah," he murmured into my hair. "That's why I knew I could find you there."

Understanding sank in. Sadly, I said, "This is a dream."

"I'm not dreaming." Lucas hugged me more tightly. "I won't believe it."

I was in Lucas's dream. Raquel had told me about her ghost attacking her in her sleep; I should've realized the wraiths could travel into sleeping minds. So I could be with Lucas but only in his dreams? It was so little, and yet at least it was something to hold on to. "Every night," I promised him. "Every night, I'll be here for you."

"It's not enough. I need you. Don't let this be a dream."

The reality around us vanished in an instant. Once again, I seemed to float very near the ceiling, looking down at Lucas, whose eyes had just opened. He grimaced and rubbed his face with one hand. In some ways, he looked even more tired than he had that morning.

"Bianca? Are you there?" he said. I couldn't answer him, but he understood anyway. "You'll always be there, I guess. Just too far away to touch."

Being with him in dreams would give me some comfort, I realized, but it would only torment Lucas. He wouldn't be able to hold on to the experiences the same way I could. More than that, I wasn't sure I could make him understand that our togetherness in dreams was real. If I visited him every night, all I would accomplish would be to make him grieve for me anew, over and over again.

Lucas rolled onto one side, punching the pillow beneath his head to provide more support. "I dreamed about you," he said. "I was in a bookstore, and I was trying to find you— I don't remember how— God, it's already slipping away. But you were there. Your being dead was all some big mistake, and I could hold you again. Pretty great dream—until I woke up."

With a sigh, he threw off the sheets and rose from the floor. He moved stiffly, and I realized he had to be sore. Just as he pulled a carton of juice from the minifridge, I heard footsteps outside. Lucas went to the door and opened it before Balthazar could even knock.

Instead of *hello* or *how are you*, Balthazar said, "You were right about Charity."

"News flash: I already knew that." The venom had gone out of Lucas's jabs at Balthazar, but apparently that didn't mean he was going to stop making them. "You find her?"

"I found someone who knows her. Which means Charity will be aware that I'm in Philadelphia soon, if she doesn't already."

"You just let the vampire run off to play messenger?" Lucas took a deep swig of juice straight from the carton. "Not smart."

Balthazar scowled. "I don't stake people the first second they could be trouble, which is one of the many differences between us."

"I guess this means you've got to run, huh?"

"I don't run from a fight," Balthazar said. "And I'm not abandoning my sister to this kind of existence."

"Nobody's making her act like that," Lucas said as he stowed the juice back in the fridge. "You ought to know that by now. Or did you know it the whole time?"

Balthazar didn't answer that question. "If I can separate her from her tribe, Charity will come around."

"What are you going to do? Just keep her locked in a room for a century until she agrees with you?"

"Yes."

"Man, your relationship is really screwed up."

"Do you have a better plan for dealing with her?" Balthazar demanded. "Staking is not an option."

"Says you." Lucas took a deep breath. "So you want my help on this kidnapping run?"

Balthazar clearly didn't like having to turn to Lucas for help, but he nodded. "You can handle yourself in a fight. And Charity won't expect the two of us to cooperate. We could use the element of surprise."

"When?"

"She'll make her move at sundown. So, a couple of hours." Like all vampires, Balthazar could sense how far away sunset and sunrise were. "The sooner we get out there, the better."

Lucas didn't need to go after Charity tonight. Really, I wished he wouldn't go after her ever. She was dangerous, and no matter how good a fighter Lucas was or how strong I'd made him by drinking his blood, Charity would always be stronger. With her tribe by her side, I didn't see how he and Balthazar could prevail.

But most of the time, I would at least have confidence that Lucas could get through it alive. Now he was exhausted and in mourning. Balthazar, blinded by his own guilt or grief or both, was foolishly taking the two of them out on a suicide mission.

Did Lucas know that? Horror overcame me as I realized that, probably, he did.

I watched him throw on a flannel shirt and lace up his shoes. Dread gnawed at me. Did Lucas think that, if he died, we would be together again? Or was his life not worth anything to him anymore? It was worth something to me. I wanted him to live and be safe and happy for both of us.

Lucas looked like he didn't care about any of that.

When he was almost done preparing, Lucas paused and went to the small drawer where I'd kept my things. His hand closed around the jet brooch he'd given me—it seemed like so long ago—and I could tell he was trying to take strength from it, the way I always had. Quickly he tucked it into the pocket of his shirt.

Oh, Balthazar, I could kill you for this. Please stop, guys, please.

Balthazar leaned against one of the wine racks, so obviously tired and sad that I took pity on him for a second. Then Lucas said, "Let's get out there."

"We need weapons," Balthazar said.

Lucas, who had never gone out for a Black Cross hunt or even a visit with me without being armed to the teeth, said only, "We'll figure something out."

They walked out the door, and I meant to follow—but I couldn't. About halfway down the path to the driveway, I found I couldn't go any farther. I seemed to be stuck there, watching them climb into Balthazar's car.

As Lucas settled into the shotgun seat, I saw his eyes narrow as he looked at the spot where I stood. As Balthazar gunned the car's motor into life, and they sped off, he turned his head away. Maybe he wondered if he saw something; probably he figured it was only a trick of the light.

Chapter Twenty-two

LONG AFTER BALTHAZAR'S CAR HAD DISAPPEARED down the road, I stayed where I was, looking forlornly into the distance. I had no reason to remain outdoors, but apparently I'd be haunting the wine cellar forever. So I'd be sick of that place soon enough.

"You're more than a little pathetic, you know."

"Shut up, Maxie," I muttered.

"How about you shut up and actually listen to me for a change?" Maxie's presence became more substantial. The first thing I could see was not her hair or her body but one arched, skeptical eyebrow, as if she were some snarky version of the Cheshire cat. "I can help you, you know. And I know the others who could help you, too. So it might be a good time to stop treating me like something you scraped off the bottom of your shoe."

"How can you help me when I'm already dead?"

It was a rhetorical question, but she answered. "Wouldn't you like to find out?"

"Okay."

Maxie took shape at last, but as she became more solid, the lawn around me became misty and translucent. Before I knew it, we were inside the wine cellar, standing near the bed where I'd died.

"That's a little more like it." Her smile looked too satisfied for my taste, but she really did have the advantage. "I figured you'd come around eventually."

"I haven't 'come around' to anything," I spat. "You guys fought the vampires for me. You won. Either way, I lost."

"You act like there was some possibility for you to have a normal life. Well, guess what? That was never going to happen. You were born to join the undead. That's your nature—who you are and why you're here. Blaming me for it is ridiculous."

"I think you've been dead so long that you've forgotten what being alive means."

Maxie cocked her head. "You're probably right. It'll happen to you, too."

Forget being alive? Never. Forgetting life would mean forgetting so many wonderful things; it would mean forgetting Lucas. And that could never happen. "You say you can help me. I suggest you prove it."

"Fine." Maxie gestured toward the little cardboard drawers where I'd kept my things. "Get your coral bracelet."

"What is it with you and the jewelry?"

"Pick up your bracelet and you'll see."

How did she expect me to pick anything up? It wasn't like I

had real hands any longer, only the illusion. Thinking I would show Maxie how stupid her suggestion was, I scooped my fingers into the open drawer—and felt the silver and coral, wonderfully solid. I brought the bracelet up and stared at the hazy reflection in the glass window of the microwave: a shimmering blue light in which a bracelet dangled, apparently suspended in midair. I was too amazed to say a word.

Maxie tossed her blond hair with a smirk. "Told ya."

"How is this even possible?"

"Material objects that we bonded to strongly before we died—like the door of your house, maybe, or a diary or in your case some jewelry you cared about a whole lot—connect us to the real world. You're lucky, too, because that's coral. Coral is one of the most powerful materials for us, because we've got something in common. Can you guess what it is?"

"We were both once alive." I touched the red coral and imagined its life beneath the sea, so long ago.

Maxie didn't look thrilled that I'd guessed correctly and stolen her thunder. "Well. All of us can use things and places like that. Since you're a born wraith, one of the pure ones, I guess you'll be pretty good at it. With a lot of practice, you might be able to do something with that bracelet. See why I told you not to let Lucas bury it with you?"

"Thanks." For the first time my gratitude was completely sincere. Instead of lording that over me, Maxie dropped her eyes, almost bashful. "What do you mean, 'do something?'"

"I've heard that wraiths like you—well, you might be able to get a physical body back, at least for a little while. Supposedly it takes a lot of practice—though. . . ."

Maxie's voice trailed off as I concentrated hard on the bracelet in my grip. I remembered Lucas giving it to me, the love between us on that day, and that made the stones seem even more real. First I willed all my strength into the hand holding the bracelet and—to my amazement—the hand appeared in the reflection. The solidity swept through me, like a warm sort of shudder, and then I stood there, my reflection identical to the way it had been a few days ago when I lived, albeit a little paler. A smile spread across my face as I knocked against the wall and heard it thump, then tossed the covers on the bed and watched them obediently flip back.

"Well, that was quick," Maxie said crossly.

"I have a body." I laughed, and it felt like a laugh. No, it wasn't being alive; there was no joy or warmth in this body, and I knew it wasn't my home. But at least I had substance again. If Lucas were here, I could hug him, even kiss him; we could talk like normal people. "This is incredible."

"You won't be able to have a body all the time. Even Christopher can't do that." Maxie seemed to enjoy diminishing my pleasure, although it was beyond her power to ruin it. "And it won't really fix anything. But at least you can get some stuff done this way."

I sighed. "This is definitely the best thing to happen to me since I died."

Then I wondered who this Christopher person was, but I

didn't have time to ask her about him. A car's tires crunched on the gravel driveway, and excitement made me leap toward the door—which I now had to open instead of floating through. I believed it would be Balthazar and Lucas returning home. Surely Balthazar had thought better of taking Lucas on a hunt tonight. Instead, I saw a sunshine yellow convertible pulling up; inside rode Vic and Ranulf.

"What are they doing back?" I muttered. Maxie peeked over my shoulder. "Oh, wait—Lucas said he wrote Vic and told him I was sick. He must have convinced his parents to let him leave Tuscany so he could come back to look in on me."

"Then he's running a bit late," Maxie pointed out.

Ignoring her, I turned and ran toward the driveway. She shouted, "What are you doing?"

"Saying hello to my friends!"

"You can't just go out there— Bianca, you're dead!"

I wondered if that meant some invisible force field or something would stop me, but it didn't. When I bounded out into the yard, Vic's face lit up in a grin, and Ranulf gave me a quick wave. "Hey there, Binks," Vic called. "Looks like you're on the mend!"

"Vic!" I hugged him tightly, and I'd never been so glad simply to be able to hug another person. He smelled like cologne, which I usually found stinky, but it was the first thing I'd really smelled since I died. Who knew men's cologne could smell so fantastic? "Oh, I missed you."

"Likewise," he said. "Sorry I woke you up. Or are you still recuperating?"

Vic was talking about the pajamas I still wore. Apparently the coral bracelet couldn't do anything about them. "It's kind of a long story. Also a weird story."

"Come on." Vic straightened his trucker cap on his head, like he was getting ready for serious business. "How much weirder could our story get?"

"You'd be surprised," I said weakly.

Ranulf straightened, and his gaze shifted from friendliness to wariness. "Vic," he said, "something is very different about Bianca."

"Huh?" Vic looked between me and Ranulf, not getting it. "She feels a little clammy, but that's about it."

"Her very nature is changed." Ranulf's eyes narrowed. For the first time, he did not look like an innocent; I caught a glimpse of the fiercer man he must have been long ago. "I do not think she is still a vampire."

"What?" Vic grinned. "All human now? Bianca, that's awesome."

"That's not quite how it went," I said. "Can you guys come inside? We really need to talk, and you have to find Lucas."

Vic started to follow me inside; Ranulf, still suspicious, came along, too, but hung back several steps. "What's wrong with Lucas?" Vic asked. "Where did he go?"

"He left with Balthazar."

"Balthazar? Your ex?" Vic's eyebrows rose so high they vanished beneath the brim of his hat. "Okay, this is getting good."

"Let's just get inside, okay?" As I gestured toward the door, the bracelet slipped from my fingers. The moment that happened, I disappeared—or almost disappeared, since a blue, smoky image remained where my arm had just been.

Vic jumped back so fast he nearly fell over. "What the what?"

"She is no longer a vampire," Ranulf said, steadying himself like he expected a fight. "She is a wraith."

"A wraith? You mean, a ghost? Bianca's a ghost? That's impossible."

Concentrating hard, I managed to close my hand around the bracelet again and will my form back into being. Vic and Ranulf stared at me, slack jawed, the whole time. Neither of them spoke a word.

Once I had my shape back, I said, "It's possible. I'm a wraith now. And, no, Ranulf, I'm not going to hurt you. The old war between ghosts and vampires—as far as I'm concerned, it doesn't have anything to do with me and the people I love."

Ranulf didn't look touched, but he didn't turn away, either.

I asked, "Now are you going to let me explain?"

Vic swallowed hard and nodded. "I think you'd better."

Half an hour later, as the sky outside darkened, Vic, Ranulf, and I sat around the little table while they took in what I'd just told them. Ranulf, who naturally understood more about the strange rules that governed the undead, seemed to be taking it in. Vic, on the other hand, looked completely flummoxed.

"Okay," Vic said, "let me see if I have this straight. You died."

"Yes." That was never going to get easier to admit, I thought.

"Balthazar showed up, and he and Lucas buried you in the backyard."

"Right."

"So there's a dead body in my backyard, which I have to explain to my parents somehow."

"I don't think they'll find it—it's behind the grounds, kind of—and, anyway, isn't that kind of beside the point?"

"Not really," Vic said. "Don't get me wrong. Compared to the rest of what's going on, it's not that big a deal. I understand that you're having a way, way worse week than I am. Okay? But that doesn't make it any easier for me to explain to my parents about the *dead body in the backyard*."

I sighed. "True."

"I suggest pulling some greenery over the location," Ranulf said.

"That's your total contribution to this discussion?" I asked.

"Yes." Ranulf appeared unruffled. "I will say what is useful. That is the only useful suggestion I have at this point."

Vic pointed at him, two finger-guns of approval. "I like a man who knows the value of words, doesn't spend 'em too cheap."

Ranulf nodded. "That is the manner in which I roll."

With that, Vic turned back to me. His expression seemed odd until I realized that I'd never seen him this serious before. "Bianca, I hate that this happened to you. If I couldn't look you in the eye and say that—if you weren't just dead but, you know, *dead* dead—I don't even want to think about it. Maybe things can't be like they were before, but—if there's a way—we can still be friends, right?"

I felt like I'd never smiled before, at least not for real. "We're friends no matter what," I said. "And you're the best person I ever met."

Vic ducked his head, surprisingly bashful. "So, how did you figure all this stuff out?"

"Your ghost helped me," I explained. "Her name is Maxie."

"What? My ghost has a *name*?"

"Why wouldn't she?" It seemed offensive to assume that ghosts wouldn't have names. We'd all been people once, hadn't we? Then I realized I was thinking of ghosts as "we" already.

"If she can appear, how come she never appeared to me?" It was Vic's turn to be offended. Clearly, he thought of Maxie as *his* ghost.

"She didn't want to scare you. Maxie?" I called to her, though I knew she'd probably been eavesdropping on our every word. "Hey, Vic wants to meet you. Come say hello!"

"I am socializing with wraiths," Ranulf muttered. "This is not a thing that is done."

To Ranulf, Vic said, "Remember what I said about social conformity being the prison of the mind?" Vic's sandy hair stuck out from the brim of his trucker cap, so unruly it made him look a little wild in his eagerness as he spoke again, this time to Maxie. "We're all nonconformists here, so, you know, drop on by."

Why did you tell him my name? I could see Maxie without

seeing her—as a vision in my mind, the same way she'd briefly appeared to me in the attic. *He doesn't need to know who I am!*

"She's talking to me," I said to Vic and Ranulf. "Not aloud. I think she's shy."

"Aw, man." Vic looked around the wine cellar avidly. Maybe he thought he might glimpse Maxie hiding between the bottles. "Seriously, Maxie, it's okay. Come say hi."

I'm not coming out there.

So far as I could tell from the tone of her "voice," Maxie felt genuinely terrified at the thought of finally seeing Vic face-to-face. Apparently his opinion meant a lot to her.

I realized I could use that to my advantage. Was that playing fair? I decided it was at least as fair as the wraith trying to freeze me to death. My best chance of getting good information from her was to ask now, while he was a witness. "She's agreeing to help me out," I said loudly. "Can you explain more about how the bracelet works, Maxie? I just want to understand."

Maxie's consternation felt obvious, at least to me. Ranulf and Vic were both staring at the ceiling, as if wraiths were dangling from above like a chandelier. Vic muttered, "I have *got* to get a Ouija board."

Well? I thought to her. *You don't want to let Vic down, do you?*

Like you even need my help, she snapped. *You can already walk around and hug people. I never could get solid like that, and look at you now. Bet you could walk around the whole day.*

"I can pretty much act naturally while I've got the bracelet,"

I said to Vic and Ranulf. I couldn't wait to surprise Lucas. He'd be so happy. Well, first he'd probably be scared out of his wits. But after that, he would see that there could still be some kind of future for us. We had a lot to mourn for; my lost life killed so many possibilities. Already I dreaded the long stretch of centuries that would follow after Lucas was gone. Nevertheless, it was more than I'd had before. "Does the same thing apply to the jet brooch? The one he took with him?"

Lucas took it along? Maxie relaxed a little; she still sounded sullen, but not as angry. *Then you're in luck, kiddo. Like I said, all the stuff we imprinted on in life, we can use in death. Not just to become corporeal—like you are now. You can also use them to travel.*

"Travel? What are you talking about?" At this point, I was talking to the ceiling, too. From the corner of my eye, I could see Vic and Ranulf gaping in total confusion.

Ever been on a subway? Then you know how it works. You can travel anywhere the train stops. The things you connected to most strongly during your life? Those are the subway stops. You can go wherever those things are.

The gargoyle. How many hours had I spent staring at that thing grimacing outside my bedroom window at Evernight? Apparently I'd imprinted on it strongly enough that I could now travel back to the school whenever I wished. There would be other "subway stops" that I could find. My world had just expanded—if not back to the freedom I'd had when alive, at least a lot farther than this one house.

"The brooch," I repeated. "Lucas took it with him. You mean—I could go to Lucas, right this second? Would I still have substance? Could he see me?"

Your bracelet wouldn't go with you. But, hey, the brooch is jet, right? You might be able to use it once you get there.

"Jet is fossilized wood!" I grinned. Jet, too, used to be alive; that meant it was as powerful as the coral.

Vic said, "Please tell me the other half of the conversation is going to make the stuff you just said make sense."

"Kind of." I summarized the situation for them as best as I could, with only Maxie's explanation to draw from. "I'm going to give it a try and see if I can do it. I need to tell Lucas we can still speak to each other—that there's still some way—"

"Yeah, get out of here," Vic said. "Lucas needs to see you as soon as possible, I'd guess."

"How do I do it?" I asked Maxie.

She sounded fainter, like she resented my success too much to hang around much longer. *You concentrate on it, really hard—see it in your mind's eye—and then you ought to get there. Might take you a few tries.*

I closed my eyes, determined to get it right away.

In my mind, I heard Maxie add, *You can hang around the living all you want. Sooner or later, they're going to forget you. And you'll forget them. You're dead, Bianca. The sooner you face it, the better.*

I ignored her.

If there was one thing in the world I could picture perfectly, it was that brooch. The ornate carving—the outline of the strange, sharp-bladed flowers I'd seen in my long-ago dream—the cool weight of it in my hand, the way it fit into my palm—

Darkness.

Startled, I tried to figure out where I was. This wasn't the terrible enveloping mist, but it wasn't any place I recognized. No lights shone, save a few bars of red that I recognized as distant exit signs. The ceiling was high—very high—and I floated near it, trying to make out what was happening below.

Then I heard Balthazar's voice echo, "Lucas! Look out!"

Beneath me I made out movement—two people struggling. They fell to the ground, limbs in a tangle. Fear pushed me downward, and I managed to get a bit closer. Still, in the darkness, I couldn't see much besides rows of seats, as though we were in a church. But Balthazar couldn't possibly be fighting inside a church—

Then I realized the white wall at the far end of the building wasn't a wall—it was a screen. This was a movie theater of some kind. Like most of the places Charity preferred, it had apparently been long abandoned. Multicolored graffiti decorated the walls, and half the seats had been ripped out.

I looked closer at the people doing battle below me. The figures pushed apart from each other, and I could see them as they faced off. One was Lucas, his T-shirt ripped and a trickle of blood on his hairline. He was breathing hard, and in his hand he held a switchblade—a weapon nearly useless against vampires.

The other half turned, so that I could see her face. *Charity.*

"You let the ghosts have her," Charity taunted. Her eyes shone like a cat's, bright and flat. "Bianca's body is rotting, her spirit is hostage, and it's all your fault."

Lucas shuddered, and I knew she'd cut him to the quick. His voice was deadlier than I'd ever heard it when he said, "You'll pay for hurting her."

"Do you even believe what you're saying?" Charity smiled. "You don't want to kill me, boy. You want to die."

I wanted Lucas to deny it. He didn't.

Charity laughed. "Don't worry, Lucas. You'll be reunited with Bianca soon enough—in your graves."

"No!" I cried—but I wasn't in the dark room any longer. I was back in the wine cellar. Vic and Ranulf were staring at me, even more bewildered than before.

"Bianca?" Vic said. "What happened?"

I grabbed his arm. "If we don't get to Lucas right away, he'll be killed."

Chapter Twenty-three

"BALTHAZAR'S EVIL SISTER, CHECK," VIC SAID AS we ran from the wine cellar toward his car. The streetlight nearby cut through the night to outline his thin shadow against the driveway; I no longer had a shadow. "Lucas and Balthazar at the end of their tether, check. Lots of crazy-ass vampires, check. Have I got the situation here?"

"Pretty much." I was relieved that I wouldn't have to explain in more depth. "I don't know where they are, though."

Vic grimaced. "Philly's a big city, Bianca. Can't you use your subway magic whatever to go back there, maybe describe the place?"

"I've been trying," I snapped. Spectral traveling required concentration, apparently, and I was far too frightened to concentrate. Then it hit me that I did have one more clue to go by, one I'd have thought of earlier if I hadn't been panicking. "It was a movie theater but one that had been abandoned a long time. Graffiti taggers had hit it hard. Does that sound familiar to you?"

To my relief, Vic's face lit up. "The McCrory Plaza Six shut down two years ago— Yeah, that's got to be it!" He turned to look for Ranulf, who had calmly walked out after us and headed to the garage. "Ranulf, buddy, you with us?"

"I am collecting items that may be useful," Ranulf called.

"Weapons." I ought to have thought of it before. "Vic, we need to be armed for this. Can you fight?"

Vic didn't look thrilled by the idea. "Uh, I took karate—"

"That's awesome!"

"—for two months," Vic continued. "When I was seven. The first time I tried to break a board, I sprained my wrist. My parents pulled me out of lessons. Doesn't count, huh?"

What was I even thinking, trying to mount a rescue party? Vic wouldn't stand a chance against a homicidal tribe of vampires. Ranulf would be strong enough—stronger than most, given his great age—but I had difficulty imagining him even raising his voice. That left me as our only fighter.

But I remembered what the wraith had managed to do to Charity before, the pain and shock on her face as an ice-blue fist plunged into her gut. Could I bring myself to do that? For Lucas, I absolutely could.

Two would be better than one, I thought. *Maxie? Maxie, is there any way you can come with us? Do some of that crazy stuff with the ice?*

Don't think so.

If you could come, I'd really appreciate it. We could talk about—about what it is the wraiths want.

You'll end up talking to us about that sooner or later anyway. Maxie. Please.

Couldn't help you if I wanted to, she admitted. *For that kind of mojo, we need serious help. We'd need Christopher.*

Who the hell was Christopher? Then I remembered the frost man, the powerful figure who had been the very first ghost to appear to me at Evernight, the one who had saved me from Charity. Was he a leader of the wraiths? I didn't have time to find out. This mysterious Christopher wasn't here, and that meant his power didn't matter now.

Don't worry. That bracelet will hold you no matter where you go. You're strong.

Maybe Maxie couldn't have said anything so encouraging if she'd had to look me in the face. It didn't make much difference at that moment. We still had only three of us to go up against Charity's tribe.

Outside the garage, Vic stared down at a small pile of stuff Ranulf had pulled together. As I came near, Ranulf said, "I do not think Vic should attempt to stake any vampires. He would be unlikely to survive."

"I would resent that if it were any less true," Vic said.

Ranulf held up a large tin of lighter fluid and a plastic lighter. "Perhaps Vic could start a fire, which would cause the vampires to scatter."

"That's dangerous for you," I said. "For Balthazar and Lucas, too."

"I agree that fire is only a last resort." He presented the tin and lighter to Vic before he went back into the garage.

"Hey, we have plenty of stuff right here!" I called, holding up the gardening stakes that could work against vampires. "You found plenty of weapons, Ranulf. Let's go!"

"Those are not useful," Ranulf said, maddeningly calm, as he came walking back out with a full-sized, long-handled ax in his hands. Before I could ask, Ranulf threw the ax at the closest tree. It spun blindingly fast, blade-over-handle, until it thwacked so deeply into the trunk that I could hear the wood groan. The handle vibrated back and forth.

Vic and I stared. Ranulf smiled in satisfaction. "The ax is useful."

"Where did you learn how to do that?" Vic said.

"Remember how I told you that the Vikings sacked my village and took me back with them?" Ranulf was speaking to Vic now; I'd never heard this story before. "All young men among the Vikings were taught to fight."

Vic slowly said, "This is why you kick so much ass at World of Warcraft, isn't it?"

We had a Viking warrior on our side. Maybe we could do this after all.

Vic drove with his foot to the floor the whole ride to the McCrory Plaza Six, which luckily turned out not to be too far away. The movie theater had never been a grand one, like the vintage cinema in Riverton where Lucas and I had gone on our first date. Red velvet curtains and scrolling woodwork had nothing to do with this place. It was a squat, sprawling building in the middle of a huge parking lot that had cracked and become choked with weeds. With the theater's derelict appearance and murky surroundings, it had become the kind of place little kids would dare each other to walk past on Halloween.

"Stay outside," I told Vic as we got out of the car. Ranulf led the way, ax across his shoulder. "If you hear one of us yell for you, start the fire. If you hear—I don't know, something else, something bad, call nine one one. Ranulf and I can't exactly turn to the police for help, but you could."

"I'm ready." Vic looked petrified, but he gripped the lighter fluid tightly. I knew there was no way he would leave his friends while we were in trouble.

Quickly, I kissed Vic on the cheek, then ran ahead with Ranulf.

I'd thought we would sneak in, but Ranulf simply pulled open the cracked glass door, which sent shards clattering to the ground. From behind the abandoned concessions stand, a figure with long, bedraggled hair instantly emerged. "What's going on?" the vampire said, clearly wondering why another vampire had just wandered up.

Ranulf swung the ax with all his might, instantly beheading her. I cried out in shock, and the sound rang throughout the whole theater. With a frown, Ranulf turned to me. "Screaming is not useful."

"Sorry!"

Vampires, alerted by my shriek, began appearing—two,

then three, then five, all crowding into the lobby. Two of the biggest ones sprang at Ranulf, who was armed and the more obvious threat, but Ranulf threw them off like they were nothing. The ax slammed into the floor, shattering dusty tile, and a vampire's skull rolled past my feet.

"You." A vampire stepped toward me, and I realized with a shock that it was Shepherd. His rust-brown dreadlocks were gone now; no hair remained on his head. Neither did one of his ears. The fire had scarred his skin so terribly that his features seemed to have melted, and his skin was the revolting color of overcooked meat. "You're the other one who started the fire."

His ugly leer frightened me—for about two seconds, until I realized, *You know, I'm already dead. There's not a whole lot else he can do to me.*

"You should've let us go when you had the chance," I said, as I fumbled with the clasp of my bracelet.

"When *I* had the chance?" Shepherd shook his head. "You've got a lot to learn."

"So do you."

As he pounced at me, I let the bracelet drop to the floor and plunged my hand—now spectral—into Shepherd's chest.

It felt like the burn of frostbitten skin when lowered into warm water, simultaneously scorching and freezing. Each layer passed through my palm, disgustingly recognizable: skin, ribs, heart, spine. Shepherd jerked upright, stiff and shuddering, clawing ineffectually at his chest as it turned powdery and blue around my arm.

He wanted me to let him go, and I was desperate to shake him off, but I knew I had to use the advantage. "Tell me where Lucas is!"

"Upstairs," he gasped. "Projection—room—"

I pulled back my hand, and Shepherd collapsed to the floor. I grabbed my bracelet; by now, all I had to do was concentrate on holding it, and I instantly had substance again.

At that moment, Balthazar staggered into the lobby. A thin line of blood marred his hairline, his black clothes were ripped, and one of his lips had been cut, but he held stakes in both hands and looked like he'd had the better of any fight he'd been in. When he saw me, he gasped. "Bianca?"

"Help Ranulf!" I shouted. Ranulf, near the doorway, was holding four vampires at bay—with a little smile on his face—but I didn't know how long he could keep that up. Balthazar plunged into the fray, and I ran. "Lucas! Lucas, where are you?"

No reply.

I found the stairs to the projection room and climbed as fast as I could, cursing every step and the fact that I couldn't yet control my powers well enough to simply appear at Lucas's side. By the time I was near the top, I could hear their voices.

"Why won't you give in?" Charity sounded genuinely sorrowful. "Without Bianca, what do you have left that's worth fighting for?"

Lucas had no answer.

I reached the doorway of the projection room, and I had to decide: Drop the bracelet or keep it? If I dropped it, I'd be better able to strike Charity; if I kept it, Lucas could see that I was still with him, and then we could fight Charity together. Keep it, I decided.

The projection room had been decorated with movie posters that spanned decades, one overlapping the other: Angelina Jolie over Meg Ryan over Paul Newman. A projector lay on the floor, and the crumpled black coils were actual, old-fashioned film—the long-abandoned print of the last movie ever to play here. Cobwebs littered every corner, so thick they might have been sheets of silk. Part of the room's front wall overlooking the theater had been punched through, leaving a gaping hole. Lucas and Charity stood in the center of the projection room, each of them bloody and disheveled. Charity's ripped jeans and ragged T-shirt might have been tattered to begin with, but I suspected some of the tears were new. Lucas's shirt had been shredded at the collar. He clutched a stake in his hand.

Lucas looked ready to strike, to jump back into the pitch of battle, when he saw me. I'd thought his face would light up in joy, but instead I saw only blank disbelief. "Bianca?"

"Lucas! It's okay, we'll be okay!"

Charity saw me. Her face didn't change. She spun and kicked Lucas hard in the jaw.

He staggered backward, not unconscious but stunned. Charity smiled, and I realized in horror that she could finish him off now easily.

Dropping my bracelet, I bounded forward, ready to punch through Charity's chest and finally teach her a lesson. But she simply ducked, grabbed something from the floor, and threw it at me.

No! The pain lashed through me, through everyplace my body would've been if I still had one and farther than that, too. Even the air around me could hurt. Blue mist closed in around the edges of my vision, and I nearly vanished from this reality altogether. I felt myself falling and striking the floor, and I seemed to shatter. Crystals of ice scattered across the floor, and the agony of breaking into little pieces was worse than anything I'd ever imagined.

And yet I was still there. I didn't even have the relief of dying.

"Iron," Charity said. "I think it was part of the projector. Nothing shuts a wraith down like iron."

Clutching the bracelet upon the floor, I tried to materialize, but injured as I was, I couldn't quite manage it. At least I was partly visible, shadowy blue light flickering upon the floor.

Behind Charity, Lucas staggered to his knees, then slid down toward the floor again. Only now could I see how roughed up he was; even before Charity's last blow, he'd been in trouble.

"Bianca?" he groaned. "Can't—can't be— Is it you?"

"I need a family," Charity whispered. "Can you understand that? How lonely I've been? My tribe—they follow me, they help me, but they aren't family."

"You have a brother." I was surprised I could speak out loud. "You could be with him if—if you would just stop—"

"Stop acting like a vampire." Charity's head drooped, and

her fair curls tumbled past her shoulders. She took a step toward me. "That's not the answer. At least now I know what to do. To tie Balthazar to me, I have to tie myself to you. That means we'll need something in common."

"Don't hurt her!" Lucas charged toward Charity, but she wheeled around in time to avoid the blow. He was still stunned, still too weak to fight at his best. Swiftly she grabbed Lucas, jerked back his head, and bit deeply into his throat.

I screamed. It seemed as if the whole world was screaming, as if there were nothing but my scream and the sight of Lucas struggling against Charity, then slumping into unconsciousness as she drank, and drank, and drank. Her lips at his neck darkened with his blood, and her body shuddered with pleasure at every swallow.

Charity finally pulled back and let Lucas go. His body fell heavily to the floor with a thud. My scream cut off, replaced by the most terrible silence.

"That will do it," Charity whispered. She gave me a pitying look, then glanced sharply over her shoulder. I realized that people were coming up the stairs, and she didn't look pleased.

Charity ran to the gouged hole in the projection-room wall and leaped out. For a second I saw her dark shape silhouetted against the white screen, but then she was gone.

It can't be. It can't be. Please, no.

I somehow managed to gather myself. More than anything, I wanted to go to Lucas, but first I went to the doorway and closed my hand over my bracelet. Instantly, I had substance again. Now

I could help Lucas. I could carry him downstairs or do CPR or help him sit up, whatever he would need.

Lucas lay still in the darkness. A few drops of his blood stained the floor, and the bite mark on his throat was gory. When I'd bitten him, the only wounds had been my fang marks. Charity had torn his flesh open.

That's okay. It will heal.

"Lucas?" I whispered. With my fingers, I brushed against his cheek. He didn't move. "Lucas, it's me. I'm here." Still, nothing.

Reluctantly, I pressed my hand to his chest, and I felt no heartbeat. Lucas was dead.

I didn't want to face it. I couldn't hide from it. Charity had murdered Lucas before my eyes. I'd come back to try to rescue him, but I'd been too late.

Oh, no. Please, no. But there was no one to beg, no power who could grant my wish to go back in time, to take back what had just happened. I was trapped in the horror of what was real and irrevocable.

The thumping on the stairs grew louder, and then Balthazar, Ranulf, and Vic burst into the room. Each of them froze as they saw the scene before them, and Vic clapped his hand to his mouth like he thought he might scream, too.

"It was Charity," I whispered. "She drank his blood. She killed him."

Vic sank to his knees. I simply cradled Lucas's head in my lap, wishing I'd had a moment to touch him, just once, before the end. It would have meant so much to me, to have one more second together. But Charity had stolen that, too. I thought about Juliet, holding the fallen Romeo in her arms; she also had returned from the dead too late.

Ranulf bowed his head. Balthazar stepped forward and laid one hand on my shoulder, but I shrugged it off.

"This is your fault," I said. I didn't shout; I didn't have to for the force of my words to be felt. Balthazar had to know this as well as I did. "You dragged him out here even though you knew he was in no shape to fight. You never could face the fact that Charity's a monster. Because of that, Lucas lost his life. Don't you ever—ever—talk to me again."

Balthazar lifted his chin. Although I could see the pain in his eyes, he didn't have the decency to walk away. "If you still feel that way in a couple of days, I'll respect your wishes."

"You'll respect them now." Could I put my hand through Balthazar's chest, hurt him the way I'd hurt Shepherd? At that moment, I could have.

But Balthazar said something that banished all my thoughts of revenge. "You're going to need help with what comes next."

At first I could hardly speak. I knew he was telling the truth—I'd known the rules since before I ever met Lucas—but in my anguish, I hadn't yet considered what would happen next. It seemed too terrible to face. "Not that."

"You know how it works, Bianca."

"Don't lecture me!" I shouted at Balthazar. "You don't understand. This is the last thing Lucas ever wanted. Ever. He would have chosen death over this. It's—it's his worst nightmare."

"Wait," croaked Vic. His cheeks shone with tears. "Chosen death—I thought you said Lucas was dead. He's not? We can still help him?"

I embraced Lucas's body tightly. *I'm sorry, Lucas. I'm so sorry. The one thing I should have protected you from, beyond anything else, and I failed.*

"Lucas is dead," Balthazar said, "but he was killed by a vampire's bite. And Bianca had bitten him in the past, so he was already exposed. Prepared."

Vic looked from Balthazar to me in bewilderment. "What are you saying?"

I whispered, "Lucas will rise from the dead as a vampire."

Was it possible that Lucas would be able to endure it? He'd hated the idea, always. But I kept remembering what Balthazar had said when Black Cross held him captive: *For our kind, death is only the beginning.*

This could be our greatest nightmare. But maybe, instead, this would be our only hope of salvation.

Nobody could speak after that. I held Lucas's head in my hands and stroked his hair. All we could do now was wait for dawn.

THE ROMANCE AND DANGER CONTINUES WITH

"Once I picked *Evernight* up, I couldn't put it down! I can't wait for Claudia Gray's next book!"
— L. J. Smith, bestselling author of *The Vampire Diaries*

CLAUDIA GRAY

THE SECOND BOOK IN THE EVERNIGHT SERIES
OUT NOW